SMALL STEPS

Other books by author:

A Day at a Time

Long and Short Stories

More Long and Short Stories

Three for the Road

Double

SMALL STEPS

short stories

Henry Tedeschi

iUniverse, Inc.
New York Lincoln Shanghai

SMALL STEPS
short stories

iUniverse books may be ordered through booksellers or by contacting:

iUniverse
2021 Pine Lake Road, Suite 100
Lincoln, NE 68512
www.iuniverse.com
1-800-Authors (1-800-288-4677)

This is a work of fiction.
All of the characters, names, incidents, organizations and dialogue in this novel are either the products of the author's imagination or are used fictitiously.

ISBN-13: 978-0-595-40099-7 (pbk)
ISBN-13: 978-0-595-84483-8 (ebk)
ISBN-10: 0-595-40099-X (pbk)
ISBN-10: 0-595-84483-9 (ebk)

Printed in the United States of America

Go where your fancy takes you in
SMALL STEPS

Old Adage

Contents

THE DAY BEFORE AND THE DAY AFTER

Love—as complex as the human mind, as enigmatic as the heart of the forest or the depths of the sea.

The three of them, Celia, Laura and Sue, were sitting in Laura's college dormitory room consuming milk and cookies, an activity punctuated by laughter. This was their evening ritual. In fact, Laura didn't think she could ever go to sleep without milk and cookies. Although in pajamas, the idea that they were emulating a pajama party of their early teens was never considered.

"What can I say? Claire has to be a bit crazy. Don't get me wrong, very nice but a bit crazy. She actually thinks that something or somebody is following her around and makes everything alright." Laura was putting into words what they all had thought at one time or another. They were actually very comfortable with Claire. She had an openness that could only be admired and was just a regular gal except for this one fixation.

The door was ajar and who should come through but Claire herself. Speaking of the devil! But they weren't concerned. They were all good friends with a minimum of backbiting.

"You are not speaking about boys, clothes, the latest complaints about the Biology Department or yesterday's quiz. So you must be talking about me."

"Of all the conceit! Besides, we are past talking about boys."

"Yeah! It's mostly about men."

"You think my stories are far-fetched. I can't stand nonbelievers." Claire laughed. Obviously she had overheard their conversation. "Once upon a time princess Claire was Cinderella Claire. She wasn't mistreated like poor Cinderella—I mean the original Cinderella. She just wasn't loved. And then suddenly a mysterious stranger intervened and at age five she was adopted by the Sandersons, who were not only very comfortable but also very loving and kind."

Little did they know of the little girl cringing in the night all by herself until almost by magic a new world had opened for her. A world of security, kindness, love.

"Whoa! Maybe you're underestimating the Social Service system."

"Laugh if you must!"

There were stories Claire couldn't tell. They really would think she was insane. There was the day when she had been walking to school, just a few blocks away from her home. She must have been in middle school. A man, who seemed very nice in the beginning asked for directions. Suddenly he had tried to drag her into his car. A vagrant, very rundown and dirty, had appeared from nowhere. His eyes were ablaze. He seized the man's arm. "No," he said. And that was that. The man jumped in his car and quickly disappeared.

🍁   🍁   🍁

He had been called Zap because he'd been a sharpshooter in the jungle war and he zapped them. From trees or hidden in the bushes. He could come and go without making a sound and then he would zap them. Ironically, it was the hand-to-hand combat that had brought his service to an end. All the blood and all the deaths were seared into his mind and he was sent home to a psychiatric facility for a long time. He didn't talk and would ignore anybody who talked to him.

Many years later, Zap tended to his bootlegging in a log cabin hidden in the woods. People thought him a hermit.

He had heard her coming—the twitter of birds had subsided, supplanted by a few distressed calls and then he could only hear the murmur of leaves agitated by the wind. He had grabbed his rifle but then he saw her. The woman looked like trouble. In rags and although young, she looked old well beyond her years. The bulge of her abdomen told her story.

"It's cold out there. I ain't going to be no trouble."

Zap's face remained adamant. He knew he looked menacing and thought that would suffice to discourage her.

"Alright. Give me a square meal and I'll be out of your way."

"In town they could take care of you."

"I can't do that. They threw me out. You should understand. They don't want you there either."

"I don't need no woman around."

He had a squirrel stew on the fire in an old iron pot. She stayed first for one day, then longer. He took her farther up the mountain to where he actually lived. Her name was Joyce. He called her Joy. The way he said it robbed the nickname of its meaning.

She didn't require much—slept on the dirt floor wrapped in a blanket. She took over the cooking and kept the cabin in order. He protested—didn't need any damn woman around. He would go his own way but come back every afternoon, sometimes with a rabbit—once with a turkey.

Not many weeks after she'd arrived she was writhing on the floor moaning.

"It's nothing. Just give me a hand."

Zap had never attended a birth but he knew what to do. Joy labored for several hours. She tried to hold back her yells behind clenched teeth but didn't always succeed. Her pained cries were those heard since time immemorial. Zap helped pull out the little baby girl covered in blood and slime. The baby's cry was muted as he held her. She was such a little thing!

"Cut the chord," Joy instructed calmly.

He took them to the hospital in his rusty pick-up truck. The middle-aged woman behind the desk had a thick nose and yellow ringlets around a flabby face. She didn't want to tend to them.

"You should try the municipal clinic."

"I have money."

She didn't seem to care. Zap looked at the receptionist in his cold menacing way, leaned over the desk and grabbed the woman's arm, sinking his fingers in her flesh. Admitting Joy and the baby seemed to be the simpler thing to do.

Of the four friends, Sue and Claire were the fair ones. Both blonde with short stylized hair they could be taken for sisters. Celia and Laura couldn't have looked more different if they'd tried. Celia was slightly overweight and had dark hair, kept long. Laura was very thin despite her voracious eating habits and had a dark complexion. No box of chocolate or cookies was safe with her around.

Their backgrounds were entirely different. Why they got along so easily was a mystery to all four. Laura came from a large family with whom she made sure to spend most of her weekends. Celia and Claire seemed to come from all-American families, parents and one sibling. Claire had the distinction of having been adopted. Sue's family was rich and socially prominent but she never put on airs and was just a good friend. There was no doubt about her family's wealth. All four had spent some time in Harrisburg at her house during their Easter vacation. The front lawn was as large as a football field. The house, more of a mansion, was attended by at least three servants. Fortunately, the parents had been friendly and warm and made them all feel at home.

❋   ❋   ❋

"What's so surprising for a Town Manager to be interested in the nitty-gritty of the town? Crime, homelessness and other problems are obviously important for the quality of life. You think that a manager just sits on his ass?"

"I wouldn't say that exactly." The chief of police smirked, "But then you're the first one in twenty years to want to walk around with a policeman and talk about his troubles."

"I know your troubles! You don't have enough manpower. Will never have enough manpower. Everything else is new to me. Don't forget that I've been in charge just two short weeks. I want to see for myself everything that affects the town. This is why we're taking this walk."

The police chief, Eugene Moss, was an undistinguished looking, unassuming man. Of average height and with a shock of gray hair he looked more like a shopkeeper. His slightly protruding belly and his casual clothes gave him the appearance of softness. More than one person had been surprised, to their regret, when they had anticipated softness. Under the softness he was muscular. Under the bonhomie there was iron and a sharp mind. The Town Manager, Hubert Comtone, was much younger. Tall and distinguished with regular features, brown hair and a permanent dark midday stubble, he was wearing a well-cut gray suit and a red tie.

They were strolling in the plaza in the middle of the village—in the middle of the plaza a Civil War statue and wooden benches, on its sides two churches and businesses, mostly store fronts.

"Sometimes the local homeless hang around here. In the winter they either come to the jail or one of the churches when it's very cold. None of them are here now. Mostly a harmless bunch. Sometimes Zap hangs around here. Also harmless now. He isn't exactly homeless. Used to provide the citizens with some of the best booze in town. Never got caught at it. Didn't need to bootleg.

Had a disability pension from the war. Then I convinced him to drop his illegal activities."

"I thought you said he was never caught."

"No, never was. It's a long story."

It was on those walks that the two got to understand and even like each other. While sitting having coffee in a diner, Comtone's curiosity got the better of him.

"I'm intrigued by this man Zap! What a weird nickname! Can't you tell me some more about him?"

"Grew up around here. Name Steven Romwhich. No family left. Became peculiar after Nam, as so many of them did. In the army he was known as Zap because he was a sharpshooter. A very good one I must say—earned medals and all that. Then after his breakdown, in the hospital some of the men thought it was a funny name for a man who was mostly silent and sometimes mumbled to himself. They kept the nickname alive. Not much more to say."

Moss and Comtone continued their walks once a week. Their growing mutual respect was almost the same as friendship and soon they were on a first name-basis. They had visited the police building, the various agencies and the sites of previous crimes. Moss expounded on the problems of truant teenagers and police techniques to prevent crimes rather than just enforce the law. Sometimes they stayed in police chief's office. Comtone's curiosity kept him interested in the story of Zap.

"This man Steven Romwhich. You obviously didn't tell me the whole story. I hear he was plenty dangerous at one time."

"Well, he never did anything terribly wrong but when still in the bootlegging business he could be violent. The Almuerzo brothers—you must have heard of them—sent some of their henchmen to close him down. They burned down his operation. They couldn't find him but then when they returned to their cars, he shot them dead…from above. All three of them. He must have been up in a tree."

"Was he arrested?"

"Hard to arrest a man when you have no evidence. The folks in town actually were quite pleased. They thought it was clearly self-defense and the Almuerzo brothers have stayed away ever since.

"There is a soft side to him too. I went to school with him. He was always quiet but he was a good guy. I talked to him after that shooting, man-to-man. I talked him into dropping his operation in the woods. Haven't had such good hooch in town after that."

"Your story sounds like a miracle or a fantasy."

"Not really, the man has a soft core, if you can find it. As I said, I knew him when we were kids. That must have helped. Did you hear the story about him and the baby?"

"Can't say that I have."

"A woman who was staying with him had a baby. Apparently not his. The woman died in the hospital. Social Services didn't want him to raise the baby. He has no patience with officious bureaucracy. Without my intervention I'm sure he would have turned violent. I was just a detective then. I played up the fact that I knew him from school days or that officious lot never would have consented to let me mediate. I told Steve, Zap that is, that his wasn't an environment for a little girl! He didn't say a thing for a day or two. I had a rough time holding back those weirdos from Social Services. Then he came out from the woods with the baby and relinquished her, without a word. He must have been good to her. She was quite upset when he left."

❦   ❦   ❦

The newspaper headlines screamed their account. Radio and TV had little else for at least two days. It had been one of those rare kidnappings for ransom. Two young women had been taken—one wealthy and socially prominent, Susan Menard, the other Claire Sanderson. The police theorized that the two looked sufficiently alike that the kidnappers had taken both to make sure. The kidnappers had threatened to kill them both if Susan's parents didn't accede to their demands or called the police. There had been a leak and the kidnapping was reported by the *Sun*.

After the initial contact there was total silence. Many feared the leak had sealed the poor girls' fates and they would not be found alive. Then there was more of an uproar. The girls had been found, in good condition. Their two captors were found dead with their throats cut.

The airwaves were rife with conjecture. Was it a falling out between criminals? Were there mysterious vigilantes? Most of the commentators relished the mystery of it.

Eugene Moss folded the paper he had been reading and put it aside. He had work to do—the day of a chief of police never ends. He shook his head. A smile was playing on his lips. He had his own theory of what had happened but nobody had asked him.

PARALLEL

It all began in the Grand Hotel Guignol, someplace on the Riviera. Of course that wasn't the actual name of the hotel but I don't want to give everything away. Some folks want to preserve their privacy. Particularly when they practice certain professions.

These days with credit-card scams on the phone and the internet, the game is no longer an art. But at one time it was.

Jessica had been trained carefully. She could play the ingenue, set up clients. More so once she had acquired some education. But she had been just as useful when she was a little girl.

Jessie had a checkered past. That's a term she'd seen in a novel, "checkered". Whatever it was called, she remembered moving, moving all the time from town to town—from west coast to east coast. From south to middle west. From resort to resort. In school she was always the new girl—she had no friends.

"It's better that way," said her grandpa. Jessie had no idea why he would say that. She yearned for friends. It didn't help that her clothes were picked by Grandpa. They made her look weird. She wished they could stay in one place longer.

Grandpa Bernie was in charge of her future. Tall, gray-haired, her grandfather could be very dignified. A man of formidable charm, he could assume many poses but never that of the trickster he was. He had always been very kind and considerate. Her parents, Martha and Tom, made occasional visits. They were almost strangers to Jessie. A middle-aged couple, they appeared to Jessie to be of the same age as her grandfather—the mother with heavy makeup and sugary ways and the father, a burly man with sparse ginger hair turning to white. There was no joy in either of them. Jay, a wayward cousin with a dark shrewd face and a bad complexion, had been in jail. He made an appearance now and again. Jessie knew that her grandfather did not approve of him. She understood that Jay was an extortionist, a blackmailer and a violent man. "If you have to resort to that kind of thing you must be pretty stupid," was one of Grandpa's sayings.

Jessie was aware that they were confidence people. She had learned the word "con man" also in a novel. Reading was her only friend. It took the place of loneliness and was the only constant in her life.

Grandpa's capers fooled people with their own greed. How to make money that wasn't earned. Grandpa tricked people who stole or tried tricks themselves. There was the scheme where his clients would bet on a horse that couldn't lose. Grandpa claimed to have inside information delivered at the last minute just before the race.

Once, the horses really had brought him a big haul. He had placed bets for several people, supposedly at the last minute. At first they entrusted him only small amounts and Jessie knew for a fact that her grandpa had disbursed the money out of his own pocket to the clients supposedly holding the winning tickets. When they finally trusted him with larger amounts, Grandpa and Jessie left town in a hurry. They had enough money for two years, although the old man didn't stop his work—that's what he called it.

"You have to keep your hand in or you lose your skills."

Jessie understood—an unused muscle "atrophies." She had read that in a textbook. School books no less than novels were also a source of pleasure. She read them all the way through as if they were fiction. They told her about a world she had never seen before.

The schemes never involved Jessie directly—a conscious effort on Grandpa's part. He didn't want her to get hurt. The one case in which Jessie became deeply involved almost by accident changed her future.

It happened in a plush hotel. Grandpa was preparing a scheme that required the appearance of wealth. He was probably charming clients at the bar, but had been gone for too long. That summer she must have been about fourteen. Trying to entertain herself, she was looking out of the windows in the hotel hallway. The scenery of the esplanade with its darkness and many lights offered a magical view of a different world. A man engaged her in conversation. Gray-haired, well dressed, he looked very respectable and spoke very pleasantly. Suddenly she found herself pushed into one of the rooms. He'd kicked the door close and grabbed her where he shouldn't. That's when Grandpa made his appearance. She had never seen him so furious. But it didn't stop him from collecting five thousand dollars. Of course, if he had waited a bit, it would have all been for naught. Jessie had been ready to knee the man where it hurts most.

"I can't let this happen again. You're going to boarding school. You still have three years of high school left. Don't you worry, it will be nice. And then to college. There is nothing like a good education to make more money."

In the fall, Grandpa wearing a classy suit took her to her new school. Jessie felt positively elegant. For a change they had taken the advice of a saleslady in a snooty store.

Finally, the world stopped spinning. At school she made friends of the kind that last a lifetime. And she could spend time studying without interruption. When it was time, Oberlin College followed and she found further challenges and discovered boys. Oberlin had been her choice. She had heard marvelous things about it. Oberlin had educated girls and students of color as early as in the 1800s!

She acquired a bit of polish—a bit of knowledge. All marketable skills.

Parallel lines! Bet you don't know what that means. Paul was Paul Inglewood III. His second cousin was also Paul Inglewood III. Get it? You'd think they did it to confound genealogists and it wouldn't surprise me none. It was indeed confusing to more than one person. The two parallel cousins also resembled each other slightly. Not so that it would confuse close acquaintances but one that could confuse them in a police description. Not that the gendarmes ever had occasion to look for either one of them. I just wanted to explain. For some reason the two branches of the family didn't know each other well. It had something to do with some sort of disagreement between two cousins. Time instead of healing, added details that were mostly imagined and a bitterness that hardly matched the original slight.

Ironically, the family of one Paul Inglewood III had been very successful in business. The father had dabbled in real estate in the days long gone when you could buy properties cheaply. If you had the patience and the courage and didn't blink, a large profit could be guaranteed. In fact the Inglewoods were considered very wealthy. Enough to have fancy cars, a city and a country home and a few servants. The other family had chosen a different path. Suffice it to say that Mr. Inglewood was a professor and Mrs. Inglewood a librarian. With two children, they were comfortable, although they had to watch their expenses all the time.

❦   ❦   ❦

There was excitement at the Grand Hotel Guignol. Paul Inglewood III had arrived. A playboy, his fame had preceded him. His face had been splattered all over the newspapers, TVs and magazines of Europe and America. Car racing. Race horses. Mountain climbing. And of course women, women and women.

Grandpa rubbed his hands enthusiastically. "This is for you my little Jessie! He's even close to your age. We should make a big hit. I'm not getting any younger and I would like to see you settle down before too long."

To many at the hotel, Paul Inglewood III was a big disappointment. He drove an expensive sports car, a Lamborghini, no less. You had to be rich to drive that! But he didn't live up to his big spender reputation. Jessie and Paul eyed each other while moving through the hotel or going to the beach. She finally introduced herself with a most demure blush. Jessie was surprised that it had come on spontaneously. There are ways of faking it. He obviously enjoyed the company of women, but soon Jessie found that she had him all to herself. Just as she wanted it.

Dark hair and eyes, Paul was slim and moved gracefully. He had a likable smile and was a good listener. Jessie had never met a rich man like that. She had been introduced to boys of her own age and the strange rituals of dating and sex at Oberlin. But this was different. She could tell. Their conversations moved freely from the serious to the jocular and he never tried to impress or dominate. Kissing came naturally. First shy and then passionate. But he never rushed her.

Grandpa was delighted, at least at first. "You still don't have him on the hook, but you're getting him there." And then later, "We should use the Cuban story. You know, you need the cash to get your mother out of Castro's jail or something to that effect."

"Grandpa, I'm a grown woman and Paul is entirely mine. I don't want anybody to butt in. I'll do it my way."

She had never rebuffed him before. Grandpa hoped she wasn't falling for the boy. That could only lead to pain and misjudgment. Grandpa had been able to avoid that trap all his life.

✺   ✺   ✺

The moment she entered her grandfather's room, Jessie knew something was wrong. He wasn't alone. Cigar smoke permeated the room and her parents were there huddled around the table with Jay, who with a sneer pasted on his ugly face had a lighted cigar clenched in his mouth. Her grandfather sat apart with a defeated expression she'd never seen before. His face was marked by a bruise that would soon turn into a black and blue mark. Fear filled her along with cold anger.

"Ah!" Jay exclaimed, "about time you came back. Here we have been waiting for you while you were screwing that asshole." No greetings from any of them. "You can play your stupid games! For a million! A couple of retards! You have the jerk. About ten million worth of jerk and you don't have the guts to go for it."

Bernie intervened, "Jay thinks we could kidnap Paul and hold him for ransom. Not a bad idea."

Something twisted inside her. She would never do anything that would hurt Paul but then she saw a gleam in the old man's eyes. Something that she recognized. It said, "Let's go for it. I'm still dealing." Jessie had seen his resilience in the past and knew that kidnapping was not something he would accept.

Sure enough Bernie took the initiative. "This is how we should play it. Jessie will take Paul with her for a few days of nooky. Then she'll keep him there at the point of a gun."

"You expect a little cunt like that to do a man's job?"

"Don't you worry your pretty head. I trained her. She'll do the right thing. Don't you worry."

Jessie was filled with dismay. She would die before hurting Paul. While talking, Bernie had scratched his cheek with his right hand. This had been a signal in their previous life. It meant: the game is on. This just reassured her only marginally.

"Jay, Martha and Tom will stay with me to arrange for the ransom request and collect the money."

In a hotel in Nice, Jessie and Paul discovered the joys of love and sex. Jessie would have enjoyed their intimacy fully if she hadn't been so worried about

Bernie. She couldn't see how he could extricate himself. That bunch was capable of murder. Finally, they received a telephone call from the Grand Hotel Guignol. Bernie's message was short, "All done. Let's meet at our safe house." Grandpa had always arranged for an alternative meeting place if something went wrong. It had never proved necessary before.

After announcing herself on the house phone, hand in hand with Paul she entered the hotel room full of trepidation. A smiling Bernie reassured her.

"Well, well, well! You still have him in tow. How did you manage that?"

It was Paul who explained with a grin, "She had to marry me. That's how." But that wasn't all. Jessie also had to explain. "I'm not cut out for what we were doing. I want a simpler life. And I love Paul."

"You know of course that he's the wrong Paul."

"You mean the one without the money. And how did you find out?"

"I figured he wasn't behaving imperially, as I expect very rich people to—so I investigated. I have known for some time. By the way, the fancy car was loaned by the rich Paul. They recently met and liked each other." And then with a smile, "I'm not a complete amateur, you know!"

"But why didn't you say anything?"

"I didn't want to crimp your style. You seemed stuck on him. I had no right to butt in, as you told me so succinctly!"

"What did you do with the kidnappers?"

"Oh, that was relatively simple. They didn't trust me and Jay was always with me. I made the contact with the family, the rich family that is, by phone. Since their Paul was right there with them they took it to be a prank. I talked our relatives into lowering the demand to two million. That I could handle. The money was to be moved into a numbered account our dear relatives and I had opened in Switzerland. Jay made the trip with me to make sure the money got there. What they didn't seem to know is what goes in electronically can come out just as quickly. And then before the transfer to see whether the system worked we had put in one hundred grand, twenty of them mine. So I turned a small profit."

"The problem is that they know you took them for a ride. They can get to us."

"Not really. Know your enemies, I say. They came for me, but the police were expecting a man with a gun. In some countries carrying a gun is a very serious offence. Our friends (I can't bear to call them relatives) didn't even have the brains to say nothing. They spilled the whole story! Imagine, they had been cheated! As if you can refer to my finesse as cheating! They deserve the sentences they are going to get just for that! And since there was no kidnapping and no evidence of an attempted kidnapping except for their confessions, the authorities are not even looking for me. Although, unfortunately, I was expected to make a statement. As you know I don't like to lie!"

Jessie let go of Paul's hand and hugged the old man who explained, "I really don't mind you getting out of the game. I'm getting too old for it myself. Maybe it's time to retire."

IMAGES

Love—as complex as the human mind, a enigmatic as the heart of the forest or the depths of the sea

Nancy met Jason Rorick accidentally. She was entering the Second Avenue Deli with her friend Joan while he was exiting. Joan introduced them.

"You're from the same neck of the woods. Jason is an Assistant Warden at the penitentiary."

Nancy knew when Joan was teasing her. Anything associated with the penitentiary was a complete no-no in Nancy's social circle. People who considered themselves better than most completely ignored the existence of the penal institution at the edge of town.

Jason was a solemn-looking fellow with a friendly smile. He was not unattractive although completely undistinguished—not at all cool in today's parlance. The formality of his nondescript suit was totally out of place in the hurly-burly of the city. Nancy knew what the solemnity stood for—total boredom.

Standing on the sidewalk with a stream of people flowing around them, they spoke for a short while. The aroma of pastrami and pickles escaped through the doorway.

"Jason is author of a book," continued Joan, "let me see what's it called…" and then with evident satisfaction, "Ah! *Punishment or Rehabilitation?* with a question mark! He is working on his Ph.D. now."

Nancy has a sudden inspiration. How to put Joan in her place and how to shock her parents so that they'd stop bugging her. They were organizing a party during her Easter vacation. Almost certainly they would try to introduce her to desirable young men. As if this was the nineteenth century and she wasn't a throughly modern twenty-two year old.

"Wonderful! We are having a party at my home this Saturday evening. Consider yourself invited. Perhaps you could come?"

"Thank you. Hum! I'm not sure...possibly if I can reorganize my schedule. They don't give me much free time. May I give you an answer later?"

"Totally unnecessary! Just come if you can." They exchanged telephone numbers and her address. After noting with satisfaction Joan's puzzled and perhaps shocked expression, Nancy promptly forgot all about the invitation.

Saturday evening, Nancy was next to the door when the bell rang. With the hubbub of the party she would have missed it entirely if she'd been elsewhere. She didn't recognize Jason Rorick and it must have shown in her face.

"I'm Jason Rorick...Second Avenue Deli...remember me?"

Nancy made a quick recovery. "Of course! You don't think I could possibly forget you, do you?"

He chuckled, "Of course not! I make such an indelible impression!"

With that settled, Nancy introduced him around and revealed his affiliation. Everybody was very polite and didn't twitch an eyebrow, including her parents but she knew there would be plenty of talk after the party was over.

The tenor of the party was mild. Except for Jason, its composition and atmosphere had been carefully tended by Nancy's parents. There were middle-aged couples and younger guests in equal proportion. The music in the background was soft and from yesteryears—white wine and champagne predominated.

Surprisingly, Nancy found little time for her special guest. Elaine, one of her young women friends, latched on to Jason. He found her a bit patronizing but nevertheless she seemed to be spellbound by stories of crime and punishment which Jason was reluctant to relate. He had met her type before, thought their fascination almost prurient and was embarrassed by it. He tried to tell as little as possible.

"You must know some fantastic stories." she insisted.

"Most of them are too dark to tell in a happy crowd such as this."

At some point, Nancy's parents gathered the group in front of the fireplace. They wanted to hear the experiences of Joan and Mike who had just returned from a trip to Paris. The two had met there a few years before, had become interested in each other and then broke up. Without planning, they found each other again in the very first spot where they had met, one at the edge of the

Seine. Almost a case of telepathy! After returning to the USA, they'd married and their latest trip had been a honeymoon.

At the end of the story of Joan and Mike, Elaine embarrassed Jason by loudly proclaiming that he had some very fascinating stories to tell. Others also remarked how they were interested to hear something from a world unknown to them. Jason blushed and protested. He wasn't a good storyteller. Besides, many of his experiences were too dark and inappropriate for such a festivity. The crowd noticing his reticence insisted.

"You wouldn't want to hear the terrible stories I can tell you."

"Come on Jason! We are not children."

"Don't complain later. Most of what I could tell you would require parental consent even for adults! Mm…Mm. Let me see…" Jason didn't seem to mind suddenly having everybody's attention. Nancy was surprised; he had appeared so reserved when the party was in full swing.

"Okay, what you are going to hear, believe it or not is a love story. Very different from the one you just heard, but a love story nevertheless."

❦   ❦   ❦

The day had been dreary and the group of juveniles had gathered in the old warehouse. The great structure was cavernous—the windows high, most of them broken or grimy. The warehouse was almost empty except for what remained after years of neglect and vagrancy. There was the smell of mold, cigarette smoke and unspeakable things. Rusty and crumbling equipment, remains of wood fires, disemboweled mattresses, abandoned clothing and condoms. The group was a gang but still uninitiated in the ways of serious crime and drug trafficking. The head honcho was known as Banger, God knows why. He was a muscular lad of about eighteen. He had his position by being strong, having no hesitation in using his considerable strength when challenged and having a jail record, petty as it was. He had demonstrated his prowess more than once with his viciousness and sometimes a switch-blade knife.

They needed something for entertainment. On other days they'd delighted in breaking car windows, stealing hubcaps or robbing any unfortunate who came their way. Perhaps they were discouraged from their usual mischief by what looked like imminent threat of rain.

One of them brought in a girl, holding her arms cruelly pinned behind her back, yelling, "Look What I found, Banger. A snoop!" She looked small and might have been about fourteen. She actually was sixteen. Poverty must have held her back. She was dressed in jeans and a t-shirt.

Whether she was snooping or not didn't matter. Scared out of her wits, she was thrown from one boy to another. One of them removed some of her clothes before throwing her to the next boy. Pretty soon all her clothes were torn off among their jeers and yelled obscenities. It didn't take long before two of them held her down while the others took turns on top of her. She was moaning and bleeding. For some reason this was too much for one of them, Billy.

"Stop that. She's had enough."

"Who's clapping his mouth?"

He was half Banger's size but he held his ground. The switchblades shone in the half-light from the fire they had lit. Where Banger was strong and determined, the little guy was nimble. He was holding a denim jacket on his left arm to stop the thrusts he couldn't parry. He was bleeding from several superficial wounds when the encounter was brought to an end by police sirens.

There isn't much more to tell. They caught most of them and, of course Billy got the shortest sentence, two years. The judge was not in a tolerant mood or Billy might have been given only parole in view of his role in the affair. He served only a little more than a year with good behavior. Her name was Amy and she came every visiting day. Pregnant she dragged herself to the correctional facility. They left together when he was released, accompanied by the baby in a stroller.

"I don't know the why and wherefores. I think nobody had ever made a commitment to either of them until then. They both must have realized they had found a kindred soul. All I can say is that they are still together."

Jason answered a few questions from the now quiet crowd. And then he said, "I must go now, I'm supposed to be at work soon."

Nancy walked him to the door. She shook hands with him. She didn't know what else to do. The words came out of her mouth without warning.

"I would very much like to see you again. Could you give me a call?"

They were both blushing. Nancy figured they were on the same wavelength. This was the first time that had happened to her and the first time she ever had been so bold with a man she had just met.

THE COMPLEXITIES OF LIFE

Amy was facing an important test: explaining herself to a mother-in-law who had severe reservations about her. It wasn't so much that Amy would be affected personally, but her future and Larry's would be very different if she were unable to be persuasive enough. They were sitting at a table in a coffee shop, Amy with coffee and a doughnut in front of her; the older woman with tea. The ambience was cheerful. Modern paintings and prints adorned the walls.

"Thank you for agreeing to see me, Margaret. I know you are not comfortable about our marriage. I'm going to tell you our story. I would like to have your respect as much as you have mine. You don't have to love me or even like me. The bottom line is we both love Larry. Don't ever doubt my love for him. We have to find some accommodation."

Amy thought that the features of the woman in front of her had thawed somewhat into a smile.

"You are very blunt. Aren't you? That I like very much."

      ❦   ❦   ❦

Amy had been in love with Professor Koenig since attending his first lecture—if you can fall in love at a distance and from the strength of ideas. Not that she would have told anybody about it. A confession of that sort would have made her the butt of jokes. It seemed so childish!

The whole class, as many as a hundred students, had expected a famous man and anticipated a middle-aged fellow. For a moment they'd thought the lecturer was a graduate student and Amy sensed a collective sigh of disappointment. But if there was disappointment, it was soon dispelled, at least for her. A torrent of ideas had flowed forth, tightly organized with arguments pro and con following. She sat spellbound. She'd been so entranced she'd forgotten to take notes so that she still could remember most of his presentation to this day. As she'd become more experienced, she'd found that the rush to write made her miss some salient points. Larry Koenig, that year the new professor, was not tall or glamorous but seemed to grow in size and attractiveness as you listened to the smoothness of his voice and the harmony of his logic.

Amy used to look at herself in the mirror stroking back her short straight hair—she was a blonde then, wondering whether Professor Koenig would like her if they met accidentally on campus. She didn't want to approach him after class. Her interest might have shown through and embarrassed her in front of her fellow students. The idea of stopping by his office had never occurred to her. She had been told her complexion was lovely, but tended to look like a little kid. Her breasts were small and her gestures, she thought, had the artless movements of a teenager. She knew she was plain pathetic but she couldn't help herself. Over time, her feelings for him faded, of course, but when his wife left him she'd discovered some remained. His wife was a statuesque beauty and Amy instinctively disliked her, although she had only seen her on campus from a distance. For a moment, Amy had felt that perhaps she should arrange a chance encounter with the professor, only to discard the idea as ridiculous. She would have risked making herself look foolish. Besides she was dating Doug at that time—not a bad fellow at all, although she'd known the relationship wouldn't last. Too often he'd liked to be the center of attention and would become peevish when he didn't get his way.

Again Amy had overslept. Not the first time. Usually, whether she was going to attend a lecture or a lab, it didn't really matter how she was dressed, whether she had combed her hair or applied makeup and nobody seemed to object to her bringing a cup of coffee or rather what passed for coffee hastily purchased at the cafeteria. But then it was the caffeine she was after not some flavor kick.

But that time it had been different. She was the student representative to an ad hoc disciplinary committee. She had been added at the last minute, in fact most of the deliberations had already taken place. The by-laws demanded student representation but they had been forgotten until somebody had brought it to the committee's attention. Amy had put her name down on the list of requests at the beginning of the term. She had written that she was willing to serve on a University committee and her preference was the Curriculum Committee. She had never been called. But then they begged her to serve on the disciplinary committee. So late into the semester no other student had been ready to accept the assignment to a new committee that was likely to require work.

She'd murmured some excuses sheepishly as she entered the room. Bummer! They already had coffee and confections laid out. She'd felt stupid with her silly cardboard cup. Thank God nobody had noticed anything strange and she set around the circle of chairs and their corresponding tables.

The woman she'd thought might be chairing the meeting looked up disapprovingly over her glasses. She was a small woman with short gray hair and regular features. At first sight she might have been mistaken for a boy. Her stern expression, forceful delivery and rather deep voice would have quickly dispelled that misconception. She surveyed the newcomer and continued talking after the briefest of interruptions. Amy let out a silent sigh of relief.

"We have reviewed the facts thoroughly and you just approved the minutes of the last meeting which summarized our deliberations. To summarize once more, Ms. Juliet Ober's accusations of sexual misconduct by Professor Koenig have been proven false. The conference where the misconduct was purported to have taken place was taped with the knowledge of Ms. Ober and the tape does not support her accusations. At the time of the supposed second incident Professor Koenig was out of town. I urge you to bring the matter to a quick conclusion. The reputation of our institution for fair play and absence of sexual harassment is at stake. I therefore move that we recommend Ms. Ober's immediate expulsion. And now I'm opening the matter for discussion."

Amy had not been given the details of the charges and she'd probably forgotten to read the minutes. She was therefore surprised by the tenor of the meeting. The familiar voice of Professor Koenig interrupted her thoughts and her heart took a jump. She had been so flustered when she had entered the room she hadn't noticed him.

"There is nothing to discuss. The events Ms. Ober describes were clearly in her imagination. If you took the trouble to interview her, you'd see that she is deeply disturbed and in need of therapy which I would recommend. I don't see how expulsion would accomplish anything except disrupt her life further."

The chairwoman was ready with a rebuttal. "I'm afraid that it would send the wrong message to the outside world. It would leave the impression that the whole matter was being pushed under the rug, so to speak. I can tell you that those are precisely the feelings of the Dean."

Koenig's voice continued to argue his point. "I think that her welfare is more important than any image problems that might be created for the University. And now we hear the truth. It's what the Dean wants. The deliberations of this committee are just for show. Sorry, I can't go along with this."

The matter had been taken to a vote and the chairwoman's view had prevailed. Amy had left with the feeling that she should have spoken up for Professor Koenig, but her mind had just been too slow.

Just before graduating Amy had heard that professor Koenig had resigned giving the explanation that he had irreconcilable differences with the University administration. Amy wondered whether the committee meeting she had witnessed had anything to do with his resignation. Whatever the reason, not surprisingly Professor Koenig was almost immediately snapped up by a university on the West Coast.

❦   ❦   ❦

In Las Vegas, the four girlfriends got together to have a good time. Amy was trying to recover from an engagement broken only days before the wedding. It had hurt her terribly, eroded her self esteem and disoriented her. They were having a late breakfast at their hotel. Nightclubbing can be exhausting. Amy surveyed the room. She couldn't understand why they had to have slot machines in every imaginable place. She was surprised they didn't have one in each cubicle in the lady's! She recognized Tracy sitting at another table. They had been in high school together. She was much changed. She looked like a model and was dressed in designer clothes even this early in the morning.

"Oh!" she said, "that's Tracy."

"Don't you dare talk to her." was the response from Lucy, sitting to her right.

"Why not?"

"Come on, you must know that she is a slut. She's been a call girl for the past few years. You can tell by just looking at her."

Amy had heard rumors to that effect for some time. Perhaps she felt that Tracy was a member of the "sorority of the rejected" and felt an unexpected sympathy for her. "So what? She's still a person."

"Well, I'm afraid if you make her your choice, you'll have to go your own way without us."

"Oh, please, don't be so melodramatic."

But that was exactly what had happened. Amy couldn't accept such an injunction. She was surprised the other two girls felt the same way as Lucy.

Amy moved over to Tracy's table.

"Remember me?"

"Oh, my goodness! Amy Fanjoy! Fancy meeting you here and in Las Vegas of all places."

They reminisced for some time. They never had been close but common experiences have a way of bringing people together even after a long hiatus. Tracy made no secret of her occupation. Amy couldn't help but express her reservations and was pleased that Tracy didn't take offence.

"I know it's well paid but it must be difficult."

"Not really. I pick and choose and don't get involved with just anybody. There is a certain element of risk but how else you can make two hundred dollars an hour!"

"You can't do it for the rest of you life."

"Indeed not! I'm planning to retire soon."

Looking around the room, Amy was shocked to see the flame of her youthful imagination, Larry Koenig sitting at a table with a small group of three men and one woman. Sometimes coincidences can be so improbable as to be unnerving. She heard later that there had been a convention in town. Professor Koenig seemed to be admiring Tracy from a distance. Amy didn't blame him. Tracy was truly beautiful and probably could have made it the entertainment world.

Amy didn't stay long at Tracy's table. When she got up she'd found that her friends had already left. The message was clear. Amy was sorry she wouldn't be able to continue with her three companions. A case of extreme stubbornness on both sides! Putting together a schedule on her own—when and where to go wasn't going to be easy. Up to then, she had left all the decisions to her companions. She didn't even know what spectacles or entertainment were available. Furthermore, there would be considerable tension with her friends since they shared a room. She decided that she'd get a separate room. Las Vegas was never that expensive! The money came from the gambling, not the services.

Amy was bombarded by a wealth of information available from brochures and even one of the channels on the television set in her new room. Somehow she'd waited too long for any elaborate plan and decided to just go to the night club attached to the hotel.

Sitting by herself, she discouraged two men from picking her up. She wasn't accustomed to strange men being attracted to her. Suddenly, she noticed Larry Koenig sitting alone at another table with a drink in front of him. He seemed as lost as she was. The irony of it all pricked her thoughts. Driven by some demon inside her she got up, picked up her drink and approached him.

"Mind if I join you? We are both lost souls." Perhaps she had found courage in her feeling of helplessness—perhaps it was the effect of the drink buzzing in her mind.

"Not at all. Please sit down."

What else could he have said? At worst he might be entertained by the novelty. She quickly noticed that he didn't have a ring on his finger, although she understood that for most men that meant nothing.

"You're Larry Koenig, isn't that right?"

"Have I met you before?"

"No. It's just magic. I have special powers, although it's not that obvious just looking at me." Her smile was meant to erase any hint of sarcasm. But then she had to explain why she knew who he was.

That moment marked the beginning of a most delightful evening. Amy forgot the humiliation of having been left at the altar—the feeling that she was undeserving and ugly. It was like waking up from a bad dream. Larry was unpretentious and funny. She was happy that her mind hadn't seized up as it usually did when she first met an attractive man. Their exchanges were light-headed but friendly. His dancing was clumsy. What could you expect from a professor? But it gave them moments of intimacy that she was to treasure.

Sometimes during the evening Larry laughingly spoke up. "I have a confession to make." Amy thought he was actually blushing. "When you first came to my table, I thought you were a call girl!" As if call girls cruised night clubs! She understood that their arrangements were much more discreet.

"What changed you mind?" In a way she was flattered. Tracy was a model of feminine beauty.

"I'm not sure you can call it a change of mind. I just didn't want to believe it!"

Amy thought neither of them had had an inkling of what was about to happen. In the early hours of the morning he took her up to her room. They were euphoric. They kissed at the door.

"Does it have to stop here?" he asked.

"That would be a darned shame."

They shared her bed and the next days were a whirlwind of courtship and lovemaking.

But it all came to an end when they had to part ways. Amy didn't want to give up her job and didn't want any of the hypocrisy that she had seen mark the brief encounters of others.

"I don't think we can maintain a long-distance relationship. Let's make a clean break."

Larry seemed sad but resigned.

It was hard for Amy to reestablish her routine when she returned home. Larry seemed to intrude into her thoughts. She'd wished she had met him under different circumstances where they could have had a chance to really get to know each other. He was by far the best man she had ever known.

She was surprised one evening to get a phone call from him.

"I have to see you. Do you mind if I come?"

"Of course not! I can pick you up at the airport if you come at a decent time. Well…I can pick you up at the airport." She felt a wave of excitement but didn't want to expect too much. She was sure that he wanting to see her was merely an afterthought.

They stood in front of each other—expressionless as the stream of the passengers moved around them. Amy broke the silence.

"If that's the best you can do, you might as well turn around and go back."

His face broke into a big smile. "I was just flabbergasted!"

And suddenly they were in each other's arms.

RAUL MEREJA

Raul Mereja acquired a low-level job in the Ministry of Foreign Affairs. Like everybody else he had gotten it through contacts. His uncle Ernesto had obtained it at the behest of his sister, Raul's mother. As far as Raul knew, his uncle had no direct connections with the Ministry. He must have followed a convoluted route to achieve his goal. Raul absorbed the news sitting across from his uncle at a sidewalk table of the café Melton on Avenida Corrientes, with traffic noises intruding into their conversation. The smell of automobile exhaust was mixed with that of coffee and cigarette smoke. Despite the hubbub, Raul could still understand the gist of his uncle warnings.

"Don't make balls of this opportunity. Don't fuck it up or this will be the last time I will help you. And you might as well drop your stupid theater group. That's for *maricones*."

Raul was very fond of his theater group and had throughly enjoyed their performances of *Dracula* and *Torquemada*, plays by Archibald Blitz, where his friend Luis (nicknamed the Fiend) had been properly horrific in the title roles. His talent could not be doubted—with a twist of his mouth and a fiery look, Luis could scare you out of your wits.

Between pronouncements, Uncle Ernesto coughed, deep in his chest, a sound that never ceased to irritate his nephew in their rare encounters. Ernesto had a dark mustache and graying hair. His dark brown eyes were invariably rheumy, possibly from the smoke of the lighted cigarette always hanging from his lip. Raul's uncle also had the annoying habit of crushing his cigarettes in the coffee cup saucer before lighting another one.

Raul wasn't expected to respond to the onslaught. Predictably, he looked bored. A wasp was perched on his coffee cup, probably in pursuit of the excess sugar he had added. He considered smashing it but this would disturb his uncle's tirade. A rather attractive woman passed and he couldn't help following her with his eyes only to snap back into his attention stance.

His uncle continued, "Then, it's understood. You'll be on your best behavior. You'll be respectful of your superiors, follow instructions etc., etc. It isn't as if you were born yesterday, although sometimes I have my doubts."

The very impressive Ministry building was more a massive palace than a public building. Its large black wrought-iron gate was open only during working hours; at the entrance, an impressive marble staircase with an elevator on one side. His supervisor at work, *Señor* Balustre, was an old white-haired man, with an emaciated wrinkled face and a voice without inflection or expression. He wore a duster over a bony body and a dark suit. He had a slight stoop and wore a visor like ones Raul had seen only in very old foreign movies.

Without directions, Raul filed documents which had no meaning for him, haphazardly at best. There were three other clerks of apparently the same rank as Raul. They were of no help. In their work, they simply followed proscribed paths that were a mystery Raul. They gathered in the middle of the afternoon to drink *mate* in a small room away from the office. There they exchanged dirty jokes and meaningless commentary. The work was boring and Raul couldn't help falling asleep every so often. He always had been able to avoid being caught in *flagrante delicto*. He often dreamed, an activity that produced surprisingly sharp images. In one, Balustre was caught in the subway and had to travel throughout the train system for days. In another, the beauteous Olivia, a neighbor in the apartment house where he lived appeared. Actually, they had been good friends until she'd grown breasts and more curves than any woman should be allowed. Now, he was lucky if she would say hello, although he had hopes for more. After dreaming about her he would wake up full of wants and desires. When not daydreaming, he worked out a system to catalog and cross-index documents on the computer. Nobody seemed to know what to do with the computer terminal in the office. Not wanting to offend anybody, Raul would make entries when nobody was looking. Displaying your skills before the uninitiated only leads to jealousy and arguments. As it often happens when you carry out a task surreptitiously, Raul got caught by no less than Balustre himself, who demanded a detailed explanation of what he was doing. Throughout Raul's account, Balustre frowned disapprovingly. The hero of our story was sure that he would be summoned in front of his superiors and summarily dismissed. Raul didn't know what would upset him more: losing the job or having to face his uncle. Whatever was to happen, he waited stoically for the other shoe to drop. Then life took unexpected turn. Newspaper headlines and pronouncements from television reporters were highlighting a scandal in the Ministry of Foreign Affairs. A million simply had disappeared into thin air. This wasn't much compared to the billions stolen by the previous administration. Nevertheless, somehow the turmoil that followed caught the imagination of the media. For some reason a government elected democratically was expected to be totally pure by citizens turned cynical and angry after the collapse of the economy that had preceded the election.

Raul followed the drama from a distance. Destiny had in mind a more direct role for him. Balustre asked him to proceed to the office of the Minister. The staff there had requested the services of a messenger. Raul was the closest to that appellation. Looking for the office, he became lost. Either the instructions he had tried to follow were incomplete or he had taken a wrong turn. At any rate, another clerk pointed him in the right direction. Raul knocked on the door and entered. The large room was white in contrast to the institutional green of the small offices familiar to Raul. Paintings and photographs from other eras adorned the walls. The furniture was dark, heavy and formal. Several bookcases with bound official-looking tomes lined the walls alongside the windows. Four men were sitting around a polished dark table. Raul recognized the Minister from photographs he had seen in the newspapers. The Minister was holding an envelope in his hand and looked very worried. He had a florid complexion, short sparse sandy hair and was dressed in a well-cut dark suit, as might be expected of somebody in his position. A younger man was dressed more informally in jeans, a dress shirt and a narrow tie.

He was remonstrating. "That goes against every precedent I know. You should at least preserve some dignity. This is really a small matter that has been blown out of proportion. You should wait until the formal investigation which can tell us what really happened."

The Minister responded, "You know better than that. A formal investigation would take forever. Then everybody would be sure that a coverup had taken place. The money will be gone, along with an effective government. At least with my resignation, the President will have a chance to govern. Anyway, I don't want to go in person. To be blunt, I was humiliated enough in the last cabinet meeting." The other man held up his hands in a gesture of reluctant surrender. Raul was unable to keep his mouth shut.

"Minister Ferghetti may I make suggestion?" The man that had been addressing the Minister turned to face Raul.

"Don't you know enough to address the Minister as Your Excellency? And who are you anyway?"

"Raul Mereja at your service."

The man became even more agitated. "What does a *pendejo* like you have to say?"

Raul knew he was messing up and his uncle would hear about it soon enough. The Minister, who had been somber until then, seemed amused.

"You have my permission to proceed, although I'm not in the mood for laughing."

"This is no joke Your Excellency. It's my nature to have ideas. I have sized up the present situation. You want me to carry your written resignation to the President. As your friend pointed out this is premature. If the money were made to reappear the problem would be gone."

"How do you expect this to happen?"

"I'd be glad discuss this in private."

"Don't you dare do that," the man in informal clothes addressed the Minister. "Not only would it be insulting to the three of us but this youth is clearly unbalanced. We are still responsible your welfare."

The words had much too much of a command in them and the Minister ignored them. He acquiesced to Raul's request. Raul and the Minister came up with a scheme. Every person with access to the computer's account numbers would be interviewed by a special police envoy selected by the Minister himself. This man, of course, would be Raul's friend Luis (nicknamed the Fiend) dressed very formally in a dark suit and displaying a most threatening and lugubrious demeanor. He would also show each person a video of the interviewee entering the computer room. The video would be recorded while the person was engaged in normal activities. Then a piece would be added with a very unclear view from behind showing a blurred figure sitting down at the computer. Poor Luis almost earned a punch in the face from one interviewee. Fortunately he was too fast. The trick worked and a million made a mysterious reappearance in the Ministry account. The Minister appeared in a newspaper headline: "What million are you talking about?" A photograph showed him with a completely perplexed look.

You might imagine that recognition and honors would follow, but these are not the ways of the world. Instead, Raul was given an even more daunting task. After all, several billion actually had disappeared under the previous administration.

Switzerland looked just like postcards Raul had seen and the views shown in the international espionage movies which at that time had seemed to delight Hollywood. With all expenses paid, he stayed in the best hotel in Geneva. He wasn't accustomed to being accorded so much courtesy. He was surprised, particularly since his French was practically non-existent and he had to express himself at times in Spanish. True, the Swiss can't handle foreign languages as well as they think they do, but at least they listen when you try to speak their language. Not like Parisians (he had heard) who make foreigners feel like dolts even when they speak perfect French.

When making inquiries he copied the performance of his friend Luis but to no avail. He just didn't have the knack. A break came, however, when he was eating in a restaurant and heard not only Spanish but the accent and idioms familiar to him. He turned around with what he hoped was a friendly smile. The men who had been talking didn't notice him until he was standing right next their table.

"What a pleasure to hear your voices. You must be compatriots!"

Sure enough that was the case. But they reacted very coldly. They weren't interested in socializing with him. One of the two had fair skin and blond hair tightly combed against his skull. Raul would have thought him German or Scandinavian but knew that wasn't true. The other was darker with receding black hair and a small mustache. Raul felt the need for a quick retreat.

"Well fellows, pleased to have met you. Hope to see you around!" he said and then left.

His effort, however, hadn't been for naught. They came looking for him at his hotel. It seemed that a Señor Aurora needed a clerk who knew Spanish to help him with his correspondence. "Whoa!" thought Raul, "I'm eminently qualified." To make a long story short, he became part of the household. Raul remembered Aurora, a dignitary of the regime that been ousted in the last election, as a tall dignified-looking man with white hair and a look of utter respectability. Aurora read letters every morning after breakfast, then gave Raul very vague instructions for answering. He expected to receive the reply ready on the following day. Aurora's correspondence was not extensive. With the excuse of using the computer as a word processing tool, Raul was allowed access to it. He was able to transfer the information communicated electronically to his computer in the hotel. It was child's play to find the passwords used to transfer funds monthly to replenish Aurora's supply. Raul guessed what the total amount funds available were and transferred them to the Ministry's account. At that very moment something caught in his throat and he emitted a sudden powerful single snore which awakened him.

That very day, the second shoe from his fated encounter with Balustre dropped. When Raul arrived at work, Balustre wasn't there. Another bureaucrat, he had never met, summoned him.

"Raul Mereja, there are several matters I would like discuss with you. Balustre informed us about your performance working with the computer." Raul felt something crashing inside him. "You undoubtedly know that Balustre retired last week after many years of faithful service. He recommended that you be his successor to reorganize our files. We expect you to start as soon as possible. The three other clerks will be under your supervision. Of course your salary will be adjusted according to your increased responsibility. Do you have any questions?" Raul probably should have thanked him for the welcome news and asked about his salary. But the simple truth was that he didn't have a coherent thought in his head and could only manage to shake his head. Sometimes there are bad days, sometimes good days. This clearly was a good day. When he returned to his apartment house, he was in a cheerful mood and entered the elevator at the same time as the curvaceous Olivia. This time he didn't feel intimidated by her presence.

"Raul Mereja," she said looking him right in the eye, "since you have taken the job at the Ministry you even fail to recognize me. You must have become a terrible snob." Raul knew she was joking because of her smile. Suddenly she was again the teasing, lively girl he had known all along. He replied, "That wasn't snobbery; I was so scared to lose my job that I became an automaton." He didn't know where he had found the courage to speak in that way but he knew for sure that everything would be alright from the brightness of her smile.

RECKONING

The day of reckoning had arrived. Ann Orbach knew what the sad outcome would be, but this was the official notification in black and white. Sitting in her office, the weak winter sun filtering through the window, she tore the envelope open, and the words attacked her. She was denied tenure and hence she had only one year more at the university. For some reason the letter brought the reality down on her. Tears flooded her eyes. She had been happy at the university. Her two courses, as rigorous as they were, were prized by many of the students. Her research had gone smoothly and she had been able to develop a unique research approach, she flattered herself to think. Now she'd have to leave and if lucky, start again from the beginning someplace else. This might even extend to her private life. She didn't have much experience with men but she had met one who seemed to care for her. For the first time in her life she had felt there might have been some permanence in her emotional life, although they had yet to go past formal dating. Jack was rather sweet and she had had great hopes for their relationship.

She had heard that academic politics could be arbitrary and cruel but this was the first time she'd felt its sting. Who disapproved of her so strongly? Who thought she wasn't up to the task? The departmental vote had been in her favor, although not unanimous. Without doubt Professor Albert Levington had had a role in her defeat. His serious countenance and ponderous pronouncements had marked him as a male chauvinist of the first degree. Besides his approach was terribly old-fashioned. In his day he had been original, a dynamo in his chosen field. Now he was probably entirely spent. Margaret, her only real friend on the faculty, had made Levington's misogynist tendency clear to her. It was a hard world for a woman to succeed especially in the face of prejudice. Margaret had been one of the lucky ones. Throughout Ann's sojourn, she had offered Ann the only strong support she had received.

After her disaster, Ann felt like a pariah. Even Margaret avoided her. Perhaps the defeat of her unconditional support was too painful to consider. Levington, Ann shunned. She was sure there would be gloating on his part.

As much as she wanted to avoid a confrontation with Levington, Levington didn't seem to want to avoid her. He caught her as she was about to leave her office. Her lectures and discussion periods had been in the morning. She had been barely able to keep going with her usual zest. Exhausted, she only wanted to be left alone and was ready to go home.

"May I have a few words with you?" Here comes the lecture and the gloating, Ann thought.

"I'm afraid I have a commitment. Another time perhaps." She had to avoid breaking into tears at all costs. In his presence, it would have been insufferable.

"Okay. But please keep in mind that I'd like to have a few words with you."

It wasn't until the following day that she felt anger. Levington must be a most insensitive bastard. He should know when to leave her alone. In the past, her temper always made her face problems head on. On an impulse she turned down the hall to Levington's office.

He yelled "Come in!" at her knocking.

In the room there were books everywhere on the desk, on chairs, in a bookcase jammed in total chaos—some books upright, some on their side on top of others.

Levington was sitting at his desk and a graduate student was next to him. He had a coffee cup at his side. They were both perusing a text in front of them.

"Oh, Ann, good of you to stop by."

The old hypocrite, she thought.

"We are almost finished. Please sit down."

Ann didn't. The few angry words she wanted to say were best uttered standing.

Levington addressed the student. "You're almost there. The content is fine. You have to smooth over the sections I marked. You need some more clarity. Don't forget that the reader is not likely to have the same point of view as yours. You can't make any assumptions about what he or she thinks or what he or she knows."

The student, a girl with a strawberries and cream complexion, blushing fiercely mumbled something and then left after making another appointment. With a spectator present it is as hard to accept a compliment as much as the implied criticism.

Levington in shirt sleeves, with his jacket draped on the back of his chair, stretched and then got up.

"Please sit down my dear. Would you care for some coffee? I just made a fresh pot. Rather strong. I have to do something to keep awake in the morning."

Ann wasn't interested in pleasantries. "What's on your mind Al." She had never called him anything but Dr. Levington. But she was now in a different mood and position.

"The news about the tenure decision must have been painful for you. Please don't be discouraged." Here comes the gloating, thought Ann. She sat down in an upholstered chair close to the desk where Levington had sat down again.

"In a university defeats such as yours mean nothing. I have known men that proceeded to a Nobel Prize a few years after having been rejected."

"So?"

"You're probably the best person in your field. Only idiots wouldn't recognize that. If you ignore the misguided, you have the potential for greatness."

Ann was flabbergasted into silence.

"Yes, I know. I have been rather harsh in our discussions. It's because I have great hopes for you. I have already sent out letters, letting prime departments in the country know about your availability and ability. I don't doubt you'll hear from them soon."

"Well, thank you." She couldn't say more, something had knotted at her throat.

Another part of the story played out later. Perhaps a secretary had wanted her to know the truth. Perhaps it was just an honest mistake. After all, when there are only two women in the department, a dim person might confuse them. The copy of a memo in her personal folder in the departmental office filing cabinet, was addressed to the Dean from her friend Margaret. Obviously, it didn't belong in her file. She was about to turn around and discreetly return it to the office when her glance caught her own name in the text. The memo said: "Ann Orbach is totally unoriginal and she hides behind the feminism that has become so fashionable these days to extract sympathy and shield herself from just criticism. In reality she has very little to offer in her field of scholarship."

The shock sent a shudder all the way to her toes. She had to sit down and remain motionless until she could collect her thoughts.

THE KNIFE

God knows why they had brought us such a gift, my sister and brother-in-law. Those were the days when fear of terrorists hadn't yet banned knives carried in the luggage of air travellers. The knife was a miniature of what was carried by a gaucho of yesteryears. The knives of gauchos were the size of the short swords carried by the Roman soldiers. Yet the scabbard and handle of the smaller version had their charm—decorated with what looked like gold and silver but was more likely to be copper and tin. The sharp blade had been dipped in grease to avoid rusting, I imagine.

The gift of a knife invited recollection of an old superstition: it expressed a wish that you would hurt yourself with it. No such thought had crossed their minds, I'm sure. They must have picked what they thought would remind me of Argentina, the country that I had loved so dearly so many years before. I had seen in Buenos Aires similar knives along with larger ones in the little shops carrying colorful goods from the provinces, all enveloped by the emanations of moth balls—woolen blankets, ponchos and *boleadoras,* two leather balls filled with heavy stones and linked by a leather thong. This weapon was used to bring down running animals or the mount of an adversary. In a clean throw, it would entangle their legs.

What do you do with such a gift? Although as large as a switchblade knife, it was certainly not a weapon, but more suited as a letter opener, a use I didn't favor. It could hardly be placed on a wall as decoration to invite the queries of admiring guests. Its nobility, as much as its impracticality, prevented its placement with the large kitchen knives. A drawer in the night table next to our double bed was finally its resting place, complementing the accumulation of old photographs and assorted broken artifacts that I had a mind to fix but never did. And it lay there for years. I never considered it a weapon. In my mind, the knife was in the category of a knickknack, not like the knives in *Mar-*

tin Fierro, the masterpiece of José Hernández and some of the short stories of Borges, which had elevated knife fights and knives to legendary levels.

One day, when I was alone in the house the bell rang. Time and time again, my wife had admonished me never to open it to strangers. Break-ins by sheer force were not unheard of in our suburban community. I took a peek from the side window. The man at the door looked harmless, a clipboard under his arm. Was he here for a survey? Collecting signatures for a petition or a candidate? I couldn't really tell. I opened the door.

Violence erupted like a sudden thunderstorm in a quiet night. There were two of them. Brutally pushed aside, I was then showered with punches and my face hammered by the side of a handgun. The sudden pain didn't allow me time to panic. The man yelled something. All I could understand was "money", uttered between clenched teeth. Down on the floor, I reached for my wallet with difficulty.

"Where is the rest of it?" one of them yelled.

The pain from a kick at my genitals folded me in two. I couldn't have answered even if I had tried. In the house there was nothing except some trinkets which passed for jewelry. While one of them dragged me along, they ransacked the house. They pulled out drawers and emptied them on the floor. One of them opened the drawer of my night table and its contents flew out along with the forgotten knife. Still bent down from the receding pain, I caught it in midair. The knife drew out of the scabbard with ease. The blade struck upward, just under the ribs. I swear it had a life of its own.

John Stewart is the famed attorney of the damned. He saved many of his clients from the death penalty before it had been rescinded by the state courts. My wife and I do not believe in taking unnecessary risks—so he was the lawyer of choice.

"Defending your property with deadly force is legal in New York State. Beside what happened could be considered self-defense. I doubt whether you'll even be indicted," he commented. "Nevertheless, you would have been easier to defend if you had used something more respectable, like a handgun or a shotgun. Knives are used as weapons by juvenile gangs and recent immigrants."

Both of us, my wife and I, badly wanted to get rid of the knife after the police returned it. But how do you dispose of a knife? It ended up in a drawer of my night table along with old photographs, artifacts in need of mending and knickknacks.

My wife returned to her usual warning. "After what happened don't you dare open the door to strangers!"

IMOGENE

Imogene had always been considered homely, an estimate she shared. The idea must have formed as far back as elementary school. Her features were quite ordinary. She wasn't fat but somewhat square. As she grew up her choice of dresses did not allow judging her shape. Suffice it to say, she wasn't considered cool. Her name didn't help either. She had never heard it used except in her case. She wondered how her mother had picked it. Fortunately it evolved from "Imogene" to "Gene", although when her name appeared on school lists it still elicited snickers.

Even as a small child, Gene felt the disappointment of her parents. The sweetness and the loveliness of children her age seemed to have passed her by, and her performance in school was adequate but didn't attract attention. Her image might have been different if she hadn't been living in a small town where reputations endure and the available choices of the opposite sex are limited. Now in her twenties nothing had changed for her except that she no longer lived in the house where she had grown up. Her two years of college had shown her the need for independence.

The National Guard unit coming back from Iraq was the reason for the festivity. The hall with its removable ceiling panels and bright fluorescent lights didn't seem quite appropriate for the occasion, as happy as it was. Gene thought its bareness was more suited for PTA meetings, zoning hearings or holiday parties. The large multi-colored hand-painted signs held by wires from the ceiling welcomed the soldiers and expressed the solidarity of the community in honoring them. There were little American flags everywhere. Wives and husbands and other relatives were jubilant—the men and women returning from serving their country were more sober. Some of the children were solemn. The parent who had been absent for over a year was not completely familiar. Television crews from two different channels were at the reception.

The two servicemen who were interviewed declared how happy they were to have been able to serve their country. One of them even indicated he was ready to go back. George Lewen had returned in a coffin weeks before and his sacrifice had been honored by an honor guard with the folding of a flag and rifle shots in the air. That didn't help his parents and his bereaved wife and two children, Gene thought. Gene was alone sitting at a table. Claire's brother was one of the returning soldiers. Best girlfriends, they had come together but Gene didn't want to intrude on Claire and her family at such a momentous occasion. Gene couldn't help noticing one of the soldiers who remained detached from the others and seemed to have become impatient with the celebration. He didn't look familiar, although all of them belonged to the same unit and she knew all the others. Eventually the unfamiliar man sat by himself with a cup of coffee. After pouring some cream in it he got up and walked toward the exit. To Gene's surprise he stopped in front of her, leaned over, a hand on her table, and addressed her. He was not bad looking but then she wasn't particular.

"All alone! You don't want to say hello to the returning soldiers?"

Gene felt her face turning red and for a moment had trouble answering. "I always sit alone." Somehow she felt she had to explain more. "It has nothing to do with the occasion."

Still leaning with one hand on the table, he continued. "I suppose that the safe-return should be celebrated. Why don't you come with me and we'll have our own private celebration."

Gene had been told that returning soldiers who had no wife or family, and some who did, were only interested in one thing. In the past that reputation would have sufficed for her to shake her head. But for some reason she did not reject him and got up. What did she have to lose? It was only later, and for only a moment, that she was alarmed. What did she know about him? But he seemed relaxed and spoke to her politely. His name was Jack Sutinew, a name vaguely familiar to her. There had been a Sutinew family at the edge of town, but they had been gone for a while.

It was already turning dark. His car was an old one—in her mind an indeterminate model. To her, all passenger cars looked much the same. She wondered whether he had stored it some place when he had gone away.

They parked half a mile away, on a speck of green illuminated briefly by the car's headlights. To talk some, he had said. She was unaccustomed to dealing with men, particularly when she was alone with them. She said little except to answer his questions. Did she work? Did she have a boyfriend? What did she do with her time? He said little about himself and nothing about the war. He had recovered in a hospital in Germany so Gene felt he might have had a story to tell. She wasn't wrong about what he was after. Eventually, he kissed her briefly and his hands wandered under her blouse and released her bra. On her infrequent dates, which were rarely repeated, this had happened before. After a while he said, "Let's go for a drink." She held his arm. "Wait a minute," she said and rearranged her bra.

With a bottle of beer in front of each of them, renewed at intervals, they continued their conversation. The bar was dim but not unpleasant. There was a buzz of voices in the background but she stopped noticing it. He touched her hands or arms but didn't go past that. It had occurred to her that he might have needed some liquid reinforcements because he was nervous, but rejected that notion since he seemed perfectly at ease while her heart was drumming in her chest. Did he like her? She hoped he did. Then he said, "Let's get a room some place."

In her mind the request was inevitable but the bluntness was unexpected. She didn't reject the idea. Perhaps it was time something like that took place. She didn't know exactly what to expect and hoped it would not be too unpleasant. She was appreciative that he hadn't proposed to go to her apartment. If they had, what was about to happen would be all over town in no time at all.

She didn't even have to get out of the car when he registered them at the motel. The entrance to their room was in the back and nobody would notice they had no luggage.

The room was large with a huge bed and lots of light. He kissed her briefly and began undressing her.

"Turn off the light!" she requested. She knew she was going to be embarrassed by their nakedness.

"Gene, that's the best part. You have to see what is happening!"

She stopped protesting and for a few moments tried to cover with her hands what he was uncovering. He was caressing her all over her body and murmuring endearments and she soon forgot what she was trying to do. He was already undressed and was holding her, his front touching her back. She felt his member crowding her. She could see her image in the mirror covering most of the wall.

"I'm so plain!"

"Don't be silly. You're beautiful!"

"Jack! I have droopy breasts and look at my belly!"

"You're lovely! Let me be the judge! Do you want to be a model instead of a woman?"

She lost herself in her sensations. She felt warm all over as both of his hands were cupped over her breasts.

"Please be gentle. I'm not very experienced."

When it finally happened she could only wonder why people made such as fuss about something so simple. His movements pleased her although she felt sore. She wished she was more experienced and had more to offer.

The second time was not any different.

"Please, let's stop after this. I'm a bit sore."

He wasn't offended. He gathered her in his arms and kissed her passionately.

"Let's leave it for next time, then," he murmured.

She hoped there would be a next time.

She had noted that on one side of his body he had a mass of angry looking scars. She had touched them gingerly.

"Please don't," he had said.

❦   ❦   ❦

Gene was glad she worked at the library. This allowed her to survive her present torment without too many people noticing. Would he call her or not? Was that the last she'd see of him? She couldn't imagine how she could have allowed herself to go so far! It just wasn't like her. He had kissed her before dropping her at her house and she hoped it had meant something.

"I'll call you as soon as I get a chance." She had heard that before and it didn't mean anything.

Mrs. Lockworth, the librarian, of course noticed. "What's bothering you girl? You don't seem to be yourself."

"Everybody is entitled to have an off-day."

Mrs. Lockworth was a very light-skinned African-American with a heart of gold and the manners of a cultured, educated woman. Mrs. Lockworth shook her head. Gene was one of her preoccupations.

"With your intelligence you should do something more than being a clerk. You could get one of those fancy Master's degrees in Communication. Computers rule almost everything nowadays."

"In due time Mrs. L., in due time." Gene didn't see what was so unusual about her intelligence and her two years of Community College.

"Such a lovely girl like you should go out more often." Gene would just smile at that. She had no ready answer. How could she explain that a plain girl had limited choices?

She had just checked out a book for a six-year-old, pleased that he had acquired the habit. She had resisted her impulse to ruffle his hair. Things were so complicated these days and everything could be misunderstood. Her heart took a jump when she saw Jack entering the library. No longer in uniform, he looked fit in a jacket and slacks. No tie.

"Can I take you to dinner?"

How could he make a date like that so casually? Why didn't he make sure that she was free beforehand?

"I don't see why not." Something inside her was jubilant.

"I'd like to go to the Horbeck Mall afterwards."

She didn't care where they went as long as they were together. She couldn't imagine why he would want to go there, it was a bit too upscale for her taste.

They had a sumptuous dinner. Their conversation flowed easily. She thought that after their passionate encounter they might feel self-conscious. Instead they were comfortable and at ease with each other. As if they had been together for a long time.

She learned very little about him. His parents had been dead for some time. He was staying with the family of a cousin he didn't know too well in a neighboring town, Tritown.

They window-shopped at the mall. She had never seen dresses so expensive, she had never paid much attention to fashions. Jack would examine them carefully and sometimes comment, "That would look gorgeous on you." That will be the day, she thought. They all seemed to be appropriate for somebody else.

Eventually, they met routinely at her apartment. She figured Jack couldn't afford a motel almost every night. She wasn't about to give up her newly found pleasure. Let the neighbors talk. She laughed at the thought that they would have trouble in reconciling her previous image with her present one. She never told Claire, usually the recipient of all her confidences about her new experiences.

Their casualness with each other precipitated their crisis. He would forget things in her bedroom or in her living room. One day she couldn't resist looking through some papers he had left behind—just a glance. She hadn't planned to read the missive. But she felt compelled to read it once she saw what it was about. He had been offered a job in California. Her fear of losing him had not been an illusion. She was crushed and her whole day was ruined. She hadn't even realized she loved him.

Dealing with her newfound tragedy was more than she could face. She had been just a sexual toy of a male predator. It was worse than being ignored, as she had been until then. Searing pain filled all of her being. She hurriedly called Mrs. Lockworth who must have sensed her anguish. Yes, she could find a substitute for two weeks.

Atlantic City had been just the place to hide in. The drabness of the boardwalk brought her little pleasure. The wind was still too cold. The roulette table brought her no thrills. The shows didn't distract her. There was only one factor to boost her spirits. The dresses she had bought after Jack had admired them, gained her interested looks from several men. She even went out with one of them, but her mind was not on any of that. In a sense, running away had been a waste of time.

A month went by. Gene had not gotten over her torment. Yet, her world had changed. Men seemed to be interested in her.

She and Claire had just parted after shopping at the Horbeck Mall, a habit she had acquired when she was going with Jack, when the unexpected happened. She found herself facing Jack. Flight was impossible, she stood rooted where she was, overwhelmed by anguish. Jack seemed as surprised as she was. His face showed concern and sadness. After a few seconds of silence the words escaped from his lips.

"I thought you loved me!"

Gene didn't know what to say. She was paralyzed.

"You're the only woman I ever cared for! What happened?"

The faintness that overwhelmed her must have shown because Jack grasped her elbow and gently led her to where they could sit down.

"I'm sorry. You don't have to explain. I didn't own you."

They sat silently before she could put words together.

"Weren't you going to go to California without telling me?"

"I don't know what gave you that idea. That would make no sense. Our whole contingent is going to be shipped out again to Iraq in another week. I was just trying to see what opportunities I'll have when I get out."

She remembered then that she had learned from Claire that their tour of duty had been extended. Her whole body started trembling. She felt defeated, useless. Just a bag of insecurities. She expected anger on his part. But that's not what happened. He took her hand and led her to where they could speak more freely.

"Look," he said, "perhaps it was a good thing that this happened. Now we know exactly what we feel about each other."

It took a while for her to relax but then she felt a golden warmth fill her. She was sorry, of course, that he'd have to leave her to go to war for a second time with all its dangers and uncertainties. She would have thought that his scars would have exempted him, but then this war was strange in more ways than one.

LIFE IS BUT A CRAP GAME

You never know what life will offer you,
like the throw of dice in a crap game.

A few days after her sixteenth birthday, Emma left home without ever looking back. Buses ran frequently and she had enough money to buy a ticket to the metropolis and survive for a few weeks. Her livelihood soon came from the streets from men who had a weakness for the young. The rules of the game were quickly learned from careful observation on her part. And what difference did it make? She had to make a living somehow. And how did it differ from being overcome by your stepfather in your own bed and having a mother who preferred to ignore what might shake up her existence? In her new life Emma became Delilah. She thought the change might help men's imaginations. Her shorts and her shapely legs served her well.

She learned to skirt certain areas. Some were territories of other women. Some were favored by the police. One of the girls, Laura, had accompanied her to see movies but that didn't last. They got into arguments about trivial matters, which made their relationship unpleasant. Emma couldn't find companionship with any of the other women. Many of them depended on drugs for their entertainment. Keeping her wits about her seemed to be too important to be sacrificed for questionable pleasure. Surprisingly, reading fiction filled some of her need. She had avoided reading of any kind when in school.

When winter came, it cut into her income considerably. Until spring she made a point of frequenting bars that wouldn't throw her out.

Emma had no real regrets. Yet a world that had never been hers occasionally flashed through her mind. A happy world with no worries, with a promise of a happy and comfortable future and with caring and protective parents. Her imagination even constructed a person blessed by these gifts, the imaginary Clarisse, named after one of her friends in kindergarten. Her own silent laughter would quickly erase these unrealistic thoughts.

She hadn't expected to be taken over by a pimp. He went by the name of Beaut. The absurdity of the name would have made her laugh, if she could have. Confiding in him had been a mistake. Confined and cruelly beaten, she eventually consented to be part of his flock. He was a tall man of color, fancily dressed in colorful clothes. Daily, he would collect his dues and. leave her with a miserly one tenth of the take. Actually, it was another man who came along to collect, a Mr. Bollomy. He'd find her on the specified corner or at the entrance of the subway if it rained. Mr. Bollomy was an old black man. Because of his pronounced limp, she could see him coming from a distance even in the uneven lights of the city's nights. His wrinkled face was not unkind but he obviously carried out his duties mechanically and didn't want to talk to the girls.

Emma hadn't been humiliated into complete submission as had some of the other girls; she still had some pride left. Obviously, she had to get out of her predicament. Before Beaut had made his appearance she had started a savings account at the Marine Bank. But her savings were very meager. Even at one hundred dollars a pop, her share would only be about one hundred dollars a night. Soon she started keeping more than the ten percent she was allowed. Her initiative cost her another beating. Fortunately, this one time it left her face intact. This was a special favor and a mark of his kindness, Beaut assured her. He wouldn't be so restrained the next time. It cost Emma a whole two weeks of work. For a while she thought she had a broken rib, but that turned out not to be the case.

That event made what followed inevitable. She noticed the hunting knife in its scabbard on the belt of a client. She always had an eye out for trouble, ready to call Moe, Beaut's muscle-bound guardian of the peace, who hung around close to the hallway. But the client didn't seem to be dangerous. His cowboy hat and boots revealed that the knife was part of some silly fantasy, as many of the men had. An idea buzzed through her head as they lay naked on the bed. No, he wasn't willing to part with knife instead of the hundred dollars. It didn't matter. By then she was standing and had the naked blade in her hands.

"Come and get it then."

At first the man was amused, his ruddy face breaking into a smile. Then furious. Then a chuckle escaped from his lips and he started getting dressed. Emma had no illusions. If he got too close she would lose. But her eyes never left him and even though naked her determined expression must have shown him that she meant business.

She didn't know exactly what would be her next step. She knew where Beaut hung out when he wasn't on the prowl. When he was leaving she stuck the knife in him. A man in his profession must always be ready, she guessed. He didn't seem badly hurt and took a swipe at her. Trying to avoid him she found refuge in his apartment, a dead end. She stood resolute with the knife in front of her.

Beaut's cruel smile was terrifying, as if he was looking forward to some fun. His hand on his flank, blood seeped between his finger; it couldn't be much of a wound. She had hoped to incapacitate him.

"So, that's it. You want to croak."

Emma believed that was what was going to happen and froze in horror. The man was twice her size, all muscle, and she had already tasted his power. The knife would not be enough protection.

Beaut advanced slowly. There was no reason to hurry. When Emma judged him too close, her knife flashed forward. The monster grabbed her wrist and twisted her arm behind her back. The knife landed noisily on the floor. The pain was excruciating. A rumble of laughter emanated from his lips.

"A ho is just a ho! A cunt is only a cunt!"

Suddenly his hands were around her neck, squeezing. He wasn't going to make it quick or easy. Gasping, she thought she was suffocating. She didn't hear the commotion behind her, but Beaut must have.

"Wait a minute, Beaut."

"Mind your own bees-wax, Victor!"

"Oh, but it is my business."

"This is serious and you ain't going to change my mind. I'll do it with no witnesses around."

"I'm looking for one of your ladies. This one seems to be perfect if she can speak right."

Emma felt the hands on her neck slacken their hold and then was thrown to the floor. Beaut wasn't deflected.

"I'll trade you. Two of my beauties for this one."

"You know you don't mean that. I'm saving you lots of trouble."

The man was very tall, at least as seen from her prone position. He was dressed in casual clothes, the kind that cost a lot, that seemed to shout "playboy, playboy!" But his expression was that of a man capable of violence. Even all her experience with men she couldn't fathom what he was about.

"What's your name?"

"Delilah," she croaked. The name must have seemed absurd to the man, Victor, who chuckled and then smiled.

"Where do you come from?"

"None of your business." Her voice was now more firm and convincing, and Victor laughed again. Victor seemed to be in control. Emma wondered who he was. Not a policeman. Could he possibly be one of Beaut's associates or bosses?

"How do you feel about making good money?"

She thought for a few moments. He didn't seem to be a pimp. If he were, she was about to make a big mistake.

"As long as it's not whoring."

"Do I look like a punk?"

Emma expected some response from Beaut but he remained silent. She shook her head.

"Okay. Then fix up your clothing and come with me."

One week later she still didn't know for sure what her new job was. Victor called her Delly and insisted that she get a whole new wardrobe for which he paid. The choices were difficult for her and his suggestions generally predominated. The prices were outrageous but then it really didn't matter since she wasn't paying. The first few times the stores they entered were intimidating but somehow she got accustomed to them and even came to enjoy their elegance and glitz.

Out in the country he taught her to shoot. The handgun was very ominous. Victor laughed.

"Just a precaution, my dear!"

The grass had been cut and there was a band of trees away from the road. The chirping of birds didn't reassure her. They walked toward the trees.

Her hand trembled when she was handed the weapon. The recoil when she shot for the first time was a bad surprise. But when she'd tried enough times, she learned to hit the targets, small cans. They would jump and land as deformed wrecks. Finally Victor was satisfied. There was a whole slew of learning that had to be done. How to take the gun apart. How to oil it. How to hide it in your clothing.

Victor was more predictable in other ways. As a visitor to her apartment, he made it clear what he wanted. Emma had expected it, knowing men as she did. He didn't treat her like a whore but more like a fancy mistress. He rarely spoke to her for any length of time but was always gentle. She tried her best to simulate passion. She thought it might be important. Well, at least it was a step forward. Certainly he was very free with his money and expected her to spend lavishly. Her savings account gained some ground.

Returning from a shopping trip, the jingling of the telephone jarred her from her complacency. The instrument was always silent unless Victor wanted something from her.

Her life had forever marked her a pessimist. Her mind was always ready to receive news that would put an end to her good times. Without greetings, Victor's clipped tones instructed her to go to an apartment not too far from hers. And that was the beginning of the next phase in her life.

She entered without knocking, as instructed. There were three men in the apartment. Their looks hardly reassured her. They barely cast a glance in her direction and had the hardened looks and the empty stares she had seen only in men she deemed dangerous. The quarters were bare. The windows were curtained and the light subdued. There were only chairs and a refrigerator. The walls were painted a strange shade of light gray or blue. Two of the men were smoking. One with dark hair and a complexion that showed encounters with juvenile eruption was sipping a can of beer. She sat down trying to attract little attention. There was only silence. All and all, it didn't look very promising for her—she had a dark premonition. Then the door opened. Victor took charge immediately. He obviously expected to be the boss. He sat down and sighed.

"I have recruited you for your skills. Starting today we have work to do."

She was supposed to visit the largest jewelry store in town: a well-dressed teenager, there to pick a ring that her uncle had promised her for her eighteenth birthday. She had to be charming but not showy. What Victor wanted were the details of the layout, the number of salesmen or salesladies, accessibility of the backdoor and evidence of a possible alarm system. Emma got the idea of what was coming down and something with the solidity of a brick settled in her stomach. If she had interrogated Victor earlier perhaps she could have found a means of escaping her fate. Now she didn't have any choice. Her knowledge of how the world functioned told her that there were no means of escape and sooner or later she'd pay for her involvement. She felt as if she was watched all the time and didn't dare make a phone call that would block Victor's raid. Why she felt as she did was not clear to her.

One of the men, the one with the bad complexion, dropped her a few blocks from the target. The jewelry store was a marvel of sparkle and lights. She wished she was on one of the shopping trips. But the knot in her stomach didn't allow her to enjoy what she was seeing. She also knew that failure on her part would bring more than a beating. She examined the rings carefully and expressed her delight at their design. The salesman was a tall well dressed man in dark clothes. Clean-shaven he looked like an aged all-American boy. He smiled at her and congratulated her on her good taste.

"I'll have to come back with my uncle! He'll be delighted!"

She did come back but wasn't allowed out of the car because she might be recognized. One of the men, Al, she had heard him called, saturnine and unshaven, remained at the wheel of the double-parked car. The other three entered the store and spread out, one blocking the back exit. It was all over very quickly and a good deal of the cash and jewelry made it into the leather sacks the men were holding. Everything was efficient and quick. Emma felt that they must have done it before. They came out of the front door and two of the men jumped into the car. Victor hesitated at the door, turned around and shot. An unfortunate salesman crumpled to the floor. The sudden report startled her. She was sure the man was the one whom she had dealt with during her visit. It felt as if the poor man had been a friend. She couldn't understand why Victor would do something like that. There had been no need. Faint and nauseous, the sour taste of vomit invaded her mouth. Al leaned over. "The slut we had before couldn't take it either. Victor got rid of her." Emma knew what the words meant when they referred to a witness to a murder. She pulled herself together. "Fuck you," she was able to say with conviction. The car, for a moment blocked by traffic, came quickly to life and roared away. They never returned to the apartment where they had first met.

The next time the routine was much the same but in an entirely different neighborhood. Just before her reconnaissance, she had a chance to slip into a bar. As far as she could tell nobody had followed her. With shaking hands she slipped her quarter into the pay phone. Dialing 911 she reported the planned raid and ran away as quickly as she could. She had read that the pinpointing of a call was very quick. She had to wait before going to the jewelry store until her hands stopped shaking. Her defection, she was aware, could easily cost her her life. Equally possible, the police could ignore it, considering it a hoax. After all she hadn't provided the date or time of the raid-simply because she didn't know them.

Like the first one, this raid was quick and efficient. She regretted that there was no police intervention. First bracing herself for a sudden onset of violence, she found herself relaxing when Victor quickly boarded the car without a final shot.

Unease and worry kept gnawing at her. The falling body of the man in jewelry store kept plaguing her mind. She felt that Victor's ways were despicable and something warned her that she would end up either in jail or in the morgue. She no longer enjoyed her shopping trips and remained in her apartment terrified that she would receive another telephone call from Victor. It was fortunate that he didn't stop in for his usual pleasures. He would have detected something was wrong. She knew the time had come for her to disappear. Going to the police didn't seem a good alternative. She didn't know where Victor lived or even his full name. Her record wasn't exactly spotless—her reconnoitering was for the commission of a crime.

Time to pack and go. At the bank, she exchanged most of her money for travelers' checks. Only a few of her good dresses would fit into the small suitcase she'd bought. The handgun Victor had given her was there in plain sight among the garments to be left behind. Should she take it? Obviously the need for firearms was over. She'd never participate in one of Victor's raids again. Reluctant to leave it behind, however, she hid it in the suitcase under the clothes. Another worry invaded her thoughts. Could Victor be having her watched? Perhaps Al had planted a seed of suspicion in Victor's mind.

She preferred the bus terminal to the airport. Flying had not been one of her past experiences. She bought a ticket for Orlando, Florida and sat down to wait for the time of departure. Sometimes it's difficult to tell whether you are seeing what you fear most or if it's an illusion. She thought she saw one of Victor' s men—the one with the bad complexion, strolling by. Her heart began beating faster. After waiting a while, she picked up her suitcase and went up the stairs as leisurely as she could. She looked around to see where she could possibly hide. At the other end of the terminal a chartered bus was about to leave. Emma joined the line of youngster, most of them with backpacks. The backpacks and her suitcase were taken and stored in the luggage compartment. After boarding she sighed with relief. There were enough seats to hide for the moment the presence of an intruder.

Before departure a young man walked down through the aisle looking at the passengers. Emma tried to turn away as if looking out of the window. Perhaps she looked like one of the other youngsters. Fortunately, she had opted for casual clothes, shorts and t-shirt, like many of the other passengers.

They made a few stops to stretch their legs. They reached their destination in the evening. The rambling buildings were a boarding school, now closed for the summer, she learned by eavesdropping. The youngsters were looking forward to sports and recreation. Her companions lugged their backpacks, the boys moving in one direction, the girls in another. Most seemed to be paired.

Emma noted one girl was searching with her eyes and seized the opportunity quickly.

"Could we room together?"

This is how she found a friend, Yvonne. Somehow, Emma found they could converse in a relaxed fashion. While emptying her backpack, her roommate kept a chatter going accompanied by laughter. Emma's responses were vague. This was the first time Yvonne had attended the camp and this is why she hadn't had a partner.

A hurried meal followed. The two girls stayed together. Emma accustomed to restaurant chains and fast food was pleasantly surprised.

The young man who had originally surveyed the passengers stopped at her table in the morning at breakfast.

"Could I have a few words with you?"

Emma knew what was coming. Fearful of what would follow, she was grateful that the confrontation and the humiliation wasn't going to be public. The man was surprisingly young. With regular features and chestnut hair he didn't seem to be angry. He accompanied her to an office and sat next to her.

"You don't belong with our group, do you?"

Emma shook her head and said nothing. For an instant she thought, this man could be handled just like the others with the most ancient and easiest of exchanges.

He smiled, "So what should we do now?"

"Could you let me stay? I have money."

"That won't be necessary. We had enough cancellations. I noticed you when you boarded the bus. You looked terrified." He let some seconds go by. "You don't have to tell me unless you want to. Let me know if you need any help. I'm the boss, Franklin Overbeck. Frank to my friends. You are?"

"Emma," she murmured.

For the first time in her life Emma found herself among frolicking youngsters close to her age. Athletics, swimming, dancing, good-natured pranks followed one another. There was a minimum of regimentation, although there was a personable counselor for each activity.

She knew that it would all come to an end soon. One night sitting outside, the half moon lighting the night, she was overcome with sadness and regret and tears filled her eyes. Suddenly Frank Overbeck was sitting next to her. Immersed in her emotions she hadn't heard him coming.

"Nothing is that bad, Emma."

She didn't answer for a while. "I guess you haven't lived enough or you wouldn't say that."

"My Grandma had Alzheimer's. There is nothing worse than that. I took care of her every day until she died. Calmed down by the spoken word, she had hope. She had fulfillment...as much as she possibly could. Nothing is completely hopeless."

Although he obviously was well intentioned, she felt like yelling at him. He leaned over and kissed her cheek, then got up and left. A frisson shook her—emotions she couldn't handle or understand.

For the next few nights she made a point of sitting in the same place. When Frank was done with his last routine he would sit with her. Usually they didn't exchange words. He'd accompany her when she returned to the dormitory. One night they were at the door of the dormitory when suddenly, two men materialized from the shadows. Emma cringed as all her fears became reality. Victor and Al pushed them into the building. She could feel the muzzle of a handgun digging into her back. In her fear she still felt relief that Frank hadn't offered any resistance which would have proven fatal. In their room Yvonne was sleeping peacefully. Victor ordered without raising his voice, "Take your stuff." Emma grabbed her clothing without any attempt to fold them. The butt of her gun intruded among her clothes.

They did the same in Frank's room and then directed Emma and Frank to where they had hidden a car. Emma was sure they intended to make both of them disappear away from the camp. They must have thought Emma was a loose cannon and Frank had had the misfortune of being with her.

"Get in," Al ordered.

Her hand wrapped around the butt of her gun under her bundle, Emma knew that it was now or never. She held back her terror. Half turning, she shot the man behind her through the clothing she was carrying. Her luck held out. The man fell without pressing the trigger of his gun. Victor behind Frank, was moving around the back of the car to reach the other side. Gun in hand, he turned in surprise, leaving an opening for Emma without endangering Frank. She imagined she was shooting at a target just as Victor himself had taught her.

The two explosions had been deafening. She found herself on her knees sobbing. It must have been Frank who took over from there. She was conscious of the police arriving but of little else.

She came to in the hospital. Frank was holding her hand.

"We'll be out of here soon. They are keeping you just for observation."

"I'm so sorry this had to happen and involve you." It took her a few moments to continue. "Please don't waste your time on me. I don't deserve it. I'm just a whore."

"Nobody is 'just' anything."

Of course she wasn't free to leave. After taking down their statements, the police took her into custody. As she was taken away, Frank smiled at her. "Don't worry too much; I'll get you a good lawyer. It will get straightened out."

The cell she was kept in couldn't have been more depressing but she was exhausted and mercifully sleep came quickly.

The following morning a woman in uniform came and brought her oatmeal. She ate it reluctantly, although it wasn't bad.

Later she was taken to an interview room. The lawyer that Frank had selected made an appearance. Emma never would have thought of him as a lawyer. He looked disreputable. Tall and bony with a narrow and long face, his pointy teeth brought to mind a barracuda. His dark suit looked as if he had slept in it. She wondered whether she wouldn't have done better with a public defender.

"I'm your attorney, Ben Berstein, if you are willing to retain me."

She would have balked, but then Frank had sent him…And she was acutely aware that she owed him. Another thought was also troubling her.

"I don't think I have enough money."

"With me it's never a question of money. Frank says you're a good person and that's enough for me. For some reason I always come out okay in the end. This way I always enjoy my work."

With that out of the way they were free to talk.

"Jail is never fun. Tell me your story."

He let her talk freely but then asked questions he had no right to ask. She was too tired and scared to hold anything back.

Berstein folded himself in the hard chair waiting to be admitted into the D.A.'s office. A personable woman came to the door with a mechanical smile. She was neat and well dressed but clearly appearance was not one of her priorities. She was the DA, not the secretary he would have suspected from her appearance.

"Come on in. I'm D.A. Remarque, Laura Remarque."

Berstein shook hands with her. "Pleased to meet you."

"You represent Emma Peroni, I take it."

"Yes, indeed."

"What brings such well-known attorney from the big city?"

Berstein chuckled. "Duty of course!"

"Don't think you can play one of your famous tricks here!" The smile took some of the bite out of the statement.

"And shocking to the opposition?"

"You've said it all."

"No, as a matter of fact, one or two were mentioned in my classes in law school."

"I didn't realize I was that old."

"Time passes quickly. But let's get down to brass tacks."

There wasn't much on which they could hold Emma. The facts were clear and Al, the survivor in the shooting, made it clear that Victor had intended to kill both Emma and Frank. Emma's role in the jewelry thefts didn't come up. Anyway, Ben Berstein was well prepared. After all she had telephoned a warning, recorded on the 911 tapes, and you could easily make a case for her having acted under a death threat.

Frank was there when she was let out.

"Frank, I told you I don't deserve your attention. I'm nothing."

"Nobody is 'nothing'". You don't even know where to go. Obviously, you mean something to me."

"I hope it's nothing special. I wasn't joking, I'm just a whore."

"You're a scared girl who has guts and never got what she deserved. Look, there is a whole spectrum of human relationships. I don't know why I'm concerned. It doesn't really matter. Perhaps you remind me of my little sister. She would have been your age by now. She died when she was ten. My parents and I were devastated."

They left together. Frank would drop her with his parents until they'll figure out what to do next.

"They'll be thrilled. They have spent much time supporting women's causes," Frank said. Emma was moved, for some reason she felt she had found her family.

ROUND THE MULBERRY BUSH

Only God knows why she had married Jack. Perhaps it was because she had known him forever. Why, they went back to having attended the same high school! They'd barely known each other then. She had been very popular and had been recognized as a bright and attractive girl, Helen. "Helen of Troy" somebody had scratched in her school yearbook. She'd appreciated the sentiment if not the scribbling on her book.

Jack was one of those boys who was invisible in the crowd. Everybody knew he was smart but that doesn't make a boy interesting. But when they met again, having left college years before and in Jack's case law school, their common past experience had brought them together.

A public defender, Jack had won a high-profile murder case, and everybody had praised his name. The indigent defendant had been rescued from the jaws of the law, basically by a clever ploy. The man's innocence was further established a year later when the actual culprit was apprehended. Jack became fashionable and very noticeable for a short while. Like a single bolt of lightning in a dark night. But that was the end of it. Helen thought it was too bad that he was courting her at that time. He seemed to be a romantic figure and he was certainly taken with her. Her mistake was thinking that he would be interesting for the rest of his life. He now seemed to concentrate on hopeless cases as a public defender turning down lucrative offers from prime firms. Helen should have known that once a bore, always a bore. One of the basic principles of life.

Their divorce didn't surprise anybody. She had asked for a Reno divorce, impatient as she was to get rid of him. Jack couldn't have loved her very much because he easily acquiesced. Helen had always suspected that he might have had a girlfriend, one of the women he worked with. As far as the divorce was concerned, there were no goodies to argue about. All the money had been hers. The fashion house she had inherited from her mother was booming. She had become recognized as the American designer to watch.

Falling into the arms of Paul Carnock had been easy. An attractive man, a man of the world, always charming, always well dressed and exuding masculinity. Basically, he had been her silent partner. She had needed capital for her expansion. In fact, they had found themselves in bed before the idea of a divorce had formed in her mind. He was as exciting there as he was in the outside world.

Ready to leave for work, she observed herself in the mirror. Her appearance, as much as her originality, was important for her work. The dress she was wearing was elegant and unique. It had the right amount of cleavage, the color a new blue-gray and its lines were sufficiently austere to bring out not only her blonde beauty but the fact that she was a serious business woman. She had designed it herself and made sure there would be no other like it for at least one year. Well before that she would discard it without regrets. Her face had acquired a few new lines lately—they were lines of worry rather than those of age. Soon she'd have to confront her anguish. With her anxiety hidden, she could fool her clients and familiars but her world was threatening to come to an end.

Paul had suddenly withdrawn his support, the ingrate.

"Look," he had said. "I have more lucrative deals to fry. They don't have the glamor of what you do, but then they don't have the yearly uncertainty either."

Helen was left with a totally innovative approach to her operation that could make or break her and two hundred grand in unbacked loans that were coming home to roost.

Forcing herself through the daily routine was not easy with her load of worry. But for the present she was able to distance herself from her troubles to do a presentable job. She looked at several drawings produced by her staff and made suggestions. She noted that Lucille who had brought her the material samples still insisted on keeping a totally unsuitable hairdo and as usual was dressed in jeans and a shapeless sweatshirt. Lucille didn't have direct contact with the customers and a boss had no right to breach an employee's privacy. She examined several samples of new fabrics. Then spoke with other employees. When she had sufficient expertise, she gave advice. When she didn't, she let her staff make the decisions. After all, they had been handpicked for their talents.

Suddenly, the feeling that she was wasting her time overcame her and she stopped. She was ignoring her real problem. She sat motionless at her desk. Thoughts and fears crowded her mind. There was one possible avenue she had been avoiding because she was too proud. But finally she decided that he extent of her quandary was such that she could humiliate herself. Her ex-husband, Jack, was at least very clever, she had to concede him that, and he might be able to come up with a possible solution. For example, her business might be able to survive a temporary bankruptcy. As time went by after the initial trauma of the divorce, the two of them had found they were no longer estranged. In fact, they had met accidentally at a restaurant a few weeks before. They had exchanged greetings, had a short conversation and they had seemed to be relaxed with each other—more like old acquaintances than a divorced couple.

Helen was not surprised that she had trouble contacting her ex. After all he was very busy and had a minimum of staff. She had to leave a message on his recording machine. But finally he'd called her back. He must have thought her call personal because he called her at home. She was reluctant to explain on the phone and they agree to meet in a coffee shop.

Jack was much better dressed than she would have expected. He was actually wearing a good suit and an attractive red tie. A new girlfriend perhaps? She had trouble getting started but finally was able to put together the facts that were troubling her. He looked at her thoughtfully.

"Two hundred grand is not a large sum."

"I have tried to get other loans but it hasn't worked out. I'm mortgaged to the limit."

"All you need is a friend financially in good standing, who would co-sign with you. You must have a friend among your many acquaintances."

"I can't really broadcast my problems. There is nothing like failure to create more failure."

"Hm! Let me think about it for a moment. How is everything else?"

She felt like crying and became impatient with him. She had humbled herself for nothing. "Well, I see you can't help."

He stopped her from getting up by holding her hand. "Whoa! Give me some time to think."

He sat there without speaking. Perhaps he had found a way of humiliating her.

"Okay, why don't I co-sign?"

"Please, give me a break! You're even more broke than I. am"

"That has nothing to do with it. You don't know my most recent develop-ment. I've joined the prestigious firm of Markowitz and Lubert."

Something must have shown in her expression because he felt compelled to explain. "I have an agreement that half of my time will go to pro-bono cases. I only half sold out!"

She wondered why she cared. Was it because being principled had been his only attraction? She felt gratitude for his offer to co-sign but she hoped he didn't think that gave him special privileges. Her opinion of members of the opposite sex was not the highest.

"You must realize that you're taking a serious risk!"

"I have complete faith in your abilities. You might have a soft core but in your calling and in business you are a tough customer."

It didn't take her long to take advantage of her new opportunity. No longer worried, now that she had solved her financial problem at least temporarily, she felt liberated, perhaps like a butterfly emerging from her cocoon. Her social life was quickly resumed although she turned down several dates. She didn't feel ready for that.

At a party she saw the woman who she thought had attracted Jack when they were still married. Helen had to concede that she was very attractive. Dark hair and a lovely complexion. A heart-shaped face and big expressive eyes. Both lawyers, Jack and Patricia had worked together for some time in his pub-lic defender days and even had to travel overnight together. The hostess intro-duced them and then went off into the crowd. Helen couldn't resist the challenge.

"Fancy meeting my ex's girlfriend." She was sorry about her pettiness as soon as the words had come out of her mouth. Patricia's dark eyes were dag-gers. She turned around and ignored her from then on.

One Saturday morning, her bell rang. She was surprised to see Patricia at her door. As soon as the door was open, Patricia didn't waste any time.

"I just want you to know that I never was and never will be Jack's girlfriend. I'm happily married."

Helen was overwhelmed with shame. How could she had been so petty? Even if it had been true she had been entirely out of line. It took her an instant to find appropriate words.

"I apologize! I was entirely out of line. Please come in."

Patricia hesitated but then came in. It took a few seconds for her expression to lose some of its belligerence. Helen felt she had to say more.

"Please forgive me. I hope I didn't cause you any problems. Rumors spread quickly."

"Not really. I don't care what people think. The only opinion I care about is that of my husband, Paul, and he knows the truth without me making any speeches. I just wanted to set the record straight."

"Can I offer you a drink or tea or coffee? I was just about to have a cup of coffee when you rang the bell."

"Coffee would be nice. My, oh my! This is quite a house you have!" Patricia allowed herself to look around. They had walked through the living room and had reached the kitchen.

Helen was quite aware how unusual her house was. She poured coffee into two cups and brought cream and sugar to the kitchen table.

"Every piece was designed by my mother. As you noted they are entirely unique. A modern version of classical lines. And all entirely practical. I love them!"

"I suppose that it's the perfect environment for a fashion designer of your reputation!"

Helen found it amazing that they could converse like old friends. For some reason they came back to Jack.

"I must confess," Patricia commented, "that I was surprised and a little insulted that Jack never showed any interest in me as a woman. But then he has some unexpected sides to him and it certainly made my life easier. I always have to be on guard in this men's world."

"Oh! But he couldn't be that different from other men! When we were married there always were unexplained absences."

"You know, his job required putting in lots of time, sometimes at peculiar times of the day or night."

"He has a small apartment downtown. His original bachelor pad. He claimed it served to isolate him from the turmoil of life. Supposedly, he also worked there without being disturbed. It would make an ideal love nest!"

"Oh, why should you care?"

"I don't know. I'm just curious. I don't believe in male virtue. Mm! Maybe I can have a look."

"I would be very surprised if you were right. And I'm a great believer in privacy. Don't do anything you might regret later."

"It can't get worse than being divorced!"

And that was pretty much the end of their conversation but not of Helen's strange curiosity. Really, why should she care? Perhaps her conviction that he had had other women had something to do with her decision to get a divorce.

She called Jack at work. He was too busy to hear her out. Her hasty claim that she needed to isolate herself from the turmoil of her work got his permission to enter the apartment.

"The super must remember you. Get a key from him."

❧   ❧   ❧

Eventually she was able to meet with Jack for dinner at a restaurant. Helen broached the topic with some trepidation.

"I have a confession to make."

"Your latest model disappointed you?"

"I'm afraid it's something much more embarrassing. I went to your retreat thinking that it must have been used as a love-nest and I would find some evidence of it. I don't know why I wanted to know."

He laughed. "You should have just asked me. You didn't find anything did you?"

"I was flabbergasted by the photographs! What is so fascinating about me? You even had a copy of the pictures that were taken for the highschool yearbook and some after our divorce."

"It's no secret that I have been in love with you most of my life...Well most of the time. I loved the girl who resigned from her sorority in highschool when they wouldn't admit an ugly and unpopular girl, or the woman who allows her employees to bring their babies to work and who set up a daycare next door at great cost, or who didn't fire a thief but transferred her to a section where she had no temptations."

Her embarrassment and surprise left her silent for a few moments. The words came out spontaneously as if they had been right at the surface. "You didn't seem to be much taken aback when I asked for a divorce."

"Appearances can be deceiving. I was devastated and angry. But then, I thought you might have been in love with Paul Carnock. And you certainly were entitled to your freedom if you wanted it. It took me a while to recover. Why are you bringing this up now? What is past is past."

"I don't know."

"Could it be that you have second thoughts?"

"I don't know. I just know that I'm very confused. If it's okay with you, I would like for us to see each other a lot. I would like us to know each other better. I certainly screwed up the first time."

"And perhaps I did too."

Jack took hold of her hand and they stared into each other's eyes. And that's how they left it, at least for a while.

TUMBLEWEED

The thought occurred to him while standing by the window. Like a tumbleweed rolled by a playful wind, life tumbles you from crisis to crisis, from one world to another.

The raindrops were coming down in fine straight lines—the outdoors dark and gray.

"God, what a dreary day to start a new life," he thought.

The trees, yet to recover from the winter, were raising their naked branches to the sky like wrinkled pleading arms. In the street, only a rare walker hurried by as if expecting a stronger downpour.

He was an ordinary man who had just broken into thirty years of life. Nothing was unusual in his appearance. Nothing distinguished him in any way. He wasn't tall and his features were far from handsome. His nose was just a little too large and the inquisitive look fixed on his face drew attention to his brown eyes. Having just moved into an apartment in a new town, he felt physically and emotionally exhausted. His surroundings as well as his new name, Randall Morgan, were unfamiliar. The walls had been painted white and looked pristine. No pictures were hung breaching the uniformity and blankness of the walls. The sealed boxes and the sparse furniture laying about contributed to the sense of impermanence.

Anything that could connect him with the past offered danger, he had been warned. But he'd had to keep a few items.

His wife, Danielle, hadn't been interested in accompanying him. "What would there be for me? All my friends are here." Including a new boyfriend, Randall had thought.

She had argued against his warning of danger, her pretty face screwed up in an unhappy grimace. "Once you're gone, the danger is gone."

Not necessarily so, he had argued unsuccessfully. The enemy may not know the sorry state of their marriage. What better intimidation tactic than to blow up a wife?

Brought back from hiding, he'd testified with a vengeance. Unexpectedly, he had found that he cared for the poor argumentative, cantankerous, disloyal woman who had been his wife. Danielle hadn't deserved such a terrible end.

Then, because his function had not ended, Randall was hidden in a more permanent mode by the US Marshals Service. He didn't feel any safer or less depressed.

Chance had played with his future. His bartending job had been meant to supplement his meager income. It had made him a marked man forever. It was one of those evenings when business at the bar was moderate. The murmur of voices. The gray expanse with subdued illumination. Randall had been wondering whether the woman at the bar was just interested in men or was actually a call girl. She was well dressed and rather attractive and didn't have the hardened look of most prostitutes. But then the variations in the sex business were endless. He had strict instructions of how to deal with them. He saw the two middle-aged men enter and distracted as he was, judged them harmless. They approached a young man sitting at a table, wearing work pants and t-shirt. The two other men wore common dark suits. The young man was drinking his second Bud purchased at the bar. Then, loud shouting and then shots and the young man laid on the floor bleeding. The two men hid their handguns. They glanced around—penetrating stares. It was all such an improbable scenario.

The characters of the drama apparently had met by chance. An old Mafia family feud, Randall was told later. Had to do more with women than with the far flung businesses of the crime fraternity. Something to do with a daughter or granddaughter. What did it matter? From then on Randall was a marked man. They hadn't found anybody else willing to testify. The police agencies, both federal and state, were delighted to be able to put two of the criminals out of business because of one careless moment where they had acted on impulse. Some of the old-timers still had too much emotion besides their cold, equally dangerous side.

The two men were tried separately. The first one was found guilty. He looked directly at Randall and passed a finger across his throat in the universal death threat. Randall was amused, what worse thing could happen than being blown to bits?

In his new world, Randall kept holed up in his apartment for a full day. He had entertained a phone call from his mentor from the Marshals Service, Louie

Gershein. Nothing to report. He couldn't explain why he had kept to himself except for quick forays into the neighborhood for unsatisfactory meals.

He spent time unpacking or just sitting around—his desire to resume his life gone. Finally he had gathered together his determination and filled the refrigerator with necessary provisions. Again he didn't leave the neighborhood, making his acquisitions in a small grocery store. He hadn't realized that such things still existed. He bought a newspaper in an attempt to forge a transition to the external world.

On the phone, Randall answered an ad and was to be interviewed for a job, restaurant manager for a chain. He could fake it like anybody else. Gershein would probably arrange for his non-existent references. He had made an appointment for the following week. They didn't seem to be in a hurry.

He had to break his pattern, start living. The modest car at the curb, a three-year-old red Toyota, had been provided by his keepers, it was supposedly his own, along with a mysteriously acquired driver's license sporting his new name. Randall finally aroused himself out of his seclusion and found the courage to go to a shopping center. The car hesitated at the start. Perhaps he shouldn't have left it at the curb so long without even running the motor. Then it coughed, its motor hummed and was ready to go. Gershein had provided him with a map of the town. Randall had no trouble finding his way. The amount of the traffic surprised him and he barely was able to avoid a truck barreling down the inner lane of the highway. The exit was easier and he sighed with relief. The huge parking lot had many openings, so he parked as close to the entrance as he could. Entering the mall, standardized music in his ears, he looked at the shops lining its innards, the fountain in the middle of a court spouting illuminated blue water interminably. Were all shopping centers made from the same mold? The glittering vulgarity was the same as what he had seen elsewhere. The shops were also the same and carried much the same merchandise he had seen before. Nevertheless, watching humanity parading through the mall gave him the feeling that he still belonged to the human race. There were all sorts of people, from the elegant to the common place. All ages. Some rushing through the corridors as if in a race. Some in leisurely pursuits or even just socializing. Not surprisingly, his eyes were attracted mostly to some of the young women. They came in all sizes and shapes. Some rounded—some long-legged with full figures, rarely flat-chested twigs. Most of them not any different from what he had observed in other malls. But now they seemed to him unapproachable.

That wasn't living of course. His mentors had suggested a job, church membership and other venues so that he'd meet new people. He wasn't sure whether he was ready for any of that. Again he found himself in the mall one Saturday afternoon. He even bought some clothes that were more to his taste than those that had been provided for him. Returning to the parking lot, he saw a little girl, perhaps three, perhaps four, crying as if she was lost. Some people turned to look at her but none of them stopped. She was wandering between the parked cars. A weeping child by herself inside a shopping mall may not be uncommon, but a parking lot held many dangers for a lost child. He looked around, her parents couldn't be too far, but he didn't see any possible candidates. Randall's recent experiences had made him very sensitive to distress. He stopped and crouched down.

"Is your mom or dad lost?"

The little girl stopped crying and bobbed her head on the affirmative. She examined him solemnly. Randall was filled with sensations he could hardly identify. Tenderness? Affection? They all seemed very improbable. He took her hand and said, "Let's go find them." She followed his initiative and they both walked hand in hand. He had seen a desk at one of the entrances labelled "Security" and that's where he was aiming for.

He was approaching the entrance when he saw a disheveled young woman accompanied two men in uniform.

"That's her! My baby!"

He was thrown forcefully to the ground and he found himself in handcuffs. Dazed and aching, he was sure his nemeses had created this diversion to get rid of him. Had he been less confused he would have been terrified.

After a short wait, a police car arrived and he was transferred to the police station. The interrogation proceeded in a special room, much like he had seen on television. Two interrogators: one civilized and one mean. The consolation was that it wasn't the danger he had first anticipated. He explained what had happened.

"The video cameras will show that you're full of shit." Randall just couldn't produce the answers that would satisfy the mean policeman who hit him repeatedly. He seemed to know how to hurt with a minimum of damage.

Randall kept saying, "Get in touch with Gershein of the US Marshals Service. The phone number is in my wallet."

Randall had to spend a night in jail. Finding himself in a smelly cage was even more depressing than the confinement of his own apartment. Although angered, he felt that eventually the matter would be resolved. Then the interrogation was resumed. Somebody must have finally called Gershein because eventually Randall was brought out of the interrogation room. He was left at his interrogator's desk without handcuffs. Before Gershein's arrival, a stocky man with heavy dark eyebrows and pale skin came by. He dropped a note to Randall's interrogator. The policeman raised his eyes in a gesture of disgust. Randall figured the missive must have something to do with the examination of the video monitors.

Randall had to wait until Gershein came to give him a ride. Nobody apologized for his treatment. Even Gershein seemed peeved.

"You had to make yourself conspicuous, didn't you? How do you think we can preserve your cover when you make yourself so obvious?"

Randall's silence was one of anger. The chiding was uncalled for and he knew that nothing could be done about his mistreatment without attracting even more attention. As he exited with Gershein, a woman suddenly jumped in front of them. He didn't have a chance to cover his face. A camera flash informed him of what had happened. The newspaper photographer had no inkling that she was putting his life in danger.

There was no question of moving again. The Witness Protection program had put enough money into his protection, Gershein informed him. The possibility that his picture, broadcast only from one local television channel, would be noticed was remote. Besides, Randall was tired of changes.

Randall went to his job interview properly dressed in a new suit—tie and all—a case of overkill. He could put on the charm and the references provided by Gershein were impeccable. The system had even manned the appropriate phones in the event his prospective employer cared to check the references by phone. After the exchange of a few pleasantries, Randall was offered a grand tour of the Black Orchid, the restaurant in question. He felt that this was a good sign. The owner was a man of about his age and Randall shared an immediate rapport. He was impressed by the man's enthusiasm and dedication to his business. In a calm moment between meals, Randall was introduced to the chef as well as the headwaiter.

When he returned home, his telephone was ringing. The voice at the other end was that of a young woman.

"I'm Sharon's mom, Joan Albright. You know, Sharon, the little girl you rescued? I'd like to thank you personally."

Randall was sure that any meeting would only bring trouble. "That won't be necessary."

"I very much would like to."

Randall tried to deflect the exchange. "How did you get my number?"

The woman chuckled. "That wasn't too hard. Your name was mentioned by the police and Channel 11. The telephone company supplied the rest of the information."

"My God," thought Randall, "now I can expect all kinds of calls."

"I really would like to talk to you. It would mean a lot to me."

Randall didn't think anything good would come of it. But how could you refuse without appearing to be a total boor?

As foolish as it seemed, he agreed to see her.

She was a small woman with a bright smile and a touch of sadness in her manner. They sat on the park bench where they had agreed to meet. People leisurely strolled along the paths. The day was clear and although the air still had a nip to it, the sun was out. Sharon was with her mom, all bundled up. Randall greeted the child with a big hello, but she gave no sign of recognition.

"That's the way of children," her mom explained. She continued, "I'm a single mom. My Carl died in Iraq last year. Some people, not too many, have been kind to me. I feel certain obligations. Besides, what happened was by in large my fault. I was at one of those stupid sales—children's clothes. I favor them because I can't afford very much. But it was stupid of me. It was more of a battle than a sale. I let go of Sharon's hand…There are so many stories of children being kidnapped. Security didn't seem to take me seriously, so I made a big fuss. I knew nothing like that had happened as soon as I saw the two of you hand-in-hand."

"Well, I don't blame you. A child is the most important thing in the world and eventually it all got straightened out."

"Could I make it up to you. Perhaps having you for dinner?"

The meals he had had so far in his new town were nothing to boast about. Besides, she seemed very pleasant. That is how it had started.

For some reason, the two of them were kindred souls. For his part Randall had never met anybody like her. It would have been hard to say what he appreciated most. Her calm and rationality. Her total lack of self-consciousness about her quiet attractiveness. He was unaccustomed to her frankness and sincerity. Falling in love with her would be easy. In fact, he suspected that he was well on his way.

But he knew he couldn't let it happen.

"Look. You don't seem to understand. I have to know. Are you interested in me or not? I'm not a youngster and I have to think about Sharon. You can't hold me in place with your cock-and-bull story about not wanting to put me in danger because you're in the Witness Protection Program. I have dealt with enough men to tell a bare-faced lie. You're just afraid of commitment. Men are such cowards."

He couldn't find a good answer. After all, even if he could prove his contentions, perhaps by involving Gershein, he still couldn't get involved. He already cared for the two too much to put them in danger. And he felt he wanted them badly. Regretfully he left after kissing both of them.

Joan closed the door after him and felt tears crowding her eyes. She suppressed her sobs. She didn't want Sharon upset.

THE SPIDER

As with most battles these days, the battle to decide the fate of the company in a takeover bid had unfolded along predictable lines. The gathering of proxies proceeded furiously with mailings, phone calls and public name-calling. Gregg, the company's CEO, had always known the outcome. But then, hidden in his defeat was a victory. The delay had allowed the triggering of the clause in the union contract establishing pensions for all employees. This is why his opponents and Gregg had fought so fiercely—several million had been at stake. Gregg had been concerned about the staff's and workers' future. In his mind, there was an unwritten obligation that he was determined to honor.

During the fight, Gregg had felt as if the whole world had been against him. His opponents in the proxy battle. Many of the shareholders, indignant about his militancy. The workers fearful of being deprived of their livelihood by a possible bankruptcy—in their perceptions not unlikely without the takeover. Only his assistant, Paula, had endured with him the tension and long hours.

To Gregg, Paula was an enigma. Why such an attractive woman stuck with him over several years was a mystery. She could have done better for herself. The debt of gratitude he had incurred was staggering, particularly since both of them at this point were surely without a job. It was probably why he had asked her to dinner at the best restaurant in town: a celebration of sorts to negate the defeat.

Preceding him as they followed the hostess, without artifice she had the grace of a ballerina which for some reason he had never noticed before. Sitting across from him, he found her dazzling. Although he had always recognized her as a woman and a very attractive woman at that, the realization dawned on him that he had never really appreciated her physical attributes. He was ogling her now, discreetly, he hoped. Usually in loose and practical clothing, for their celebration dinner she had chosen the occasion to show her best—a tightly fitting dress that emphasized her feminine attributes—perfect make-up and her chestnut hair gathered in an attractive composition.

After perusing the lengthy menu, they had ordered. The waiter had ceremoniously uncorked the chilled bottle and. the two of them partook of the champagne in little sips. Champagne is best enjoyed cold and in small doses.

Paula looked at him with an amused expression. "After all these years this is the first time you've looked at me as a woman."

Gregg was amused. "Should I apologize for my libido showing through?"

"No, you should apologize for not noticing me before."

Gregg was deeply embarrassed. "I wouldn't say that it's the first time I've noticed."

To tell the truth he didn't know how to respond to her challenge and he suddenly felt that he was in unknown territory. Inordinately fond of her, he didn't want to offend her. Yet he didn't know himself what the answer was. Luckily she intervened and laughed.

"Well, let us enjoy this moment but you must admit you owe me an explanation!"

Gregg felt himself blushing—a reaction he hadn't had since he had been a little boy.

The food was outstanding, the conversation light. Paula had a talent for satire and mimicry. The scenario she constructed had the company under new management headed by Mrs. Gold, the secretary close to retirement who thought she had a special role in issuing commands to other secretaries because of her seniority. In Paula's account, Mrs. Gold only understood precise instructions, coming directly from God, containing a version of the ten commandments stretched out by the bureaucracy to resemble most closely the constitution of the state of Texas with its hundreds of clauses and codicils covering all details of life and death on earth and beyond. The mimicry was so perfect that Gregg couldn't have kept a straight face if he'd tried.

But then their conversation followed a more serious vein. Gregg realized how little he knew of her personal life compared to the events of his life with which she was well acquainted. His failed marriage, his eight-year old daughter who he adored and saw whenever possible. And in the years just after his divorce, the hopeless affairs usually ending in nothing.

Paula didn't mind revealing her background. To believe her, she had been an all-American-girl whose greatest disappointment had been not being accepted onto the cheering squad in high school for being too flat-chested. College followed, where she was too shy to make a significant mark, although her grades said otherwise. Her proneness to disastrous romances finally led her to concentrate on a career in a man's world.

At her door it seemed unfortunate to abandon their easy going exchanges. Her invitation to go up with her was quickly accepted. With a mischievous smile she quoted, "Come with me, said the spider to the fly."

Although his feelings for her had always been very strong, they had been in a business environment. The quick transition from friendship to romance was an enormous surprise. Inevitably, at some point he took her in his arms for a light kiss which turned into a torrid embrace and they became lovers.

Stretched out on her bed with only a thin sheet covering them they spoke softly.

"I thought you were joking about the fly and the spider!"

"I have to confess that there is some truth in that saying. I have been wanting to trap you for quite some time. But why are you bringing it up? Do you have a complaint about my performance?" she asked in mock seriousness.

He chuckled. "I have to be very careful with what I say if I wish to survive. No, no, I'm quite happy with the performance. I was just wondering who was the spider and who was the fly."

"You are just lucky that I'm not a black widow. Not even a widow at that."

In the morning they showered together, but Gregg insisted on going to his apartment to shave and brush his teeth. They arranged to meet at a diner for breakfast.

Over breakfast, Gregg felt compelled to return to a topic he had been happy to avoid just a few hours before.

"We have known each other for some time but most of it hardly counted. I know and you know what a disaster office romances can be. And then we weren't always free."

"Gregg, don't let me tease you. That's all I was doing! What was, was and what is now is now."

"Tease me all you want. But some things have to be talked about. I realized you weren't somebody for a casual dalliance. And when I first knew you I had just emerged from my disastrous marriage and divorce. I think I got over that mess just last night." To his embarrassment he managed again to blush.

"Look, I have a similar story to tell. I became interested in you only recently. Before that, in my mind you were a good friend but as a man a definite risk. At the company picnic you were so distraught about the little kid disappearing and so relieved when he was found in the family car, of all places, that I saw for the first time that you were somebody who was capable of caring more than about figures and balances. I have been in love with you just for a few months. Yes, you don't have to look surprised. I hid it very well. I was just biding my time as we spiders are so good at."

TIT FOR TAT

Harmony Falls was a small dusty town. It certainly wasn't harmonious and there were no waterfalls anywhere to be seen, just a dry riverbed full of stones. Cooper sized up the town at a glance as he stepped off the stagecoach. The full sunlight of a bright day made him flinch. A hotel, three bars on one main dirt road. Some alleys and stables. A jail. A bank. One church and cemetery perched on a hill. In the air the smell of cattle and horse droppings. The heat of the day presaged discomfort.

He couldn't be too particular. This was as far as his finances could carry him. He wondered what name he'd go by. He preferred to be called Coop by his friends—if he had any friends left. He figured Cooper was common enough even if he didn't want to be recognized. Harmony Falls was remote enough from his previous world.

He'd have to figure out where to stay although there didn't seem to be many choices. Then the next thing was to relieve himself and then get something into his protesting stomach. Although tired and achy from the long trip, he'd have to take care of his immediate needs and figure out what he could do for a living.

He had had long conversations with a travelling companion, Bunion Wells, who also alighted in Harmony Falls. He was a Nosy Parker and Coop had had to avoid giving too many answers which might have revealed his past. Coop was alone without friend or foe, except with his luck he would likely develop an enemy soon enough.

He lifted his carpet-bag and entered the hotel. The bag contained a change of clothes, a derringer and a Colt six-shooter in a holster and boxes of cartridges for both. He had acquired them after he'd realized he had to be on the run. It seemed he could wear the Colt at his side—everybody else in Harmony

Falls did. The derringer was just a flight of fancy. He was sure it was too ineffective to be of any use. Not that he was planning to use either gun.

The hotel entrance was pretty bare. He had to announce his presence with a yell. A little middle-aged man with a bald pate, incongruous pink cheeks and sparse gray beard strands came out. The transaction didn't take long. A few dollars exchanged hands.

"You're lucky," said the little man "if the court was in session you would have to share a bed." Then with a sneer. "One time we had the defense attorney, the prosecutor and the judge in the same bed!"

Coop entered the dining room if such a little dumpy room could pass for an eating establishment. There were other men present, all in western attire but Coop didn't pay too much attention to them. His mind was on other things. The steak didn't taste bad but was as tough as leather. The baked potato was overcooked. But who was he to complain?

It had been a long time since he had had to earn a living. When in his teens he had run away from his Uncle George's house and joined a circus. There were several horses, two elephants, a zebra, a lion and a tiger. He found the animals and their training fascinating. Circus life was a hard but in many ways exciting. *Dante the Magician* had taken him in. He only let Coop do tricks that he himself couldn't handle any more, such as the disappearing act where Coop had to climb out through a small hole into a hidden compartment. Dante did teach him card and conjuring tricks and allowed him to practice sleights of hand for hours on end during the evening. Of course that wasn't all. Whenever the circus moved, Coop had to help with taking apart or setting up the big tent—moving heavy equipment and the planks and supports that served as seats. An exhausting life. These were all tasks and skills that in his present situation wouldn't be at all useful. Yet he certainly wasn't ready to turn himself into a cowboy and he was left with essentially no alternatives.

When Coop was still a teenager, Uncle George, a small gray-haired man with a little beard and an unhappy countenance, had traced him. "Listen my boy. We have disagreed in the past about most things. You're my only living relative. There is nobody else I can leave my money to. Nobody else that can take care of me in my old age. Nobody else that I could care for. I would like you to stay with me again."

Coop learned to live with his uncle. For some reason he didn't find him as difficult to take as he had when he was younger and more rebellious. Coop had quickly learned about instruments, investments, commerce, good business practices. None of those of any help now, either.

✦   ✦   ✦

Evading one predicament by escaping to Harmony Falls, Coop found himself in another. The man, Coop heard him called Herb, had decided to perse-
cute him. Why, Coop had no way of knowing. Herb hung around the bar and
gambling joints. Dressed entirely in black, Herb was big and threatening. His
gun was known to have killed more than once. Besides a naturally bellicose
nature, rumor reputed him to be a hired killer. He had just returned from a
trip carrying out a task which most observers in town considered to have had a
violent theme.

"How can he get away with killing. Don't we have a sheriff?" Coop had
enquired. Simple, he was told, Herb would provoke a fight time and time
again. His fists were powerful and if the object of his attention could be drawn
into a quarrel, his speed with a gun was fatal. The altercation could be about a
woman, cheating at cards or anything at all.

Herb made a point of making derogatory remarks about Coop whenever
they were in the same place, usually where they played cards. He particularly
took issue with Coop's clothing, more suited for a minister than a real man.
Coop never answered. He had persisted in wearing a frock-coat and eschewed
western garb for no particular reason. But once it became a bone of contention, he could hardly do anything different.

Coop approached the sheriff. A tall, bald man with a gray handlebar mous-
tache. He didn't seem too concerned about Coop's quandary. "I can do nothing until something happens. He's never committed a crime. He is always the
second one to draw. You don't like it: leave town." Coop suspected that the
sheriff didn't want to have to confront a notorious killer.

Coop befriended the owner of the hotel where he was staying—a surprisingly attractive woman despite encroaching middle-age shown by threads of
gray in her rich brown hair. Myrtle would frequently make an appearance
while he was eating and would stop at his table to chat. He probably had more
to say than the average citizen of Harmony Falls. Unfortunately she confirmed
the sheriff's diagnosis.

Coop wasn't about to accept being forced out of town. His prospects had
just started to brighten. He had begun to organize the ordering and distribu-
tion of merchandise that would arrive at the railroad head and from there
transferred into town by cart for over eighty miles. He had found it commer-
cially rewarding. Leaving was not an attractive possibility. He started practic-

ing drawing his gun from his holster as quickly as he could. Despite his previous experience with sleights of hand, which also required speed, he imagined himself hopelessly slow.

But was there any point in playing by somebody else's rules? Coop might have lost some of his previous suppleness and sense of timing—but could it all be gone? Many of the tricks he'd had to carry out for Dante also had had heavy risks. Could a gunfight be that much different?

The occasion came soon. Coop normally wouldn't have played cards in a group which included Herb, but the man inserted himself at their table.

After a while, Herb looking straight at Coop announced, "He's cheating!" The accusation was ridiculous since Coop had been steadily losing even if it was only by small amounts. Coop figured that a resolution might as well be then rather than when he was ill prepared.

Coop didn't know exactly how to proceed. Perhaps an insult would merit a gunfight. He had heard coyotes have a reputation for cowardice, although he had also heard that among Indians they had a reputation for stealth and cleverness. "Coyotes always lie," he said through clenched teeth. He had no idea whether his improvised insult would be sufficiently provocative or perhaps induce Herb to shoot him on the spot. Herb threw the whisky in his glass on Coop's face.

"I'll meet you outside." The die had been cast.

Coop knew how to move deliberately and with apparent calm while his insides were churning. Facing Herb in the street, he knew he had the advantage since Herb in order to justify Coop's murder would try to draw a fraction of a second later than Coop. Coop moved his right hand toward his Colt an instant after his left hand under his coat grasped the derringer and fired twice. For good measure Coop threw himself toward his left but no bullet materialized from Herb's half-drawn gun. The impossible had happened. Herb was down. Coop got up, replaced his firearms and flicked his hand repeatedly on his clothes to dislodge the dust. It wouldn't do any good to show how shaken he was. Killing or seriously wounding a man wasn't something he had previously considered possible. If his life hadn't been at stake, he would have avoided the whole experience. From that moment on, Coop was notorious. He was relieved that his trick hadn't been detected.

❧   ❧   ❧

As disturbing as he found the thought of treating everybody in the Golden Chariot to free whisky in celebration of Herb's defeat, it was expected. Who was he to stop merriment? Sitting next to him, Myrtle chortled. "How did you manage that, big boy?"

"My illusionist and teacher in the affairs of the world told me, 'Do the unexpected' and 'remember people are distracted enough when watching so that they see only one hand if they expect the action to come from there.'"

"You must have had a very interesting past. Nobody is supposed to ask questions. But you are making me unusually curious."

"I'm sure that after a few shots of whisky, I'll be telling you everything about my past. I haven't been with a woman in a long time. I'm sure you can be very persuasive."

Myrtle laughed again. "Try again, big boy. There are two bordellos in town. I'm sure you'll find them very accommodating."

Coop smiled, "You misunderstood my meaning completely."

"Did I?"

"Do you really want to hear a very sordid story?"

"Only if you feel you have to tell me. But don't make it too sad or I might cry."

Coop didn't know why he felt so comfortable with Myrtle. Comfortable enough to speak about the past he thought had been buried forever.

"Some of my story is as old as the hills. Some probably goes back to some Greek tragedy."

"That's what I like about you. You're so learned."

"Learned my foot. I think that under it all I'm just a chump."

There were two men vying for the same woman. For some time Coop thought Don and Laura were very close. Then quite suddenly, Laura seemed to prefer Coop. The two of them married soon after. She was a sweet and tender woman. He couldn't believe he'd been so lucky! Returning from a business trip he found Laura gone. Their bedroom was covered in blood. God knows who had killed her and taken her body away. The shock and the pain didn't allow him to think.

The police decided that Coop was the culprit. They came to arrest him. Before he could be restrained, Coop jumped through the window. At his age two floors weren't easy to clear without damage. He had learned to make such jumps in the circus but his younger joints must have been stronger then. The pain after landing he could endure and fortunately he didn't break any bones.

"You were with a circus? You're full of surprises!"

"I was very young then. Fortunately some tricks you don't forget."

There wasn't much more to tell. He knew the town and its hidden recesses like the palm of his hand. The pursuers hadn't had a chance. And then he'd found himself in Harmony Falls having abandoned a thriving business and a small fortune.

"Did you love her?"

"Yes. I still do. That's what made everything so overwhelming. Otherwise, I might have tried to fight the charges."

"There is nothing more foolish than a man in love. But I think you did the right thing by leaving. That is certainly a very sad story but you seemed to have survived well.

"My story is less interesting. The rumors seem to favor that I was a painted woman or a madam but they are very wrong. I spent my life living hand to mouth. Nevertheless I was able to save some money. I bought the hotel with a loan to support my daughter Barbara—the way she deserves. That's when I decided to send her to a fancy boarding school in the East so she won't have to subsist the way I had. These days, without an education you can't rise from the ground. It's bad enough to be a woman.

"But let's go back to your story. My dear Coop, you indeed need a woman. Let me read the tea leaves and examine the past and the future in some detail. It is of course possible that your wife was killed by person or persons unknown although it makes no sense. But it may not be the case at all. You were talking about a small fortune?"

"When my uncle died he left me his business and more than I could imagine."

Myrtle's forehead creased by thought lines. "Let's try this on for size. Laura is alive and well, possibly with Don. If you didn't have such unusual talents and an affinity for jumping from open windows, you probably would have been stretched at the end of a rope. Then your fortune would have been hers when she returned at her leisure."

Coop was rigid with shock. "That's totally absurd!"

"You might be right—after all I don't know Laura. But life has taught me many lessons. Don't forget that women see a different and much uglier world than men. In fact, since the rope didn't do its job, your trouble with Herb might come from the same source."

"How could that be possible?"

"Are your sure that no one followed you here?"

"Yes…No." Although the possibility was highly unlikely, suddenly he couldn't shake his memory of his obnoxious travel companion, Bunion Wells. "Well, it's highly unlikely."

"Unlikely is not impossible. Fortunately, this whole question can be tested easily enough."

"What do you mean?"

"If my idea is correct, if you were to die she would reappear suddenly."

"Well, thanks. So I have to die?"

"Not for real, dummy. You were talking about your illusionist teacher. Can't you fall from a horse without hurting yourself?"

"I did help with such a routine once."

"If you can do that, I can arrange for a lot of spilled blood and make you disappear in the innards of my hotel. It shouldn't be too hard to arrange for a burial in the middle of the night without a body."

"Hey! If you're right that might work. But you may be totally full of beans. And wipe that smug expression from your face. The odds still are that you're totally wrong."

❖　　　　❖　　　　❖

Coop was rather embarrassed to have to wear women's clothing to exit unnoticed from Harmony Falls. He was unable to change into masculine attire until he had reached Carson City. He was amused to see that the outfit Myrtle had chosen for him was more appropriate for a cowboy.

The first item of business when he reached town was to see his lawyer, or rather his uncle's lawyer—a canny man who quickly drew up a will in several copies. Coop left his estate half to a charity for orphans and half to Myrtle. His life thereby assured, he first went to the police with his lawyer and then home.

❖　　　　❖　　　　❖

Harmony Falls, September 17, 1889

Dear Coop,

Thank you for your letter of August 28, which just arrived. I would have given anything to see the red faces of the police department. Your description of how a sweet loving woman could suddenly turn into a vixen was not unexpected, although I'm happy to hear that she wasn't able to scratch your eyes out. I still think that giving her five thousand dollars to assure a divorce due to adultery was too much. You're just too soft.

I thank you most sincerely for your offer to partner in the hotel and provide funds for an expansion since the railroad will soon reach town. However, we would end in bed (that is the same bed) and love and business don't mix. I learned that in my past, although I relish the lovely girl that I was left with. I'm willing to accept a loan for said expansion.

If you're still rich and less prone to accidents when my Barbara (now fifteen) reaches a marriageable age, I'll gladly consider letting you court her. The rest would be up to you.

Love (in moderate amounts)

Myrtle

COUNT YOUR BLESSINGS

Mirella came running into the house, letting the screen door bang shut. The weather had been temperate and she had been allowed to play outside with her friends. What can a mother do with a little girl of ten who just ignores what you tell her? Ready to discipline the child—as if it would do any good—Celia saw the distress on her little face and held her tongue.

"What's the matter Mira?"

There was no mistaking the tears in her eyes and her mother followed Mirella who hastened up the stairs to the sanctuary of the her room. There must be a better way of mothering, Celia thought.

In Mira's bedroom she enveloped the little girl in her arms.

"What's the matter, honey?"

The tears were now accompanied by sobs and Mira said nothing for a while. Then between sobs came the words.

"She said…she said…Grandma…is a very bad woman."

"Who said that?"

"Paula."

What's that crabby little kid up to now, thought Celia.

"What would Paula know?"

The sobs had stopped.

"I told her she was a total retard and she's not my friend any more!" After a pause, "Mom, what's a harlot? What's a scandal?"

Well after all these years! Celia was amused more than upset. The little girls were intent on making her life difficult! "Some day I will explain it to you. But what do you think about Grandma Carmen?"

"I think she's super!"

"Well, then that's all that is important, isn't it?"

Mira solemnly bobbed her head in affirmation.

"One of these days Grandma will tell you her story. It's her story."

❧   ❧   ❧

As if carrying fifty thousand dollars in certificates for a delicate business deal in Albany were not enough, the instructions had been switched on him. Albert Morrison, communicating by telegraph, asked him to go to Saratoga first. Paul had to inform his associate's mistress that Morrison was unable to come and then he was to offer his services to soften the blow. Paul had seen Carmen, also known as Preciosa, only once at a party from a distance. He had judged her a real beauty, much younger than he would have expected. Dark and with very expressive eyes, Preciosa was also graceful in movement although a slight limp was noticeable. He didn't know anything about her apart from the fact that she had been an actress. How could an old coot like Morrison, and married at that, secure such a playmate? Not that Paul begrudged him. He thought too much of him for that. As curious as he was about her charms, still Paul resented his assignment, firmly believing that business was one thing and one's personal life another and the twain should never meet. He owed too much to Morrison to refuse outright.

Saratoga Springs was an unknown to Paul. Taking the waters, gambling and attending horse races, he remembered as being popular occupations there. It was favored by the scum of the earth as well as the very rich. The train he took was filled with holidaymakers and disgorged the boisterous crowd at the Saratoga station where coaches carried passengers and belongings to the Broadway hotels. Ignoring the bustle, he walked his small suitcase in hand. The direction of the carriages pointed the way and he knew the town wasn't very large.

He understood that Preciosa was staying at the Grand Union Hotel and he had used Morrison's name in the telegram making reservations there. The town looked crowded and Paul doubted he could have obtained a room otherwise. As he entered the hotel, he noticed women and men strolling by, bedecked in finery. He scoured the crowd looking for her, knowing that it was a hopeless task. He was relieved to find out that his trick, using Morrison's name, had worked and he could stay at the hotel.

The certificates were concealed in a secret compartment in his leather suitcase. He hid the sturdy cardboard pouch containing them on the underside of the table in his hotel room, securing it with tacks. For some reason he didn't trust the hotel's safe. The reputation of the town as a haven for tricksters couldn't be easily dismissed.

Morrison had insisted that he carry a Derringer. You can't carry such a large amount of money without some extra precautions, Paul was told. Although the device was small he found it uncomfortable—an unfamiliar weight where there usually was none. He was forever worrying wether it showed through his clothing or that he would accidentally drop the loaded weapon with a loud if not fatal result. He doubted its efficiency. He was more familiar with the more common Colt six-shooter and could fire it with some precision. He didn't even know whether he could handle the pea-shooter. It was a relief to entrust it the small firearm in the hidden part of the suitcase. Although not very secure he quickly forgot its existence.

The hotel's desk had informed him of Mrs. Watson room number. That was the name Preciosa used. Apparently, she wouldn't be in until later so he waited until people started sauntering into the sumptuous dining room he had scouted earlier.

A maid opened the door when he knocked gently. He identified himself as an envoy of Mr. Morrison. He was informed that Mrs. Watson was not available yet. Did he wish to return later?

When he returned and was admitted into the room, his eyes quickly confirmed his previous impression—with her dark looks she was stunning.

"What possibly could have detained him?" Paul couldn't tell whether Preciosa was angry. Her smile was bright but unrevealing.

"I really don't know. He didn't tell me."

"And what are you to do, aside from quelling my wrath?"

"Supposedly, I am to offer you my services. Perhaps make reservations, buy train tickets. Whatever would be helpful."

"I'm not a child. What I need is a dinner companion. I made reservations—I expected Albert to be here by then."

Paul was unaccustomed to escorting a beautiful woman. With her on his arm, they entered the ornate dining room. She had insisted on his changing to more formal clothing.

"Well, at least it's an improvement!" was her response when he reappeared. Apparently what was good enough for business meetings would not do for the dining room of Saratoga Springs's Grand Union Hotel. He felt conspicuous both because of the inadequacy of his apparel and the ostentatious nature of the woman he was escorting. Besides her physical attributes, the lines of her dress and its material proclaimed good and expensive taste and a well-supplied purse. He knew that eyes were following their progress to their table.

The waiter quickly took the order they had chosen from the showy menu. Paul had expected the conversation to falter. It didn't, but it took an unexpected turn.

"So, you are one of Albert's henchmen?"

"I would prefer to be called an associate."

"Well, you do his dirty work."

Paul laughed, "I wouldn't call it that! This is the first time he has asked me to do him a favor and I wouldn't call having dinner with a beautiful woman dirty work."

"But you don't approve."

"I wouldn't say that. I just don't like to mix business with personal matters."

"You don't approve of me."

"Who am I to approve or disapprove?"

"Personal matters! Albert's private life. Albert's little tart!"

"Don't be so harsh on me or yourself. I know being stood up is never a pleasure. I'm sure there is a good reason. Don't be angry, it doesn't take you anywhere and don't take it out on me!"

"I think this was a mistake after all. Perhaps you'd better leave."

Paul was hungry. His travel had prevented him from having a decent meal all day. He toyed with the idea of laughing off her dismissal. It would at least gain him a meal. But his reticence at being where he wasn't wanted, prevailed. He wondered what had caused her strange behavior. Until asked, he hadn't expected to have dinner with her but still her sudden dismissal bordered on the appalling. She would probably set people gossiping about his sudden departure, likely not what she wanted, he thought, amused.

"Well, I'll be here probably until noon tomorrow. I think I need a good night's sleep. If you need me you can find me. I'm staying at this hotel. I used Albert's name."

He got up, trying to exit in a dignified manner, feeling incredibly awkward.

That evening, he made preparations for his departure on the following day. The certificates were back in the little suitcase and the Derringer ready to be hidden at his waist. Where else could he put it? A knock on the door distracted him. He cautiously opened it a crack and then opened it wide. Mrs. Watson's maid was obviously embarrassed.

"Madam wishes to see you before you leave."

He wondered what she could possibly have in mind. It seemed to him that she had made her position clear, but he followed the maid.

Carmen opened the door eagerly.

"Oh! Thank you for coming. I really should have come to you but I was too embarrassed. I want to apologize. I was rude and frankly a bit stupid. You were just trying to be helpful to me and Albert. Let's sit down and chat for a while...unless you have to leave."

"I'm leaving tomorrow before noon but until then I'm at your disposal."

"Well! Thanks again." There was silence for a minute or so. "I wish to explain myself...No, don't stop me. I know I don't have to. But there are very few people I can confide in. The gossip is entirely wrong. I love Albert, and that's what is most important." She paused her thoughts directed inwards for a moment. "You might know the story. I was a celebrated actress—the toast of the town. I was really very good as an actress, not just attractive. Gentlemen of wealth were waiting by my dressing room. They paid tribute to me in flowers, gold and diamonds. I had several meaningless affairs. That was permitted. I wasn't considered a tart then. It all changed when the scaffolding fell on me at a rehearsal. Both my legs were horribly damaged; it was thought irreversibly. All the gentlemen who had adored me suddenly disappeared except for one. He was a shy middle-aged man who had always stayed in the background. He came by a month after my accident. He was appalled to see me immobilized. I had been turned into a circus freak by a twist of fate. He forced me to hope and took me to the Orthopedic Dispensary and Hospital. It was a very painful period and he was there for me—for the long period of treatment and then rehabilitation. We didn't become lovers for a long time after that. He was very unhappy at home. He was already supporting me financially and I didn't see why not. By then I loved him as I have never loved any man."

She stopped talking and Paul noted her eyes brimming with tears.

"Thank you for telling me all this. I feel privileged. I've never doubted that you love him. So do I for that matter, even if it is in a different way. For me, he is all the family I've ever had." Without knowing why Paul thought he had to explain himself. "You must have heard of the Truwill family. We were filthy rich. When my parents died unexpectedly, I was a totally spoiled youth and had more than anybody could ever need. It's hard to believe now, but I went through the fortune very quickly. Bad investments, heavy drinking and gambling. Albert had been a friend of my father. He found me dead drunk in a gambling joint. He had me cleaned up although he knew that anything more would have to come from me. He made a deal with me. At that time investing in cattle in the Dakota Bad Lands was the rage among the very rich. Albert owned a ranch, the *Double M*. He had been looking for a manager. If I could fill those boots until the ranch became solvent, he would finance any business enterprise I might want to start. Broke and sick with no dignity or hope left, I knew then that I had to accept or I'd be at the end of the line.

"The first year was the hardest year of my life. I could ride a horse better than most but that was about all. I had to learn the ranching business from scratch. Fortunately, the foreman was a tolerant soul, and I really wanted to learn. It took a while for the cowboys to accept me as a man. I had to work next to them, cover myself with dirt, wrestle with the cattle at branding time and go along on the roundups and the drives to the railroad with whole days and sometimes nights in the saddle. I went with the fellows to town, to their drinking holes. I never touched a drop, although sometimes I trembled with craving. A rather big and belligerent man noticed that I wasn't drinking—taunted me and poured whisky all over me. I knocked him out with a single blow. Just pure luck and a bad temper. After that I was considered one of them by one and all. I learned how to shoot a rifle and a Colt six-shooter. I went on hunting parties although I didn't care for the hunting. It was the adventure, the hardship I was after. I even killed myself a grizzly, a huge monster.

After three years I was a different person. I owe Albert a new life, a new me. I must have gained thirty pounds of muscle. Sunburned, I no longer looked like a pale and weak kid. I haven't touched whiskey or gambled since my times in the Bad Lands. On my return, Albert kept his promise, although at times I have to work for him when he has a delicate mission. And that I guess is the end of the story. In some ways not very different from yours."

Paul was amazed at the account that had poured out of him. He had never disclosed his past and inner self so thoroughly.

They sat thoughtfully for some time before Paul got up, gave her a hearty handshake and was on his way.

As terrified as Carmen was, she put up a struggle. Everything seemed to move in slow motion. She was fighting off the rag soaked in what she recognized as ether. One of the two men was trying to hold the rag on her face, while holding onto one of her arms. She hadn't cried out. She wished she had while she still had all of her strength and didn't feel dazed. Suddenly, everything moved at dizzying speed. She saw Paul's face without understanding what was happening. A quick succession of two deafening shots and the two men were down. She moved and took a deep breath of undefiled air but her legs folded under her. An arm supported her. A raucous and suffocating crowd had formed in the hallway.

"What happened?"

"Were those firecrackers?"

"Get out of the way! Can't you see the lady needs air." She felt herself lifted and after an uncomfortable conveyance was dropped in a chair in her own room. She fought back the vomit that was forming in her throat. She could still smell the ether as if it had become part of her.

Paul was on his knees in front of her. "Breath deeply. You'll be alright soon."

She felt like asking what had happened but didn't have the strength or the will. But the answer came anyway.

"Somebody doesn't like you. Two villains tried to kidnap you."

Sudden concern moved her to ask, "What happened to Martha?"

"Your maid is still out. They must have gotten to her first."

"Is she going to be alright?"

"I think so. Don't worry about her; we are taking care of her."

She felt immense relief. It didn't occur to her to ask why the two men had wanted to kidnap her or what had happened to them.

Paul opened the window. The night air was cool and pleasant and she could hear the revelry outside.

Then she heard Paul's voice, "I'm staying until Albert gets here. He should be here by noon tomorrow. Until then you'll have to put up with me."

Carmen felt that he must be smiling. For some reason she felt reassured.

Back at his home, several days later, Paul received an unsigned perfumed note. In a fine handwriting, it said "Thank you."

There was no mystery about what had happened to the two villains. One had been hurt badly by Paul's shot. The other had carried him out through the service stairs. They were never caught.

Paul opened the door to his house trying to be as quiet as possible. No point in waking up Alfred or Nellie, the live-in servant couple. Alfred would insist on being available even though Paul didn't need anything except to crawl into bed. The train trip and the arduous negotiations had been exhausting. His clothes stank of cigar smoke. Why cigars and bourbon always had to be part of negotiations he had no idea. The familiar hallway was reassuring. As usual when Paul was to come back late, the gaslight was left on. The painting of a Hudson river scene on the wall still pleased him immensely. The faint scent of feminine perfume alerted him that all was not as he expected.

Alfred, dressed punctiliously in his butler outfit, appeared silently from nowhere, confirming Paul's suspicions. He must have stayed up waiting for Paul's return.

"Good evening, sir. A Mrs. Watson arrived right after dinner. She is now in the parlor. I hope I did the right thing."

Alfred wasn't easily rattled. His capacity to act on his own was a quality Paul appreciated. Paul smiled and gave his approval. "Good evening, Alfred. You did the right thing as usual."

Whether it was the right thing to do he had no idea. He hadn't seen the lady in question for months, since their encounter in Saratoga Springs.

"I took the liberty of offering her a drink. She chose brandy. I hope that wasn't improper."

"That was fine, Alfred."

As he opened the door to the drawing room, he noted that the room was lighted and a roaring fire emanated a pleasant warmth. Both the gloom and the chill of the room had been vanquished. Alfred had thought of everything.

Preciosa turned toward him—she had been standing close to the fireplace, glass in hand. Paul was surprised at the knot forming in his throat. She was so lovely! He finally was able to greet her.

"Mrs. Watson! What a pleasure!"

"You know my real name is Carmen, or Preciosa if you're in the right mood. You don't have to be so formal."

Paul smiled. "I'll make an effort to be more spontaneous."

"You must be wondering why I'm here. I haven't seen Albert for some time. I understood he was sick. I have had no news and have been quite worried. Do you know what's going on?"

"He is ill. I haven't had any recent contact myself. I will try to find out for you. Please sit down. Perhaps we can chat for a few minutes."

There was a brief silence.

"You might wonder why I care so much. Albert is all I have. It hasn't been all waiting for him. He gave me life anew. There were also some good times. I went to Europe with him twice. The European world more often than not treated me as his companion, for a change."

"Yes. He's told me about your trips."

They spoke then of the theater scene in New York—the political corruption of the city, where who you knew was more important than what you knew in acquiring government jobs.

Although it wasn't one of his duties, Alfred saw to the horse and the carriage so that Paul could take Preciosa home. Paul knew Alfred would have found it unacceptable for his boss to carry out those tasks. But, aside from being tired, Paul wouldn't have minded. Handling horses had been part of his western experience.

❦   ❦   ❦

Two years later, at Albert's funeral, Paul spotted Carmen at the back of the church. Understandably, like himself, she couldn't be included with the family and intimates. In his own case it was because he had contributed too much to the family's welfare. Nobody likes to acknowledge a debt of so great a magnitude. Besides, none of them knew him very well. Obviously, Carmen would have been an embarrassment precisely because she had been Albert's true love in his waning years.

Dressed in black, lovely as ever with lines of sorrow on her face, she seemed immensely distraught. Wasn't it ironic that the two people who knew him best and perhaps loved him the most were left out of his family's inner circle?

Paul hardly listened to the studied eulogy that left out all that was meaningful. Albert's financial success—the acquisition riches hadn't been his great accomplishments. Benefactor of so many causes—his great heart, his concern for people was what had made him a great man.

At the end of the ceremony he hastened to reach Carmen before she disappeared.

"Paul," she said, and then hugged him and buried her face on his chest. She lifted a sad face laced with tears. "They wouldn't let me see him—take care of him. It took him a long time to die."

He felt great sympathy for her. She wasn't likely to have any meaningful emotional support. "Is anybody staying with you?"

"Just Martha."

"Come with me. You shouldn't be alone at a time like this. We can pick up Martha and a few things at your place." Carmen didn't voice any objection and joined him in the carriage. He was amused to think that neither one of them had to conform to so-called respectable behavior. They could do what was right without any second thoughts.

"You know," she explained, "I still have acquaintances from my theater days but they are not friends."

The following two weeks were the closest to what Paul thought of as domestic bliss. Still sad, Carmen would reminisce. The theater had been the only scene she'd ever known even as a small child.

"All his life Father set up the stage whenever a new play was planned. I never knew my mother. People mentioned I looked like her and like her had a fiery temperament. They thought she was Spanish from Sevilla. I don't know if that is true but it certainly helped me with my acting career. It so happened that the opera *Carmen* had just been shown in France and for some reason, the theater people decided to call me Carmen. I caught Lester Hewlitt's eye when I was sixteen. He was the heart throb at that time. Still is as far as I know. I was no match for him. I became well known quickly as an actress and his mistress. My future might have been entirely different if that hadn't happened."

There were some light moments to talk about. A recurring problem in her career had been dealing with the incredible amount of floral offerings she received every day. The problem was finally solved when she sent them to the local hospitals and hospices.

Once, somebody had sabotaged her dress at the last minute just before she was to enter the stage for a new play. With a long ribbon trailing her, Carmen had saved the day by transforming the play, an overly dramatic work, into a satire. Her performance, including pratfalls and an exaggerated strange accent, was considered by the critics to be a masterpiece of comedy. She was just conscious that she had avoided disaster.

Carmen had expected Paul to return for dinner. She had taken a few bites but was too worried to have an appetite. Now two hours later she had a hard time explaining to herself the anxiety she felt. Even Alfred, his impeccable self moving like a ghost through the house, seemed upset. It wasn't like Paul. Sure, a myriad of possible events could explain his delay. Perhaps his negotiation had taken too long and they would get a telegram explaining the circumstances of his lateness. Perhaps the train was simply very late. Surely that wasn't impossible.

She had been fretting for some time when she heard the key turn in the lock. Paul stood on the threshold. Something unexpected and powerful took possession of her. "I was so worried!" She found herself in his arms kissing him fiercely.

He responded to her kiss and looked at her bewildered.

"What is this all about?"

"I was so worried!" she said again.

Now it was his turn to do the unexpected. With her in his arms he headed for his bedroom. Alfred, discreet as always had disappeared.

The next few days were bliss for both of them. Certainly it was not something Paul had experienced before. He was therefore surprised to find her sitting in the parlor almost in tears.

"What's the matter?"

"I don't think you want to hear it. It's just that this will not do."

"What do you mean? The two of us? Our relationship? Do you mean you don't want me?" He couldn't understand.

"I want you, very badly. That's part of the problem."

"I love you too. So what's the problem?"

"Paul, I would like to be like everybody else. I would like to have a husband and children."

In his youth he had been warned about women tricking men into marriage but he rejected the thought.

"Carmen, we'll never be like everybody else no matter what. We would be rejected by polite society!"

"That's nothing new for me. I need children. I need to love and be loved. I'm thirty-two years old. I want it all now. But perhaps it's not realistic."

"You'd be taking a big chance. I've failed every woman I've ever been involved with. I had the best of intentions but I just couldn't give enough. I'm afraid of failing again."

"You are talking about your drinking and gambling days, aren't you?"

"Who's to say that I'm really changed?"

They were sitting in the her Grandparents Truwill's parlor. Grandma had knitting on her lap, Mirella now sixteen was sitting next to her.

"Well, I still wonder why those men tried to kidnap you."

"We still don't know. Perhaps they wanted money. They might have known that Grandpa was carrying a large amount of cash and they thought they could extract the money if they held me. Perhaps Mr. Morrison's wife wanted to scare me away. Perhaps somebody wanted to get even either with me or Albert. It doesn't really matter does it?"

"Well Mira, now that I have told you my story, what do you think of your Grandma Carmen now?"

"I think you had a very rough life but a very adventurous and glamorous one. Not a dull one like mine!"

"All I can say is all is well that ends well. You'll have plenty of adventures. I hope not as wrenching or scary as mine."

Somehow Mira felt more grown up than she ever was and her affection for her Grandmother now included the feeling that Carmen had also become of one of her best friends.

TWISTS AND TURNS

Alice was telling Susan about her latest divorce, her third. To Alice the world was a battleground for the war between the sexes. In that day and age proving adultery in part of the spouse was needed not only for a divorce but for a woman to have an appropriate settlement. So when the spouse was unfaithful it was a game of cat and mouse. Alice had a favorite detective agency that specialized in such matters but for her third encounter it took forever to cook his goose, as she said, although Alice used a different calendar from other mortals.

Sitting in Alice's overly ornate living room over tea and cookies, Susan chuckled sympathetically or shook her head at the appropriate moments. She had heard the story before but what are girlfriends for? Now in their middle thirties, the two of them had known each other since high school. Alice was blonde in an obtrusive and daring way. Her figure was remarkable for a woman her age. It had served her well and had made her wealthy via the three successive marriages and subsequent divorces. Why she still favored the little town rather than the lights and excitement of the big city was a mystery. Perhaps it was a case of the fish in the little pond syndrome. She certainly had no local potential rival.

In contrast, Susan was dark with remarkably expressive eyes and a figure that still turned men's heads even after three children. In the little industrial town the social divisions were fierce, but Susan had always found a way of ignoring them. Her immediate family had been as blue collar as it comes, but when little she was cute and when she had grown up, she had heard it said that her appearance was stunning. Whatever the truth was, she was regarded as something special. She thought with irony, it had made her the target of men who wanted from her more than she was ready to give. She had been quick to learn the rules of the game.

Despite a college education she was stuck in an office job in the factory. She had come to the owner, Dwight Lapasse's attention when the office manager had tried to fondle her breasts. The fool received a powerful slap in return, and his dentures flew off for several feet. Not contended with his fiasco, indignant, the man had tried to get her fired. Dwight had interviewed her. He was a hand-on boss and he fired the manager.

That wasn't the end of it. A few months later Dwight tried to date her, an experience not unfamiliar to Susan. He must have had his eyes on her for some time. She knew only too well where this was likely to lead her to. Besides an employer had too much power over an employee. She demurred without rejecting him entirely. He finally asked her with tears of frustration in his eyes. She hadn't meant to bother or hurt him and she finally condescended. If he thought this would lead them to bed, he was grossly mistaken. After a few months of dating he proposed. She examined the pros and cons before giving him an answer. Young despite his position, tall with brown hair, he was not handsome but certainly presentable. She had discovered that he was a kind and thoughtful man. He liked children and many of the things she approved of. The money was a favorable factor, although not in her list of musts. Besides, she had become very fond of him.

She became Mrs. Lapasse in a wedding that in the little town was an object of gossip and surprised exchanges. Her family was sure that she would regret the move. "Stay with your own kind" was the family motto that had been bent enough when she had decided to attend college, a family first. They were not entirely wrong. Susan felt that his wealth always stood between her and her husband. Somewhere in the back of his mind, she surmised, he never knew for sure that money hadn't played a role in her decision to marry him.

Alice knew Susan's history but nevertheless tried to have her reveal some more.

"Did you ever have to deal with a detective agency?"

A flash of mischief crossed Susan's mind. Her story was not what Alice would have expected.

Dwight was always respectful and she was sure he was in love with her as she was in love with him but somehow they were somewhat distant from each other. Susan came to suspect that he was having an affair with a girlfriend from his past.

What should she do? Follow Alice's example? That was not acceptable to her. She had never left the field without a fight. A divorce was a total defeat unless she had been convinced that their marriage was hopeless. It wasn't hard to find the evidence using Alice's detective agency. Although bad enough, the photographs the detective was able to provide were only consistent with a dalliance and not infidelity, but they suited Susan's purpose. Dwight broke down in tears when she faced him. He was not very good at deception. He told her that he wouldn't fight a divorce but that he truly loved her. What had happened was a fluke and it would never happen again. Susan had already found out that he had broken up with his paramour. Nevertheless, she placed all the photographs and negatives one by one on the coffee table in their living room.

"You know," she said, "with these I could easily become a rich woman." And then she tossed them into the fireplace where after an instant they caught fire and were devoured by the flames. "I want you and nothing else. But I want all of you and I don't want to share you."

Somehow that was the last time they had any difficulty.

Alice shook her head. Susan knew that her friend thought that she had made a mistake. But she knew better.

PAYBACK

Arthur was a big hearty fellow who laughed a lot because he thought the world was full of oddities. He had found out a long time ago that when he did something wrong "what goes around comes around." He had never done anything bad but frequently he had been thoughtless or simply stupid. He thought this basic playback rule applied to himself. He wasn't sure whether it was a general dictum valid in other people's lives.

He didn't know exactly what ill wind had started the whole unpleasant process in his life. All he knew was that he and Irma just tolerated each other. In a marriage, there is generally some disappointment when both partners have arrived at middle age with no real accomplishment to speak of. His philosophy had always been to live and let live, and he accepted what was happening.

He didn't know what had brought Irma to such extremes. First she had acquired a lover, Ike. The man wasn't much of a specimen of the human race. Thin, with sparse gray hair and a thin hooked red nose, he certainly wasn't attractive. But then Arthur wasn't in a position to judge. Arthur himself, mostly bald, with worn out skin and a substantial pot belly was not a gift from God. Furthermore, he had never tried very hard to improve his lot. Although he could still eke out a living for himself and Irma, the hardware store he had inherited was buffeted by the unfair competition of chain stores. What he liked was the interaction with people. He delighted in his ability to show them how to bypass plumbers or take care of small household problems. He also repaired small appliances and window screens. When explaining something he would expound in a style resembling a lecture. This irritated Irma no end but didn't seem to rile his customers. In exchange he was allowed by his audience to converse about anything and anybody from good-natured gossip to football games. He was considered a good guy.

Irma entered the house with Ike while Arthur was at home. Arthur thought that was too much, well past his tolerance level.

"You two get the fuck out!"

Ike pulled out a big black handgun. "You're the one who's going to depart."

Arthur wasn't sure what was going on. He decided they were trying to scare him. Maybe they wanted to relieve him of some of his money—the few thousands inherited from his Aunt Agatha.

"Don't forget that what goes around comes around."

Irma was the one who replied in anger, "You can just stop with that shit. You just imagine you have all the answers."

Ike took over again. "Get undressed and get into the bathtub."

"You are going to drown me?"

Ike hit him with the side of the handgun. "You do what I tell you or I'll blow your balls off!"

Arthur was beginning to feel scared although he still had hopes of getting out of his trouble. Irma turned the faucet on as soon as Arthur, stark naked, had sat in the bathtub.

"Hey! That's too hot!'

"In a minute you're not going to care."

Ike had a radio in his hand and Irma plugged it into an electrical outlet next to the sink. Arthur suddenly knew what they were trying to do. It was an old ploy. They thought he'd be electrocuted and Irma would inherit Aunt Agatha's money.

"That goes to show how stupid you two are. It won't work."

Ike threw the radio in the bathtub. The relay of the outlet clicked shut and nothing happened. Arthur knew that he owed his life to the State of New York which had mandated that outlets in bathrooms click shut with a sudden surge of current. The radio and part of its cord were in the bathtub and soaking wet.

Arthur forced himself to laugh and then spoke in his "lecturing voice". "That's the outlet with the relay. If you want electricity you'll have to use the other outlet on the wall. But I have to warn you it won't work either and it's dangerous." The second outlet was away from the sink and was one of the original ones in the bathroom which had been put in before the safety rule had been introduced.

Ike holding the wet radio that he had rescued from the bathtub, sneered and ordered Irma to plug it in.

The electricity from the wet radio jolted through Ike and he fell to the floor. Irma must have gotten a smaller jolt from her contact with the wet wire, but the fuse in the basement shut off the electricity in time and although stunned, she seemed to have survived. Arthur, dripping, slowly got out of the bathtub. He didn't want to slip on the wet floor. He went to the phone, called 911 and quickly slipped on his pants and shirt.

Watching them he was pretty sure Ike was dead. He figured Irma must have left fingerprints on the plug, leaving no doubt about who was responsible for what had happened.

Before the-ill fated attempt to murder him, Arthur had been tempted to lecture them on what would happen before they tried it, but he'd been sure they would have ignored him. It was a case of what goes "around comes around." He knew now that it is a universal rule.

THE NIGHT OF PAIN

Bart knew he had lost his gamble when he saw the dark shadow of two men emerge from between the cars in the parking lot. They looked massive and menacing. He'd always thought he could handle himself in a fight but he knew now that that was an illusion even if he had been faced by only one of them. Bart's kick was ignored and he was quickly slammed to the ground. The pain from heavy boots hitting him was excruciating until he finally passed out. In the instant before he'd lost consciousness he'd wondered whether he was going to survive.

In the hospital he had trouble remembering the details of the encounter. Not that the police could have done anything about it. He still ached all over. He was told that he had lost several days during which he'd been unconscious in a coma from head injuries. With his tongue he could feel several teeth missing. He had been informed that his penetrating backache signalled a damaged kidney. Although that was his most dangerous injury, several broken ribs and a broken leg were also part of the package. For some reason an old macabre joke came to his mind: "Other than that Mrs. Lincoln did you enjoy the show?" referring to the events at the Ford's Theater.

Despite the pain it didn't take long for his mind to assemble the facts. He had released evidence of fraud involving the mayor. Why beat him up? His testimony was not necessary; the evidence he had provided was all that was needed to send the man to jail for a long time. However, the beating had not been totally unexpected. He had moved to a neighboring town and his address was known to only one person.

The psychological pain was almost as sharp as the physical distress although it didn't hit him with full force right away. He had trusted Norma. He didn't know whether he had loved her too but he had been willing to share at least some of his future with her.

❦   ❦   ❦

Bart didn't know exactly why he had become involved with Norma. A small woman, her russet hair, big brown eyes and heart-shaped face gave her an elfin appearance. Bart found her appealing. She laughed at his jokes. She made it clear that she liked him. Never having finished high school, her prospects were restricted by her lack of education, but she had dreams for her future. Working as a waitress at the Luna Café, where Bart had first met her, was not unpleasant but she thought she wanted more and would have liked to move to the city with greater employment opportunities.

Bart found their uninhibited lovemaking exciting. She knew exactly where to touch him, where to caress him, where to grab him with passion. She squirmed under him, bit him and would quickly move in rhythm with him. Her moans and yells added to their exhilaration.

She was a good listener and would interject at the right moments. "You have all those documents to turn in the crooks. But these are important men. Won't that be dangerous?"

"Sure, but somebody has to do it."

❦   ❦   ❦

They had made a pact. He had judged it too dangerous from him to stay. His testimony was not needed. Norma wanted to improve her life. They'd go together. To avoid detection, she would go by plane. He'd provide the ticket and some cash which would be delivered to her on the day they were leaving. He wanted to leave as little time as possible between the purchase and the departure to lessen the chances of being discovered. He would go separately by car. They might have a man at the airport who could recognize him. He didn't have to rush. He would slide her ticket and bills under her door. Due to the weather the airplane was delayed by two hours.

❦   ❦   ❦

The bastard was like every other man she had ever dealt with. After lifting her hopes, after taking from her the loving she was so good at, Bart had left her with her life once more in shambles. Why he had lied to her, she couldn't understand. Waiting for her ticket and money, she had been overwhelmed with anxiety. The plane she was supposed to take certainly must have arrived. She kept looking at her watch. And she would have to reach the airport and go through security in record time. There was no point in waiting any longer. She had been betrayed.

She walked down the corridor, her quarter ready for the payphone. The number for City Hall was still on the wall from the time the landlord had failed to provide heat.

"That will fix the son of a bitch," she murmured. The tears came to her eyes. She had hoped. She always hoped—only to have her plans shattered.

It was only when she'd left later, to find out if they would take her back at the Luna, that she saw the envelope at the door.

❦   ❦   ❦

Bart looked up at the good-looking nurse.

"How are we doing today?"

He didn't think the question required an answer. As she injected something into his drip, his mind wandered.

We all act within a framework laid out by our life experience. Norma's had been twisted by life. He couldn't hate her even if he tried.

MURDER IN THE UPPER PENINSULA

The murder of a judge always attracts the attention of the media, particularly after the notorious murder of Judge Lefkow's husband and mother in Chicago because of her earlier ruling against the murderer.

Judge Stephen Hallway had been found shot to death in a hunting lodge he used to frequent in Michigan's Upper Peninsula. The absence of the weapon, thought to be a .38 handgun, indicated murder and not a self-inflicted shot. The death had occurred a few days before it was discovered making the investigation difficult. There are no cabins or houses next to the lodge which is in a wild area. The murder triggered a massive manhunt including the Michigan State Police and the FBI. At first, it appeared an escaped convict was involved. Marco Laurenz had broken out of jail not too far from where Hallway had been killed. Laurenz was a convicted murderer, an ideal suspect. However, no connection could be found between him and Judge Hallway. And why would such a man erase fingerprints or even kill for no apparent reason? Nothing seemed to have been taken and Hallway's car was intact in the driveway. Dirty and hungry, Laurenz was eventually apprehended. After his capture it became obvious that he hadn't been even close to the lodge. He hadn't gotten very far from the penitentiary and had hidden in a derelict hulk in the back of a farm.

The notion of the involvement of a person previously convicted by the judge was also dismissed after painstakingly examining each suspect. Many were in jail. Some had obviously been far from the Upper Peninsula at the time of the murder. One or two couldn't be traced but their offenses had been minor. The possibility had to be left open, but was considered unlikely.

Suspects with a less obvious motivation from among Judge Hallway's familiars became more prominent in the police investigation. For some reason, Jack

Artson hadn't really thought of himself as a suspect. Although he had what might have been thought of as a motive, there was no other indication that he might have been involved. He imagined that it was routine for the police to look at all possible romantic attachments and hidden motives. This is what they did, of course.

One of the facts that the police undoubtedly explored was that Jack's wife, Penny, had been having an affair with Steve Hallway; this had been discovered by Jack several months before. The whole situation had been too painful for him to face head-on. She and his little daughter, five-year-old Amanda, were the only ones that really counted in his life.

Steve had been Jack's friend since middle school and his companion in many youthful escapades. A personable fellow, he had been a dashing young-sters of great promise. When still a teenager, everybody knew that Steve was destined for greatness. He was the father of two boys who Jack cherished along with Steve's wife, Daphne. The involvement of the two spouses in an adulter-ous affair seemed impossible even though Jack knew it to be true. Daphne, of course, didn't suspect anything, he was convinced. Her love for Steve had no doubts or reservations.

Penny herself had raised the issue with Jack as she mentioned divorce, just a few days before Steve's death. Despite having known of their involvement for some time, it was just as if he had been hurt twice, the pain assailing him with increased intensity. He remembered her expression, on a familiar face that sud-denly had become that of a stranger. What she had said must have been easier to say since she appeared to now have developed nothing but contempt for her husband. It must have made it easier for her to confront the facts, he thought. How could that somber face that he had often seen full of merriment, at times with eyes full of love, express abhorrence so effectively?

The police interrogation had been rough but Jack quickly became con-vinced that they had no evidence implicating him or they would have disclosed it to strengthen their arguments. There were intimations he had been seen at the lodge, but Jack had concluded that these were just tricks—part of their interrogation technique.

Even Daphne was a suspect. Jack had hurried to her as soon as the news of Steve's death had been broadcast. Her countenance was ice. The boys had not responded to his endearments. His world had been destroyed entirely. Jack had dreaded for some time the moment Daphne would find out about Steve's infi-delity. She had been so wrapped up in her love for Steve that she was undoubtedly very vulnerable. He was sure the police had not been too kind in the questioning.

Who had killed Judge Stephen Hallway? There was no satisfactory answer. Was it his wife Daphne? His lover Penny? Or the jealous husband of Penny? Or somebody else entirely? Daphne and Penny had weak alibis but their involvement was considered highly unlikely.

❦   ❦   ❦

The nightmares still shook Jack to his core. The same nightmares at night or in the daytime: blood and daunting pale faces of the dead.

It seemed to him that his anguish over his father's death had come back after all these years to haunt him with undiminished intensity. Only eleven years old, he had found his dad dead by his own hand, blood and brain matter splattered over his desk. It had begun the most terrible period of his life. Shock, fear, guilt were intermixed. Like all boys he had occasionally driven both his parents to distraction. Was that what had pushed his father to his ultimate fate? His mother, overcome, couldn't offer any solace or support. It had taken most of his young years to come to terms with what had happened. No small role had been played by his nanny or governess of several years, Mrs. Parday, a tower of strength and common sense—a lucky break at an unfortunate time. Now there was no Mrs. Parday. Steve's death and its consequences had torn the protective sheet he had woven around himself—he felt never to be repaired.

Sometimes guilt, which he had always considered a useless commodity, overwhelmed him. What counted, he had always felt, were not the sins of the past but the promises of the future—his and of those he loved. But what future did he have now? And what if he were to be barred from his only child, Amanda? He'd have lost the only love that counted.

The hate that he had evoked made his life even harder. His own wife's hatred, her face pinched in pain, regret and loathing. Steve's widow, Daphne, was puzzled and in anguish. Who was he to have played God?

The question entertained by police and acquaintances was a natural one. Had he killed Daphne's husband, the man who had been his best friend and later his wife's lover? The common sense of the authorities said yes, but proving it was another matter. Every year the two men would go hunting together around that time and they favored the very lodge in which Steve's body had been found. But aside from the possible motive, there was nothing that proved

Jack was the killer. The car tracks had been mostly erased by the rain. Finger-prints were lacking, although their presence wouldn't have meant much since Jack had been on the site in the past. The removal of those traces confirmed that a murder had taken place. Had Jack been there? Supposedly, Jack had been roaming the countryside miles away. All that could be said with certainty was that the car he had rented had not accumulated enough mileage to take him to the Upper Peninsula. Jack himself was not very cooperative and despite his anguish he was able to keep himself together. Having an excellent lawyer also helped.

The DA, inexperienced as he was and overeager to be part of a much publi-cized case, had had the misfortune to lead the prosecution to a predictable end. He must have hoped that eventually forensic evidence would prove Jack's guilt. Instead, the accused was found not guilty. There was hardly any evidence for conviction.

The case remained unsolved. Although the murder case against Jack had fallen apart from lack of sufficient evidence, the strong smell of suspicion still lingered around him. His wife, Penny, refused to see him—a divorce was pend-ing, and Daphne refused to talk to him even on the phone.

A reporter for the *Daily Star*, Doug Taylor, had contacted him for an inter-view. With the trial ending with a not guilty verdict, what did he want? Jack could have refused to see him but that went against his grain. Somehow he had to rebuild his future, perhaps just in his own mind, although he could not see how talking to a reporter would help. How could Jack exorcize the demons that tormented him?

After receiving the unusual request by phone, Jack suspected that Taylor might have become obsessed with the case—in his mind Jack was the mur-derer who had gotten away. The news was old, well past the headlines that had stopped a few months before. Yet if he had also interviewed the stricken women, distraught and convincing in their beliefs, they could have easily per-suaded him of Jack's guilt.

Doug Taylor was not what he had expected. He was a quiet, polite man. He didn't resemble at all the stereotype of a reporter. Well dressed and groomed, he was the image of rectitude. His questions were mostly routine and rather gentle compared to the brutal police interrogation. Nevertheless, his column discussing the case was not at all favorable to Jack, from its title, "Did Jack Art-son get away with murder?" to the text which discussed evidence that had not been spotted by the police. Jack had borrowed a car from an old woman who had raised him. The short mileage on the car he had rented on the day of the murder meant nothing since there had been two cars.

However, even in his dismay, Jack didn't hate Taylor. The man had to make his living. Nevertheless the report made his life even more difficult. At work, he was asked for his resignation. After all, regardless of talent, a PR company couldn't have a possible murderer in their midst. Jack understood and made a point of saying good-by to all his work companions even if the encounters were clumsy and embarrassing. He had spent several pleasant years with them.

❦   ❦   ❦

For a long time, Jack had thought of himself as impervious to despair. After all, at a tender age despite the pain he had eventually found the strength to survive the suicide of his beloved father. Somehow, one evening he found himself in the *Rainbow Pub and Bar* as if attracted by a magnet. His office mates often spent time there before dispersing in the evening. On weekends they were not likely to appear. When he was on his unprecedented third whisky, a woman approached him at the bar and sat next to him. He thought he was past the age to attract women in search of thrills and didn't consider himself particularly attractive. Suddenly alert, he rued the fuzziness of mind that wouldn't allow him to focus on what was happening. It took him a while to figure out who she was. Sharon McCoy was in the same field as Doug Taylor except at the television end of reporting. Jack had had frequent contacts with her in the past as part of his job. With clean-cut good looks, she was considered very attractive. He should have been suspicious of her intentions but in his mind he saw the woman and not the reporter. She had always been fair to him.

"Jack, I hate to tell you this, but you look terrible!"

Jack spoke slowly to form words clearly but still slurred them."What else is new? I only had three shots."

"Well, something is troubling you and obviously you're not a drinker despite your profession."

"Ah! My much maligned profession. But I guess I'm not a drinker."

"You shouldn't let things get you down. You'd better come with me. You need somebody to talk to and a few cups of coffee."

There was no point in resisting her inducements and he allowed her to lead him to her car, her hand guiding his elbow.

Sitting in her cheerful, small kitchen he found the freshly made coffee strong. He noted that she had remained attractive despite the passage of time.

It certainly must have helped her career on television. After a while, he seemed to revive. Sharon sensed this and was ready to talk.

"Tell me what's troubling you."

"Why bother, anything I tell you wouldn't be for publication anyway."

"That's okay. You don't have to tell me anything. I'm not after a story. We have known each other for a long time, I grant you in some respects not so well, but probably better than you think. I know some essentials about you that other people might have not discovered. You don't lie and you don't play around. I have known for a long time that you're one of the few decent men in this world. I also owe you. When I was starting out, you always spoke to me kindly and at length. You gave me the courage I needed and you are the person who gave me the information that started me on my first big story. You didn't expect a reward…I didn't have to go to bed with you and you didn't even expect gratitude." And after a while, "We can just spend some time together. I'll listen if you have something you wish to tell me. Just remember I'll always be on your side."

"Everything is dark, including the fact that I lost my job. It's eating me. It's an ugly story. I'm willing to wager you'll be sorry you let me talk."

"Jack, I'm not the naive, innocent young girl you knew years ago. A reporter sees an ugly world."

"You might have wondered whether I killed Steve Hallway. I don't even know whether I could be a killer. The story started probably a long time ago, but on that day with a phone call from Steve. I was at home, alone. You might have heard that Penny left me. He told me he was at the lodge, couldn't take it anymore and was going to end it all. This was followed by what sounded like a shot. I yelled in the phone. It didn't help. Should I call the police? I just didn't know what to do. Penny had taken the car so I had to rent one. It took some time to make the arrangement. The only car I could get at that time of night was from "Rent a Clunker". It rents used cars. That was a big mistake. I was outside Pinsapoke when it stalled and the battery seemed discharged. I couldn't restart the stupid machine. I had to thumb my way into town. Fortunately, Pinsapoke is where Ellen Parday lives—an old dear. When I was a child she was my care giver. She stood between me and total despair after my father killed himself and my mother wasn't able to cope. Well, to make a long story short, I borrowed her car, also an old wreck, but one that worked. I reached the lodge after a total of three hours. Steve's car was in front. I entered with trepidations; I think my heart had jumped into my throat." Jack stopped and looked around the room without seeing anything and then continued, "He had killed himself alright. It brought back the time when I found my father dead. Again I cried like a child. The feeling of loss, guilt, despair returned just as when I was a child. I must have been motionless for a long time. I was confused. I picked up the phone but then I felt, who could I call? The police? For some reason I was reluctant to do that. Steve's wife, Daphne? My wife, Penny who had…well had been involved with him? You must have read some of the accounts of the trial. Nothing seemed to be right. I couldn't bear the idea of how Daphne and her children would be affected. I even felt sorry for Penny. Suicide is such a strong and ugly message." His mind wandered while he sipped the strong coffee.

"You must have figured out the rest. I took the gun and later disposed of it. I erased all fingerprints. I destroyed the suicide note which simply said in his own handwriting, 'I can't take it anymore.' At that time I didn't even realize that I was setting myself up for a case of murder."

Sharon insisted that he spend the night in her spare bedroom. For the first time in a long while he was able to sleep undisturbed by dreams. In the morning, he was greeted by the smell of coffee, bacon and eggs. Sharon enveloped by a robe greeted him cheerfully.

"I have to leave pretty soon. I have to cover the Boston marathon with my people. But I want to say something. But eat first, then you can take a shower. I already have and I'm ready to leave."

Jack attacked the breakfast with enthusiasm. He knew that even if only temporary he had found a psychological shelter. Sharon waited to speak until he was finished.

"It's none of my business. Feel free to tell me to drop dead if you resent what I'm saying. I can't take seriously your getting fired. You can't keep down talent in your line of work and you'll find something soon. It seems to me that the key to your survival is Penny and Amanda. You'll have to tell Penny what happened. I'm sure it will hurt her but it can't be avoided. Hallway probably couldn't handle simultaneously, the affair and his marriage he cared for so much. But Penny should find out what really happened. And you need to get your relationship on some kind of solid ground. You have your daughter and her future to think about."

Jack grunted and was unable to say anything. He knew she was right but he didn't know whether he'd have the courage to carry out her suggestion.

On the phone, Penny refused to see him.

"Penny, our future and that of Amanda depends on us talking and there are other considerations as well. You must have heard that I lost my job. We have to figure out what to do to survive financially."

At the door Penny was somber. In anticipation of fireworks, Amanda had been sent to stay with Penny's parents. He had been denied even the pleasure of seeing her. Giving his little daughter a hug and receiving her unconditional love would have meant a lot to him.

Penny didn't say anything. Dressed in black slacks and a dark blouse, she left the door open, proceeded to the living room and sat down. She seemed to have aged in the short while since he had seen her last. Her short brown hair was in disorder, the way he hadn't seen in a long time. Jack followed and sat at a distance.

"I really have to tell you what happened. I don't know whether you'll believe me. I'm not following any particular agenda. I don't know where our conversation will lead us. Believe it or not, I was holding back the facts because they will hurt you. But I think we have to face facts or eventually suffer even more."

Jack proceeded to tell his story.

Penny listened until he was finished without a change of expression. Then her face became contorted, "You bastard! Get out!"

Jack left without looking back. He didn't know whether she had believed him or not. All he knew was that he had failed miserably in making contact with another human being.

He walked and walked as if it could distance him from the darkness. Well, Sharon had been wrong and he couldn't see what awaited him except pain and monsters roaming his mind and not ever giving him peace.

When he finally returned to the little apartment he had rented, the emptiness depressed him even further. There was nothing except for the bed, one chair and a phone with an answering machine attached. The answering machine light was blinking. He wanted to ignore it. He had enough troubles. But something pulled him toward it. Penny's voice reached him. He had to play the tape twice before he understood what she was saying.

"I'm sorry! You're right, we have to talk. Give me some time. It just hit me very hard. I think you told me the truth and I do feel like shit."

Jack sat down on the bed. There was some hope left in life yet, he decided. Two persons who had been close could still talk to each other rationally even after they had been torn apart.

PLAYING CHESS WITH THE DEVIL

Chapter 1

Alone, Karen was stretched out in bed, the fingers of her hands interlaced behind her head, her thoughts just drifting in reverie, her eyes staring into space. The sun, bright in the spring morning, was only partially kept out by the heavy curtains she had drawn. The chirping of birds was easy to ignore when her rambling thoughts dominated.

She knew she was privileged. The youngest of four sisters and one brother, nobody expected her to have a steady function. Before they had left the fold, Annie or Abigail, her two oldest sisters, might have asked her to help—setting the table, or cutting cloth or preparing something in the kitchen—but most tasks were carried out by servants. The two beloved sisters had married in the fall in a double marriage ceremony. Karen missed them. That left only Margaret, Meg, one year older. The two sisters had an ambiguous relationship. Known far and wide as the two pretty young Framingham girls, they were friends yet had been rivals for attention all of their lives.

Karen simply wasn't satisfied with her role in life. She had completed her stint in finishing school in the city—French, Italian, manners and social graces were hardly satisfying. To her father's indulgent amusement, she had been considered somewhat of an unwelcome challenge at Mlle. Esperance's school. Now at home, horses, card games and entertaining guests just wasn't enough. Occasionally, of course, theater and balls in the city enlivened her life. The summers spent at Oyster Bay or Cape Cod were also beginning to grate. What she could do while there was quite limited. The funny attire she was to wear while bathing in the sea limited movement and sailing alone was not considered proper for a woman. If she had a purpose in life, it escaped her. Supposedly, eventually she would marry, but she knew that even that would not be sufficient for her.

Her parents were quite contended with her role as the youngest pretty girl, although she really was already a woman, eighteen years old. It was time she was taken seriously. Why, she had already gone through the coming of age ritual, the debutante ball at the Fifth Avenue Hotel in New York City! She and her retinue had had to travel all the way from their estate at Arrowsmith. Fortunately, the private train compartment was comfortable. As they usually did when on an excursion to the city, they'd spent the night at their *pied-à-terre* as Father called their modest city house.

Everything had had to be just right for that grand occasion. They all had fussed about her dress and even more about her manners. She was supposedly 'flighty'. That's what they called her tendency to call a spade a spade. Well, she'd been asked to dance more than she would have wished. Her shoes hurt, she later explained untruthfully to her intimates. She had to admit that she had never looked so attractive, with her light brown hair—the mauve chiffon for some reason brought out the clarity of her complexion and the violet of her eyes.

That excursion into the external world had led to her first and so far only courtship. Handsome and rather sweet, Albert was terribly boring. He was supposed to be a great catch. Polo, card games, hunting and his days at Harvard dominated his conversation. His visits at Arrowsmith soon stopped. She must have been 'flighty' again, she considered with a chuckle. Couldn't blame him for stopping his visits as he'd had to travel some distance to be met by a most ambiguous reception. After that, Karen had to withstand the extensive reproaches of her mother and sisters. Father was just amused.

The guy her brother Robert had brought home for a weekend visit, Judd Holloway, was at least intriguing, although she wasn't sure whether she liked him. Apparently he and Robert were fellow students at Columbia College, but not in the same class. Not handsome, he nonetheless definitely was an attractive male presence. With receding auburn hair, moderately tall and muscular, he didn't correspond to the image of Karen's dreams. Although not supercilious, he had an air that seemed to proclaim that he was a man satisfied with himself. To top it off, the twinkle in his dark eyes had a way of surfacing at the most unexpected moments.

Judd had a disturbing way of fomenting and then enjoying disputations. Perhaps that's why he wasn't boring, like every other man Karen knew. He had argued at the dinner table, disturbing the serenity of the ritual. Occasionally, he would glance at her as if he were testing her reactions. The twinkle in his eyes didn't help. She hoped nobody had noticed that under his covert scrutiny, she was blushing. He had argued that women should be well educated in colleges just as Columbia's president had been advocating. There were already some newly formed women's colleges such as the Mount Holyoke Seminary, the Wellesley Female Seminary and Smith College.

"Why in the world would women want to waste time in such institutions?" Bernie, one of their guests, had taken issue. Bernie was the son of family friends of long standing. One of Robert's contemporaries, he was considered by the family to be the informal suitor of Margaret. Karen thought that she saw a silent nod in her father's countenance accepting the latter argument. She knew that Father made a point of not intervening into discussions of the young. Mother remained unresponsive. As usual, she didn't express an opinion in public unless asked and nothing changed in her benevolent expression. Karen wondered whether she might have not been listening.

"Why shouldn't education be as important for a woman as it is for a man?" Judd asked.

"Oh! Come on! You know the answer to that. A woman will get married and have a man take care of her."

"What a novel idea!" Judd's amused sarcasm had been unmistakable. After a brief interruption he continued, "A woman can make a contribution to a marriage aside from her reproductive role and raising children. Look at the case of Abigail Adams. Her ability to run a farm when John wasn't there, as well as her sound advice to her husband are well known."

"Come on! That was an exceptional case!"

It was time for Karen to intervene. "Does that make the rest of us of the female sex, nitwits?"

Bernie blushed to the roots of his dark hair. "You know that's not what I meant."

Judd wouldn't let go. "One of these days women will be able to vote. They should be as well informed as the men."

"Do you mean that you agree with those insane troublemakers in the Suffragette movement?" Robert hadn't had the good sense to stay out of the argument.

Judd seemed much amused. "That's another question entirely. Mark my word, eventually they will have the vote."

Somehow the argument was not continued. Karen couldn't remember exactly how or why.

It was on another visit, this time with just Robert and herself present when Judd had espoused the organization of the Iroquois Federation. Not only had it heavily influenced the American Constitution defining a federal government, but in some ways it had surpassed it with the prominent role of women, the universal vote and essentially the distinction of town meetings now so cherished by the New England states. It wasn't that he had dominated the conversation. He politely listened to what Karen or Robert had to say and was impressed with Karen's linguistic accomplishments—she could read and speak French and Italian. It was simply that Judd's opinions, even if politely and carefully stated, were so outrageous that they stuck in her mind.

In time, Karen learned more about the mysterious Mr. Judd Holloway and found him even more intriguing. Although she was not an eavesdropper, a good deal of information came her way, through the air, so to speak. When servants were not present, conversations in the family were rarely guarded and sometimes in the heat of the moment the voices were raised. Father was talking to Robert in his son's bedroom a few doors away from Karen's.

"I'm not ever going to tell you who your friends should be. You're a grown man. But I can tell you, your friend Judd is not welcome in this house. It's not just the nonsense he spouts. He comes from entirely the wrong background. Even if the Everetts decided to sponsor him, it's a fact that his grandfather took care of the horses on their estate and his father profiteered during the Civil War. How they got Judd into Phillips Exeter Academy is anybody's guess. And then on top of that he's a pugilist. I can't think of a more degrading occupation."

"Father, he's not a pugilist. He's a student at Columbia College. He just fought Tiger Sherman on a bet that he would last ten rounds. And he did. At fifty to one, he collected a pretty penny in bets. And that's the end of the story."

Karen had only a vague notion of what they were talking about. She had heard about bare-knuckle fights in barns or tavern courtyards which only men were allowed to witness. Some of the fighters could be hurt badly and the betting was heavy. Sometimes the police would raid the locales since the encounters were illegal.

Intrigued, Karen later tried to extract more information from her brother, who could never resist his little sister's charms.

"Karen, why do you care about how the two of us met? We are both in Columbia College!"

Begging, cajoling, finally had the desired effect. When she was little, he usually would end by saying, "You're so cute, I can't resist you." This time it was different, she had to promise never to reveal the information to a living soul. "It's no secret that I have gambled. You heard the arguments I had with Father. Well, I don't gamble any more. I got a real scare. I was with chums from college. We all drank too much. We went to this club in Water Street in the city. It's no accident that these places are called "hells". I lost a good deal of money at cards and as soused as I was I still knew that I had to stop. I'd thought a promissory note which I suggested would let me get out. But it didn't. The manager accompanied by a bruiser kept pushing me back, urging me to play some more. He wanted me to try the roulette. I was totally lost and confused. And then this guy joined us. As cold as ice. His eyes as hard as nails. I don't know how he knew me."

"'This is my friend Robert. He'll sign your chit and he is leaving right now,' he said.

"That was Judd. I only knew him by name. He had boxed some and the manager of the gambling joint and his companion knew him as 'Chopper Holloway'.

'Certainly Mr. Holloway'.

"After I signed the chit, which specified paying monthly in small amounts, Judd assisted me back to my boarding house. That night it took me a while to recover from the drinking. You won't believe the headache and torments that greeted me when I got up the following day! And I will never gamble again. I invited Judd for the weekend because I thought I owed him."

Chapter 2

The missive Karen received from Judd wasn't a total surprise. She hadn't been wrong after all—the discussion at dinner on his last visit had been, she thought, a misguided attempt to interest her. The note was dropped at the carriage house and one of the men brought it to her from there. Judd must have known from Robert of the interdiction against formal visits.

She decided to meet him at the gate as he requested for a "country frolic"—whatever that meant. He was there, manning a cabriolet drawn by a spirited horse. She accepted his hand to board the carriage with some misgivings. After all, she hardly knew him. But then she also felt that she had already made a commitment by being there and certainly his behavior toward Robert had been commendable.

She wondered what the two baskets in the carriage were for. They went some distance, they stopped and then on foot ambled into the woods. The day had been hot and she appreciated the coolness among the trees. Soon, she felt comfortable being with him.

"Was all that you said about women's education and suffrage, just to impress me?"

He laughed, "I can't deny that entirely. I certainly got your attention. But that doesn't mean that my remarks were not my thoughts on the matter. I have two sisters and I'm saddened that their chances of being happy are quite limited by the barriers the world has built around them."

Their conversation was pleasant. Judd let her steer their chat in whatever direction she wanted. He was by turns serious and at times funny. Karen was amazed at how relaxed she felt with him.

Later, they ran through the woods hand in hand, laughing like two children and carrying the baskets. At a clearing they picked strawberries. Tart and yet sweet they had an aroma all of their own. She couldn't resist popping some of them in her mouth.

Boarding the carriage again, Judd insisted on going to a farm he knew. The wooden rustic tables and benches in the yard told her that this was a place not visited by the kind of people her family would associate with. It gave her a feeling of adventure. Judd explained: the farm, mostly dairy, had found it profitable to double as a place where people could be served the very things the farm produced. A girl came and looked at Judd who simply said, "The usual!" The fresh whipped cream complemented the strawberries they had picked.

She couldn't resist inquiring, "You seem to be familiar with quite a few of nature's secrets in this neighborhood!"

"Not surprising. I grew up a few miles from here and I did a good deal of wandering when I was a kid. I grew up on the Everett estate. They have no grandchildren and they developed a liking for me."

All and all, when Judd dropped her at the entrance to her family's estate, she felt it had been an afternoon well spent.

She wondered whether this was a well rehearsed routine Judd had practiced with other women and was surprised by the stab of jealousy she felt.

Another time, he had brought some cold chicken and white wine and they lunched on a blanket he had brought with him. The two of them arranged to meet whenever he was free. He would send a note through Michelle, the maid Karen knew best. They would meet next to the estate's coach house. Their meetings were invariably pleasant.

They were together a good deal. She was surprised that nobody had noticed her change of routine. In the past, she had usually invited some acquaintance, usually a woman she had met at Mlle. Esperance's school, to spend some time with her at their Arrowsmith house.

Chapter 3

Karen rued her childish impulse. She had given in to her curiosity as well as to her resentment of the limits imposed on women. Now the crush of people, the smells of the smoke from cheap cigars and the stench of the latrine, together with the presence of the ever-used spittoons in Harry Hill's Dance Hall, sickened her. Bottles of what she presumed was whisky were frequently tipped. The hubbub of many male voices was punctuated by profanities and obscenities she could hardly understand. John Sullivan was to fight Tiger Sherman.

A fight was no place for a woman. In fact they weren't allowed in. Judd had warned her but she had dismissed his protests. Judd didn't think it was a fit place for men either, if they could avoid it. And there was always the possibility of a police raid since the fights were illegal. She had claimed that she could bribe one of the grooms to take her if Judd was unwilling. The possibility of being immediately dismissed if the escapade were discovered wouldn't have allowed any of them to do anything that daring. But her ruse had worked and under protest Judd had agreed to take her when a fight was scheduled.

The prohibition against women could be easily circumvented if she wore men's clothing—some of Robert's discarded old clothes would serve. Her hair could be tied so it wouldn't show under a cap.

Judd had insisted on darkening her face and her arms with cinders and oil.

"You are just too clean and too fair!"

Karen had fought the suggestion but when she finally gave in, the touch of his hands was pleasurable—she didn't know why. She had no idea that it had taken every bit of his strength to avoid kissing her.

When the two fighters came out, first Sullivan and then Sherman, the cheering and catcalls were deafening. Sullivan was definitely the favorite.

The men around them were openly placing bets. One disreputable looking man with strange red hat kept yelling, "Ten to one for Sullivan." Many of the spectators hastened to place their bets and received script in return. It was a totally unfamiliar world.

Karen would have hidden had there been any place to hide. Judd presence next to her, at least quieted some of her fears and revulsion. He'd touch her gently. He couldn't permit himself anything more considering her masquerade as a boy.

The make-shift ring was surrounded by heavy ropes and had a floor of rough wooden boards. Sullivan was clearly the better fighter although they were both formidable. The idea that Judd could have competed in this kind of encounter was hard for her to believe.

The match was brutal. Blow followed blow as the combatants seemed to dance away and then toward each other. The yelling of the crowd was deafening and punctuated each attack, each good punch. For some reason she hadn't expected the spectacle that assaulted her senses. Perhaps she had thought it would be more graceful and there wouldn't be any blood.

Sherman had a cut over his eye and a bloody nose after the first round. Karen was relieved by the sound of the bell. Nausea permeated her and she wasn't sure she could witness any more. Judd must have sensed her discomfort because he took her by the elbow and pushed her through the crowd, she assumed to a hidden exit.

Suddenly, all hell broke loose when men in police uniforms with bludgeons quickly surrounded the ring. With yelling and fighting behind them, Judd pushed her through the door just as a policeman was approaching, his club raised. "Run." She felt his gentle push as he put some money in her hand. She didn't dare look back to see what had happened to him. She was lucky to find a hackney a few blocks away. She flashed the money when she saw the reluctance in the driver's face. It was lucky that she had brought the keys for their Manhattan house with her, mostly thinking that she would change into reasonable attire and wash at least her face and hands before going back to Arrowsmith. She would have hated alerting the caretaker who might relay her visit to her parents.

Shame and concern for Judd dominated her thinking for the next few days. She had behaved badly! There was no way she could contact him. Until then she had never understood the expression "sweating blood", which she had heard after a groom had quieted down a horse gone wild, possibly from a sting of a wasp in its eye. A two-day old *Sun,* left in the living room by her father, had a report of a police raid on a boxing match at Harry Hill's Dance Hall with little detail but much moralizing against fights and gambling.

She was finally presented with a note from Judd. She found herself trembling as she approached the stable, the site of their rendezvous. She ran to Judd who seemed little changed except for a discoloration on one side of his face.

She found herself repeating, "I'm so sorry…so sorry."

Judd's arms enclosed her. "It was an adventure. I could have done without the twenty-dollar fine and tangling with a policeman, but it was almost fun."

She disengaged herself. "You were right. It was a horrible spectacle. I never should have talked you into it. What happened is really all my fault. I can't imagine what would have happened if the police had arrested me!"

Their meetings were interrupted when the family moved to Cape Cod for the summer. Karen didn't find it congenial because aside from entertaining and visiting acquaintances, there wasn't much she liked to do. She was allowed to return after a month. Her father left as well with the excuse that he had to tend to business. Karen suspected that he also was bored.

How Judd had found out that she had returned was a great mystery to her. But he had and it seemed as if she had never left.

He seemed interested in her experiences.

"Swimming?" She couldn't figure out what he meant.

He laughed. "Can you swim?"

"It's fun. But what do you mean?"

"Well, the Hudson is practically next door!"

"Oh no! You're not going to get me to wear those funny clothes women are condemned to wear."

"I wasn't thinking about that at all!"

"Wipe that silly grin off your mouth. You're not going to get me to shed my clothes either!"

Judd laughed, "There was nothing further from my mind! How about wearing some regular clothes a man would wear out of water. Surely you can dig up some from your brother's discarded collection as you did for our pugilistic adventure."

Karen didn't think it was fair for him to bring up that unfortunate episode.

"Don't be silly! I'm not that harebrained. You must have heard some fanciful stories about me. None of them true!"

But they did go swimming.

For some reason she was convinced she could trust him. She found a way of changing behind a bush from her bizarre man's clothing to her feminine attire.

The following week he escorted her through the woods as he had done on their first adventure together. "You have to see this. It's just the right time of day."

She was about to ask what it was, when they stepped to the edge of a meadow, a meadow of gold—a carpet of yellow flowers brightened by the sun.

"What a view!" She never would have expected a man to admire it or thought that she could admire it!

Chapter 4

Michelle had never been temperamental. But suddenly, she was unable to follow even simple instructions and would break into tears when admonished. Karen and Michelle had always been very close. Michelle was only two years older than Karen. What on earth was going on?

One day the unmistakable marks of a beating showed on her face. This could only have happened on the previous day, Michelle's day off.

Karen questioned her severely, looking at her directly, "Your boyfriend?"

Without answering Michelle broke into tears.

"Well, you can just drop him. Just don't see him any more."

It took several days for Karen to break through Michelle's reserve. She couldn't accept Karen's advice because she was with child. This was beyond Karen's experience or capacity to help. She would have taken it up with her mother, but she was afraid Michelle would be dismissed forthwith.

Karen could never understand how a woman, even one as ignorant as Michelle, could allow a man to abuse her.

The matter was resolved unexpectedly. Karen and Judd had arranged to meet by the gate close to the coach house. The late afternoon was already darkening in the early fall. The foliage of the trees, red and gold, lovely in its brilliance offered a visual delight. It was as if the majesty of the summer and early fall were saluting them with a spectacular, last minute farewell. Arriving late—her mother had engaged her in conversation—Karen saw a most disturbing scene. A bear of a man was hitting Michelle and yelling obscenities. The poor woman actually fell to the ground and painfully got up again. Karen was indignant and somewhat scared. What could she do? Her loud protests were ignored completely.

Suddenly, Judd appeared from nowhere. Stepping between the two after he had ordered the man to stop, he was himself attacked. Karen swallowed hard. The situation seemed to go from bad to worse.

Judd's movements were in a blur. Right fist followed left in a flurry of blows. The man was down with Judd towering over him.

"Don't ever come back. If I ever see you here or you beat her again, I'll come for you. If you're lucky, I'll be with the sheriff."

The man then slowly got up, turned away and ran off.

Again Judd took the initiative. "Let's take her back to the house. Maybe we should get a doctor."

"Please don't!" was Michelle's plaintive cry.

As uncomfortable as she felt about talking to a man about an intimate matter, Karen had to explain. Stepping away from Michelle, she spoke softly.

"It's not that easy. She's with child. I just don't know what to do!"

"First of all she has to be taken care of. Perhaps a doctor should see her. We might be able to keep her secret until we figure out what to do. Her family might be able to help, or we might find help either in the city or in Albany."

Michelle cried out, "Oh! Please, I don't want my mom to know!"

Judd thought he had to reply, "We...you don't have very many choices."

Michelle insisted she hadn't sustained too much damage and the situation could be ignored for the moment.

The poor woman had no family except for her mother, Kate Trovon. Judd and Karen found out where Michelle's family was from. Fortunately it was in a town on the Hudson just a few miles away. Judd proposed that the two of them try to find Mrs. Trovon.

"Judd, why should you get involved? Michelle is my responsibility."

"Well, sometimes the presence of a man is useful and we are friends, aren't we?"

He didn't have the guts to mention that on his part, what seemed to be developing was more than friendship.

The two of them went to meet Michelle's mother. The town had a main street and a row of houses on each side of the road and a dock bustling with river boats. There were two hotels and many bars. Judd had found out by asking the right questions that one of the main businesses of the town was prostitution, held as a respectable profession probably because of the money it brought to the town. He hoped he could keep that knowledge from Karen and wished they could have avoided their trip entirely.

They found Mrs. Trovon at one of the two hotels where she was working as a maid. Every aspect of the woman seemed unpleasant. Dressed in dark and ugly clothes she had a permanent scowl on her face. Karen introduced herself with a good deal of trepidation. The woman exuded antagonism.

"And what would Miss Framingham want from me?"

Karen explained the situation as gently as she could. Mrs. Trovon's hatchet face was adamant.

"She got herself into trouble. That's her problem. And the Framingham's. They should have taken better care of her. Don't bother me with this."

Judd intervened, "Some people might say that the pear never falls far from the tree."

"What do you mean by that! I'm a respectable woman!"

"We propose something very respectable. Your daughter could join you with her expenses and your time paid for."

Karen was silenced and flabbergasted. After Mrs. Trevon acquiesced without the details being settled, they left. In the carriage she found herself speaking out.

"What on earth got into you? Where are we going to find the money?"

"Well, there are two possibilities. You can discuss what's happening with your mother and see if she can take over in this matter. She seems to be a very rational woman. A servant getting into trouble is not such an unusual situation. I doubt that she would throw her out or ignore her plight."

"I'm not at all sure. She can be very intolerant for what she feels is immoral behavior."

"Good for her! But this is a bit different. I'm sure she has a heart. And it's not much money. I will be glad to provide the money if that doesn't work."

"You? Why should you? And where would you get it? Are you that rich?"

"I have a knack for making money. You must have heard about my legendary luck."

Karen imagined that he was referring to his bets on his fight with…What was his name? Tiger something. She was embarrassed to have obtained her information in a devious way and felt her face blushing fiercely. Fortunately, Judd didn't seem to notice.

Karen had to wait for her mother's return from her summer vacation. Her mother's response was a surprise after all. Karen concocted a story that she had contacted Mrs. Trevon with Robert's help. She didn't like lying, but these were not ordinary circumstances. She hadn't made up a story since she had been a little girl.

"You should have discussed this with me first. These are problems I should deal with. You should keep yourself free of these entanglements. Servants are servants. None of your concern." But her mother followed the path they had prepared.

Chapter 5

That summer and early fall had been one of the most pleasant in her life. Yet Karen had reached a decision which although essential, troubled her. She knew she had to stop seeing Judd. He was beginning to mean too much to her. It wasn't that she had detected something wrong with him or was afraid of her parents' disapproval. She simply wasn't ready. Perhaps she really wasn't as grown up as she thought.

A confrontation and the trepidation accompanying it could be avoided if she simply ceased seeing him without warning. But she felt she owed him. After all, they had been the best of friends for a while. Even avoiding a face-to-face meeting with a letter wouldn't be right.

They had met supposedly to explore the countryside on horseback. Judd was standing by his horse.

She faced him but couldn't keep her eyes on his.

"Judd, I think we should stop seeing each other."

She looked up to fathom the silence. He looked surprised. This had come out of the blue. She had expected anger. She looked into his eyes and only saw sadness and something that looked like affection. He wasn't going to make it easy for her. How could she explain her confusion? There was nobody in the whole world that she liked more than him. Couldn't he see that he was beginning to mean too much to her?

"Judd, I'm just not ready. I'm not ready for marriage. I'm not ready for anything that happens between a man and a woman. We would be heading there. I don't think we can just be friends. I'm sorry to be such an idiot and coward."

He allowed the silence to stretch out and then took her hands. "I don't think you're an idiot or a coward. What you're saying, as sad as it is, has a lot of truth in it. I'll make myself scarce. Don't forget me if you ever need me for anything. I'll always be your friend."

Tears welled in her eyes. Suddenly he kissed her on the mouth, a passionate kiss. She was too startled to respond or push him away. He jumped on the horse, waved at her and trotted away. With him gone and nobody else present, she allowed herself to cry in desperate, unexpected sobs.

Chapter 5

Four years of college had provided Karen with a world of scholarship and serious pursuits, entirely different from the one she had known. The experience was in many ways a revelation. However, she hadn't appreciated the accompanying discipline such as compulsory chapel attendance or the formality of the classes. She was considered admiringly a feisty trouble-maker by her peers, but fortunately always within the limits of acceptability. She found the challenges to her mind invigorating like nothing she had found in her life up to then.

After graduation she found herself adrift. Women were only permitted menial jobs. There were no openings for her talents or education. Yet she was driven by her need to use her God-given capabilities. She didn't care how. Fortune had favored her in such a way that work was not required for her survival.

She found the pathway she was finally forced to follow demeaning, but she had to adopt it through necessity. A woman of her class could busy herself with charitable works with impunity. Sure enough, in the instances she knew about they were merely indulgences. A way of saying, "I'm better than most. See what I do?" But Karen had something else in mind. Couldn't one actually accomplish something? There was no question in her mind that women, especially those not of her class, were often abused or abandoned to a cruel fate. Could they be given a helpful hand?

Mrs. Wholeworth was one of her mother's friends who was engaged in charitable works. Perhaps she could provide some insights. An effusive woman, she overdressed—all flowers, plumes and color, Karen had always liked her. Mrs. Wholeworth was loud, never stinted words and had her heart in the right place.

She was delighted to have the daughter of an old friend seek her advice but she was not encouraging. "When I was younger I also wanted to make a difference. Mr. Wholeworth gave me a helping hand. But I soon found out that what I was doing just scratched the surface. The number of poor people crammed into unsavory tenements and the hundreds and hundreds of abandoned children roaming the streets is truly appalling. I was happy to do what I have been doing, but I know that it doesn't amount to a hill of beans. Nobody has been worrying about the poor abandoned women! There is an evil in our society that will take generations to remedy."

Karen wasn't to be discouraged so easily. Wouldn't it be possible to set up a shelter that could solicit funds and then provide housing and benefits for abandoned women?

"Oh, my poor girl you set an impossible job for yourself! But I would be glad to do what I can to help you. I'm not completely without influence...or money, I might add."

Karen and Mrs. Wholeworth started to hatch a plan to provide shelter for women who had no place to turn to. In their campaign the aim of their effort was never made too clear. They still didn't know enough about what the obstacles and problems might be. Karen found herself very effective in extracting pledges from the very rich. After all, she was young and pretty, came from a prominent family and had Mrs. Wholeworth as a mentor! Unfortunately, it all meant that she had to attend a multitude of parties she had tried to avoid religiously in the past.

Karen had moved to the city into an impeccably above reproach boarding house for gentlewomen. Her parents had strongly opposed the move. No respectable unmarried girl of her class would abandon her family home. The argument that what was good for her brother had to be good for her wasn't acceptable. But she had stood her ground. The claim that was most persuasive was that she was of age and was to earn her living. She would be drawing a salary from the foundation once it was formed. Karen never raised the issue that her earnings couldn't possibly suffice. Her parents wouldn't consider her living without the amenities they were accustomed to.

At one of the parties, Karen saw a ghost from her past, Judd. The shock of recognition coursed through her. Her feelings were ambiguous and confusing. He had been a good friend, perhaps her first love. She wasn't quite ready to face that possibility even after all these years. Supposedly you can never forget your first love. Yet she felt like hiding from him. Reliving her past and all the emotions it could bring out was not appealing. Fortunately, he seemed to be unaware of her presence. But then, pique wrestled with her other feelings. Perhaps he hadn't even recognized her. The past might have no meaning for him. Eventually, her curiosity got the best of her. Her eyes searching for Mrs. Wholeworth found her in a deep conversation with an older man, white-haired and impeccably dressed, probably a prospective donor. As soon as the two of them parted she walked over and asked, "What is Mr. Holloway doing here?"

"You know him?"

"Not really, he was a friend of my brother." She hoped her matter-of-fact tone covered her embarrassment.

"Well, I don't know. He's one of our small contributors." After pause she continued. "He could be here on business…I sure hope not. He's with the Police Commissioner's office."

"What do you mean?"

"That's his job. Although it's rumored that he has some money from his investments in railroad stock. I wouldn't know anything about that. I can't think why anybody would do anything so menial. Police work! But still, he is a charming young man and there is no Mrs. Holloway. God knows why." The last judgement was offered with an air of disapproval that made Karen smile internally.

Chapter 6

Many of Karen's girlfriends had married right out of college, right after graduation. Karen knew that was not for her. She liked to flirt but had never reached a stage of intimacy with any man other than Judd, and that was in the distant past. It wasn't that men didn't find her attractive. Steve Lowett had been more insistent than the others. He still persisted, although she gave him little encouragement. The truth of the matter was that Karen found him immensely attractive. Handsome and facile of tongue, he could argue on any topic. Karen could not deny that she found him physically attractive, but she resented his possessiveness. For some reason he thought Karen was ready to marry him at any moment.

"Of course," he opined sententiously, "you'll have to give up the silly notion of working."

She finally said in no uncertain terms, "Look, I'm definitely not marrying you, much less give up my work."

"You're just being patronizing. What are you going to do with yourself? You know that eventually you will have to marry. I'm the man for you. I know you enjoy being with me. Don't deny it!"

Chapter 7

After Karen had left for college, her sister Meg had married her longtime boyfriend Bernard Truall. Karen had been happy for her, although she couldn't think of a duller fellow. The wedding was a memorable affair with a radiant Margaret, a well attended ceremony and partying.

They settled in a brown townhouse in Manhattan's Union Square. On schedule, a baby followed changing Meg's view of the world. Her whole universe centered on the care and well being of little Cynthia. Karen was surprised to find her sister so quickly converted into a matron. Five years later another baby, Tom, followed. Meg felt constrained and dazed with little time to herself despite the nanny, servants and sisters eager to be of help.

Meg had heard of an opera being produced at the Academy of Music, *Lucia di Lamermoor*. For some reason she became obsessed with the idea of attending. Bernie made it clear that he considered it a worthless pursuit. A respectable woman was not expected to go to such a function alone and convincing Karen to accompany her quickly became Meg's fixation.

Karen was reluctant to go. For a change she shared Bernie's view. She had heard about opera and although music pleased her, she couldn't understand how mixing theater with music could produce a pleasant experience. However, eventually she accepted the inevitable. Her sister's heart seemed so set on going!

The theater was bright and attractive. It was hard to believe that all those lights wouldn't start a conflagration. The people crowding its hallways were dressed in formal finery. In the box they shared, which isolated them from the crowd, Meg's enthusiasm was contagious and Karen became excited by the prelude. When the curtain was raised she was dazzled by the singing and realized how wrong she had been. Voices and music blended harmoniously, but she found the theme disturbing, if not entirely unfamiliar—she even understood some of the sung Italian. Women had been subject to men's unscrupulous ambitions for too long and the story resembled some of the lesser contemporary tragedies she had heard about.

The final act and arias moved her and she found tears coursing her cheeks. Whether this was because of the reenacted tragedy or the quality of the music she wasn't sure.

In the hallway while exiting after the last act, the presence of Judd facing her caught her completely by surprise. A very attractive young girl was with him. Was Judd robbing the cradle? Karen judged her to be about fifteen.

"Ah! The Framingham sisters. What a pleasure!" His broad smile signaled that he actually meant what he had just said.

Meg was quick in correcting him. "Actually, Mrs. Truall and Miss Framingham but it's certainly a pleasure to meet you here."

Judd smiled. "I'm not always up-to-date and everybody knows that socially I'm totally inept."

Karen decided not to be embarrassed by the remnants of her tears and quickly wiped them with her handkerchief.

Judd continued. "This is my little sister, Laura. I had to explain the story to her and now she's a bit embarrassed because she has been crying at the ending."

How insensitive! Just like a man! It's just what her brother would have said when she was that age, Karen thought. And was he teasing her as well? She had just wiped the traces of her tears a moment before! Her intervention was quick. "I'm always delighted to meet a kindred soul! I was crying all the way through! We both must be sensitive and perceptive."

Noting that the girl was blushing Karen couldn't resist touching her arm affectionately. "I hope we'll have a chance to talk one of these days."

They spoke for a few minutes. Karen tried hard not to look at Judd directly but found the encounter awkward. She didn't know why. In the conversation, Meg's wedding and Karen's college experience were quickly disposed of. Karen was surprised to find out that Judd knew about her association with Mrs. Wholeworth.

"A very important endeavor." He had said.

After that chance meeting Meg was full of curiosity and speculation. "Are you seeing him?"

"Don't be absurd, I haven't seen him in years. He was Bob's friend, remember?"

"He seems to know you very well. He wasn't able to take his eyes from you."

"I'm not responsible for anybody's idiosyncracies! For goodness sake. He's a man. Nobody can figure out what silly thoughts might be going through his head."

"Well, he certainly seems interested in you. If I were Steve I would be concerned."

Despite her denials Karen was not displeased by Meg's comments about Judd although she wished her sister had left Steve out of the conversation.

Karen would have liked this encounter with her past have ended there, but she hadn't counted on Meg's tenacity. Meg had organized a garden party at her house.

Fortunately, the weather was good—no rain or cold. You have to give Meg credit, she thought. The garden at her Union Square house was one tenth the size of that of their parents at Arrowhead but she had managed to make it look attractive and comfortable. The weather had conspired with her to make the party possible. There were flowers everywhere, some on the tables where guests were sitting. At least two dozen people were talking animatedly. Meg was the first person Karen saw as she entered the garden, but her smile died on her lips. She saw Steve at one table. Judd was standing not too far away talking to a woman Karen didn't know.

"Meg, you sure managed it. Steve is the last person in the world I wanted to see."

Meg was not fazed and the smile on her face didn't falter. "You should keep me *au courant* about your love life. It's a total mystery to me!" And then with a saucy smile, "At least I got Mr. Holloway here for you!"

Karen groaned. "I don't know why you're making my life so difficult!"

"I'm doing nothing that any good sister wouldn't do. I'm just trying to increase your popularity with men."

"I bet."

Her encounter with Judd was actually quite relaxed.

"I'm told you work in the Police Commissioner's office. What do you do, catch crooks?"

Judd smiled in the same way she had found so appealing years before. "Not exactly. Currently, we are trying to devise a system to choose police personnel by merit rather than by who you know. Every politician says they favor a merit system but they hate us for trying. The chances for success are minimal. Frankly, it might be a complete waste of time. But I suppose it's important to try."

Somehow she had to reciprocate by discussing her endeavors. "We really don't know exactly what needs to be done. Perhaps something along the lines of Newsboys Lodging House or the Children's Aid Society. On top of it, you can't help women unless they hear about you and are willing to accept help. We are trying to keep an open mind until we become more involved. Possibly, churches would be willing to refer clients to us."

"You'll be dealing with a cause which collides with a variety of prejudices. I wish it weren't so for your sake...or even more for the sake of the women of our city. The idea is that women belong in the home and if they are not there it must be their fault. Hard to believe, but that is what passes for thinking."

"I sure hope you're wrong!"

"So do I!"

The very few words exchanged established that the two were still close in their concerns. Somehow she felt that despite the superficiality of the contact, they had regained some of their friendship that had dissipated over the five years that had elapsed. With the exception of Mrs. Wholeworth, Karen hadn't found many truly sympathetic souls even when they contributed financially to her endeavors.

As she might have expected, their exchange in Meg's garden didn't please Steve, who must have been watching them. As she was leaving, he accosted her and managed to whisper through clenched teeth, "I see you're replacing me with that nonentity!"

Karen limited herself to glaring at him. Words wouldn't suffice.

Chapter 8

Karen hadn't expected Judd's comments to be so prescient. But there it was in black and white—an article in the *Sun*. "The Reverend Bucklerod attacks the formation of a Women's Shelter as a misguided attempt which would invite the propagation of the ways of street women!" Karen was even surprised to see such a thing in print. She knew well what the euphemism "street women" meant and realized that even the paradoxes of the English language conspired against her.

The good reverend was scheduled to present a talk on "The Decay of Virtue and Common Decency in our City". Karen didn't hesitate. She would attend the talk and accost the speaker after his talk and explain what the actual goals of their shelter would be.

Toward the end of the talk the good reverend did speak about the latest threat to virtue and decency. He actually used the word "harlotry". Then added that the search for financing was headed by a respectable and unimpeachable woman, Mrs. Wholeworth, well known for her good deeds, but obviously misguided and a young woman of dubious reputation who had a dark past and questionable morals.

Karen was flabbergasted by the personal attack. Paralyzed by shock she couldn't move even after a few innocuous questions, the audience began to leave with a scraping of chairs. She couldn't understand why the man had assailed her so viciously. He might just as well have used her name. What could possibly make him talk that way? And what did he mean exactly? From the tone of the presentation, it implied that Karen's questionable morals amounted to sexual misconduct.

Walking back to the boarding house where she was living had the quality of a nightmare; although she hardly noticed her surrounding and was surprised to eventually arrive at her room. It wasn't until the following day when anger replaced the pain she had been feeling.

This reverend was a monster, certainly not a man of God. What could she possibly do in her defense? Who would help her out of her morass? Totally exposed, she couldn't defend herself alone—surprisingly she didn't know enough about the world around her. She doubted Mrs. Wholeworth would understand what was happening—understand the malevolence of the attack and be able to offer some advice. Meg would be pained but could offer little support. She belonged to a totally different world. Karen was terrified at the notion that her parents would hear about it sooner or later. She knew they would be tormented by memories of her unconventionality and wonder whether she actually had gone too far. The irony was that she was practically without experience with men. She had allowed only Judd to get close to her in a relationship which had never developed past the bounds of simple friendship. But then he had been a good friend and now shared some of her values. For a while, even if it was so many years before, she was daunted by the fact that she had turned him away possibly unkindly. She tried to recall every word said, every nuance on his face on that unfortunate day when she had ended their friendship. Surprising, she remembered the incident well. Perhaps under his present amiability there was poison? Many men, such a Steve, couldn't stand rejection. Perhaps Judd was cut from the same cloth.

She knew that she had no choice. Judd was her only hope. She arranged to meet him at Meg's. Her concerns poured out of her as soon as she was alone with him, sitting on the same sofa. Meg had found a convenient excuse to leave them.

He looked at her with solicitude, she thought but without the level of sympathy she had hoped for.

"It's my problem. I thought you might help but you don't have to."

"Karen, don't jump to conclusions. I'm just thinking. I'm slow. I want to come up with something useful not just silly pronouncements."

Karen felt her eyes unexpectedly filling with tears and was surprised to feel his arm around her as he continued, "It might have been many years ago but we shared something priceless. I'm not about to forget it."

"You know," she felt she had to say, "except for you, I have never been involved in any way with a man. You're the only one I have even been alone with."

Judd seemed to ignore the comment. "In my past experiences I have found that attack is the best form of defense, particularly against unadulterated slander."

Relief came to her. In the back of her mind, she really hadn't been sure that he would believe her. "That's easy to say…"

"You know me better than that. This is what you should do. First, you have to talk to your parents. Let me come with you. After all I'm a protagonist in this drama. If they understand, they can get you a lawyer of repute. I have one in mind. And then you can sue for slander. The law has been fairly severe in New York."

"Oh, Judd! How can I possibly do that? I'm a woman alone, attacked by what might well become a wolf pack."

"That's why you should try what I suggest. One wolf doesn't make a pack and remember, wolf packs are not known for their courage, just for the danger they represent."

At Arrowsmith, facing her parents with Judd at her side, Karen was practically trembling. They were in the room her father was using as a study. Several comfortable chairs, a desk and a table with a few books piled on it. She couldn't tell how they were taking her story. She would give anything to have them on her side, but the account of what had actually happened was a bit unbelievable, she realized. Her father's face was expressionless. Karen was afraid of looking at her mother.

"Let me see if I understand this. Before you went off to college, you and Mr. Holloway were good friends and saw each other secretly for several months. But nothing inappropriate happened between the two of you. And you think this relationship is what the Reverend Bucklerod is probably talking about. You know there is a reason for conventions. Look how you could avoided this whole thing if you had seen each other openly. And is it really true that nothing happened?"

"Mr. Framingham, I know it's hard to believe now. But you made it clear at the time you didn't approve of me and I was taken with Karen. I don't know if that is an excuse but it is a fact. I'm not sorry for what I did. Karen's chastity, sorry if my frankness makes you shudder, is a fact. To be frank with you, I was in love with her and I didn't want to do anything that would hurt her. It might not be what most couples attracted to each other would do, but that's what we did."

"And why are you here now. What do you feel now?"

"I wasn't quite sure for a time. After all five years is a long time and people change. But as this unpleasantness started developing, I realized I still love her." After a short silence, "It's only fair to tell you that whenever this is over, I will court her as best I can and if she consents I will marry her whether you like it or not."

There was complete silence for a moment.

"At his point, I must say we would be relieved if you would take her off our hands, as much as we love her. But I have no idea whether she will accept you."

As surprised as she was with what she was hearing, Karen was relieved to hear her father chuckle. Looking up, she also saw her mother laughing.

"What do you think we should do?" her father continued.

"As I told Karen, attack is the best defense. I can't understand why this is happening but there is no need to analyze it. As you know in this unkind world it's not only Karen and her endeavors who are endangered but your family's reputation as well. I think a lawsuit for slander and defamation of character is in order. In New York state, the law has been very severe in these cases."

"Anything else you would suggest?"

"I understand Mr. Summerman is available. Your social prominence and the publicity of this lawsuit would be to his liking and he would take the case. He hasn't lost a case in a long time."

"God! Publicity is the last thing we want."

"I'm afraid that's out of your hands!"

On the train returning to the city Karen and Judd sat side by side. With their minds full of their thoughts, the clatter of the wheels on the rails and the vibrations were easily forgotten. Karen touched his arm shyly.

"If you felt that way about me why did you wait so long before saying it."

"We really weren't in the same social circle. When I heard you were back in the family fold, I thought you might be engaged to Steve Lowett. Then don't forget that I never was entirely sure of why you broke up with me."

"Judd, I really haven't been very fair to you. The least I can do is be as frank as you have been. I don't think you'll have to court me when this is over. I do love you, even if it took this mess to awaken me. I'll say yes if that's what you want then. But keep in mind that by then I might come out of this as used merchandise."

Judd put his arm around her and chuckled. "Used merchandise? Interesting analogy. For me you'll always be the young charmer so full of life whom I met so many years ago!" Judd continued, "Can I then claim that we are engaged?"

"I would have preferred to have my parents announce the engagement after all this was over, but I have no objection."

"It would allow me to participate openly in our counterattack."

They were silent after that but they both felt that something momentous had been settled between them. They held hands for the rest of the trip.

Chapter 9

A confrontation with Bucklerod occurred soon enough. The lawyer, Mr. Summerman, Judd and Karen had gone to the parish house and requested to talk to the Reverend. He refused to see them. The slight and sad looking woman at the door was clearly embarrassed.

Summerman provided the right words to open the door for them. "We are about to file a lawsuit for slander and defamation of character. Perhaps Reverend Bucklerod would like to hear what we have to say before seeing us in court."

The Reverend received them in his study where he was sitting behind a ponderous desk weighed with books and papers. Summerman introduced himself and proceeded to introduce Karen and her fiancé. The antagonism and hate in the Reverend's face was clear to them.

He opened the discourse. "You're wasting your time. I'll fight sin whenever I find it. The activities of this young lady will have nefarious consequences. If I hurt somebody from a prominent family so be it."

It was Judd who responded. "You are totally mistaken and your error will expose you and your congregation to ridicule and expense. We'll be happy to settle for a public apology and the sum of 20,000 dollars."

The Reverend had turned purple. "Of all the impudence! I have direct testimony of the behavior of this vixen. A whole summer of wanton behavior! You'd better get out of here before I have you thrown out."

Karen winced at the insult but wondered who was there to throw them out. The slight smile in Judd's face puzzled her.

"Thank you very much for your help, Reverend. It was a pleasure."

In the street it was Summerman who remonstrated. "I told you it was useless. He thinks he has instruction directly from God Himself."

Judd smiled again. His response was as arcane as his smile."Not a waste of time at all. If you were only arguing the case in court I would agree with you. But when you are playing chess with the devil you have to match him move by move."

Chapter 10

Karen was not attuned to a waiting game. She called on a rather cold Mrs. Wholeworth and told her that it was best to defer their activities for the moment. The older woman's response seemed to be a guarded relief, hidden by politeness and wishes that everything would turn out well for her cause. The parting hug was no consolation. Karen had hoped her friend would be more supportive. She was then left with time on her hands. But it wasn't totally wasted as Judd would spend most of his free time with her. Their rediscovered love made some of the waiting bearable and they had so much to learn about each other! Due to the nasty accusations they had to spend it in the public eye, usually in the boarding-house's parlor. Judd supplied her with novels and she was reading even more than when she had in college.

The Reverend had revealed some of his nasty secret. Karen's supposed indiscretions were to have happened in a single summer. Mentally surveying all the summers of her adult life, Karen and Judd had concluded that as they had originally suspected, the summer in question was the one during which the two of them had seen each other. They then tried to screen out who might be the Reverend's source of information. The stable hands were quickly discarded. That left Karen's favorite maid, Michelle. Karen would have been surprised if she was involved. She couldn't see how knowing the source of her problem would be of help. Presumably the Reverend was ready to call a witness—perhaps Michelle—when the lawsuit proceeded.

Sitting in the courtroom, Karen recognized it as a man's domain. Meg had offered to accompany her, but Karen felt that her sister was needed more by her family. If it weren't for the presence of Mr. Summerman, she would have concluded that everything was already lost. Once before Judd's presence in Harry Hill's Dance Hall had sustained her. This time, he had left to try to find out what or who had created the crisis and to see whether anything could be done. He had begun to tell her what he was going to try but she'd silenced him. "Don't tell me. It just would raise my hopes and set me up for disappointment. Let's just hope that I will be vindicated by the court."

The atmosphere of the court felt vaguely and unpleasantly familiar. The cigar smoke was not as heavy as in the Dance Hall the day of the fight but she still found it annoying. The absence of the Reverend was puzzling, although his lawyer was there—a tall sallow man with white hair who looked like respectability itself. Karen, who hadn't caught his name, thought of him as Mr. Respectability. To her dismay she was told he was reputed for his devastating punch at the end of the proceedings, where he would produce surprise witnesses with dramatic effect.

When Judge Prucent entered, all those present had to stand up. The judge in black robes addressed the audience after the noise subsided.

"Today's case is the suit of Miss Karen Framingham vs. the Reverend Bucklerod alleging Slander and Defamation of Character." He enunciated each syllable carefully. "The defendant requested that the case will be decided by the judge and not a jury as is his right. The Reverend is well known and respected, I might add." Karen thought she detected a sneer directed toward her. "Miss Framingham comes from a prominent family. This will then be a high visibility case. Hence I will not tolerate any disruption. If the noise interferes with the proceedings, whoever is responsible will be ejected immediately."

Karen felt that they had lost already. She wished Judd was there. She hoped he'd be back soon. She felt helpless without him.

The proceedings alternated between droning and dramatic moments. The heat and the dull routine of the proceedings made her drowsy and yet anxious. It was so stupid! It wouldn't have been hard to establish her virginity, although the thought upset her. Besides Judd had insisted that it would have been humiliating. Also, the Reverend would argue that this fact was not significant. He probably thought sins came in all kinds of colors and shapes.

Summerman had an impressive presence, she had to admit to herself—tall, with graying hair, a respectable paunch and a well-cut dark suit. He apparently was expected to speak first. He got up with a flourish. Then he proceeded with a few kind words about the Reverend. He was a man of God dedicated to charity and rooting out evil, but unfortunately misinformed by his friends. The Reverend had characterized Miss Framingham's charity as an enterprise to aid women of ill repute, either by design or accident, even using the word "harlotry"to describe them. What an unfortunate mistake! If anything, the charity would rescue unfortunate women from a life of sin by offering shelter and alternatives to their livelihood. True, the place of women is in their homes but circumstances, including deaths in the family, sometimes expose them to outside hardships and dangers. Also, in attacking the morals of Miss Framingham, the Reverend was making a colossal mistake for which he should apologize forthwith. She was recognized as a woman of virtue, from a very good family and motivated purely by the most praiseworthy charitable impulses. Mr. Summerman was ready to produce witnesses who would support every one of his contentions. The lawsuit was a last resort. Miss Framingham had graciously offered to forget the whole matter in exchange for an apology and correction by the good Reverend despite the pain she had suffered from these unjust accusations.

The proceedings were interrupted for a lengthy lunch break. This only increased Karen's discomfort. She herself was unable to eat. Summerman had escorted her back to her boarding house and Karen sat in the parlor alone. She was alone because she had discouraged the presence of her parents and sisters.

The proceedings were started again in the afternoon. The heat of the day made the events even more uncomfortable. The Reverend's lawyer stood up and addressed the judge and the audience.

"My honorable and learned colleague, Mr. Summerman, undoubtedly means well and certainly must be convinced of the truth of what he is saying. Unfortunately, he is mistaken. Miss Framingham makes no distinction between virtuous women and sinful women. The street women she is proposing to aid would be for the most part prostitutes. Who else are roaming the streets of our fair city, shaming all of us, law-abiding God-fearing people? As for Miss Framingham's morals, I will show you that they are sham. I'll present one witness with special knowledge. Contrary to Mr. Summerman's evaluation she will be shown to be far from virtuous. Her conniving ways were able to hide her true nature. All sources of corruption and sin must be rooted out. I much regret that her very respectable family will be hurt by these facts but we must root out all serpents living among us."

It was then that Judd pushed his way through and sat next to her. The insulting presentation was hard to take. His presence calmed her down.

On the following day, Summerman called several witnesses, some from her college days. Mrs. Wholeworth was a reluctant witness, obviously not wanting to be in court. She explained clearly enough the basis for their effort and the altruistic nature of her and Karen's motivation. Karen would have hoped for more enthusiastic support but that was not the impression conveyed by Mrs. Wholeworth's testimony.

Mirella, her college roommate, testified at length. How Karen seldom went where men were present but always to chaperoned events and always was back well before the curfew. Dear Mirella! Karen was particularly grateful. They had never been close friends. Now Mirella was married and lived in Boston. Her testimony must have been at the least inconvenient. Karen vowed to get in touch with her and express her gratitude after the lawsuit was over. Many of her friends or acquaintances were not available, having scattered away from the city for summer vacations.

Somebody from the Police Commissioner's office gave a rundown of known cases of abandoned and abused women in the past year.

The next day it was time for Mr. Respectability to call his witnesses. He was late. When he sat down he seemed shaken and unwell and he hesitated.

"Well?" asked the judge impatiently.

The lawyer asked for permission to approach him and with Mr. Summerman walked to the bench when the judge beckoned them. There was silence in the court, probably because this was a most unusual development.

A buzz of voices started when the two lawyers left the bench. The judge banged his gavel.

"Please be silent." With silence reestablished, Judge Prucent started again. "Justice," he said, "is a complicated process and eventually reaches a just settlement whether finding an individual guilty or clearing him as the case might be. Civil suits such as this only need a satisfactory ending. There has been a new development. The Reverend Bucklerod authorizes me to state that he apologizes for his remarks about Miss Framingham and her charitable endeavors, the result of some false information he had received. His congregation will pay Miss Framingham's Women's Shelter twenty thousand dollars as way of making up for the unfortunate incident. Apologies will be printed in tomorrow's *Sun*, *New York Herald* and *New York Tribune*. As a consequence, Mr. Summerman acting for Miss Framingham has agreed to drop the suit as long as the terms of the agreement are followed. Case dismissed!"

Voices were raised in a collective din and several men sitting in front, probably reporters, ran off without looking back. Elated and surprised Karen turned to Judd who squeezed her hand. He simply smiled and said: "Checkmate." Karen could hardy hear him over the commotion of the crowd.

Chapter 11

Karen took Judd by the hand and led him to her room in the boarding-house. After all she had gone through, she didn't care at all about her reputation. Alone they kissed passionately. Karen broke the silence.

"We have so much to catch up with! I'm tired of all this chastity. Do you realize that we have kissed, I mean really kissed only three or four times? First tell me what happened. I'm totally non-plussed! We can get a bit more emotional later."

"You really want me to waste our precious time alone telling you all that?"

"That will make it easier to forget the quagmire and think about the two of us."

"Well, I followed the leads we had. I started with the Reverend. I got a list of the parishioners. Not as easy as it sounds. And then I tried to find what had happened to Michelle by contacting her mother, Mrs. Trevon. That part was easy—the old witch hadn't moved and got stuck raising the child! After a good deal of vituperation, I was told where I could find her miserable daughter. The two approaches converged. It turns out that Michelle is a maid in the Lowett's home, Steve's parents. In addition, the Lowetts are congregants of the Reverend's church.

"So I found her and talked to her. She blames the two of us for ruining her marriage prospects. Imagine, we were so terribly unkind to her boyfriend! It goes to show you the differences in people's perceptions. I thought the two of us had saved her life! I told her I would recompense her amply for our unfortunate role in that affair if she would leave town immediately. It's my impression that she went upstate."

"Wow! Isn't that interfering with a witness?"

"Was she going to be a witness? Well the Reverend's lawyer didn't list her as one. They might have been saving her as a big surprise. I don't know. Perhaps she was waiting for a monetary settlement. Regardless, nothing I did was either unethical or illegal. I never spoke to her about her role as a possible witness."

"I still don't understand. That took care of my 'moral turpitude' but what about the accusations that I would create a haven for prostitutes?"

"I think Mr. Summerman had made a convincing enough case that they thought they would lose in court."

From then on Karen's time and thoughts were filled with more important items than the need to defend herself.

JANE'S TROUBLES

In the hospital, they wouldn't let Jeff see Jane even after they had accepted his lie, that he was her husband. Jane's sister, Maureen, was pleased that he was able to go to the hospital immediately. She would follow as soon as her husband, John, came home to take care of the kids.

Jane came out of the operating room after two hours of surgery. She had been in a car accident. While waiting, all he could feel was anxiety. After a sympathetic intern had hinted that Jane's injuries, although serious were not life-threatening, Jeff had relaxed somewhat. The silly TV on the wall was flashing advertisements and meaningless chatter. The silent, uninviting vending machines and a payphone complemented the banality. There were two other persons in the well lighted room—both cloaked in pain. One, a middle-aged man, waiting to see his wife after a hysterectomy; the other, a young woman silent and somber in her painful vigil.

The reassurance from the intern didn't mean that Jeff stopped worrying, but after hearing the optimistic forecast, he was capable of rational thinking again. One thing that had probably been in the back of his mind for some time was now clear to him. He was irrevocably in love with Jane. How else could he explain the pain that paralyzed him? Knowing she had been hurt, he would have gladly traded places with her. If she would accept him, he was ready to commit himself.

❧   ❧   ❧

The events that led to that moment in the hospital waiting room played over in his mind while he was waiting. One never knows where a trivial happening will eventually lead.

Arlene was Jane's roommate. Jeff and Arlene had just started dating, but that didn't justify stringing him along or lying. Claiming a sudden onslaught of flu, Arlene had cancelled their date to attend a dance. Nothing can make a man feel more foolish than finding himself at the door of his supposed date with a bunch of flowers, and watching her gracefully entering the car with another man. In a light indigo gown, she'd looked stunning. The flowers he carried were meant to bring a measure of grace to her supposed illness.

After witnessing her departure, he resisted the impulse to toss the flowers away in anger. For him they had been an expensive extravagance. Well, Jane, Arlene's roommate, was probably in and would provide the necessary water and jar to keep the flowers from wilting prematurely. He was not about to take them home with him. Anyway, he had expected that she, not the patient, would come to the door. Jane always seemed to be in when she wasn't working or in class. He had liked her even on his first contact with her when picking up Arlene. He also had shared at least one course with Jane in their freshman year. Although he hadn't exchanged many words with her, he thought she had no pretenses or artifacts. Perhaps she could enjoy the flowers meant for another. He suddenly felt how absurd the situation was and suppressed a chuckle before ringing the bell. In jeans and a shapeless sweatshirt, Jane opened the door promptly.

"Oh, Jeff! I'm so sorry. Arlene isn't here!"

"I know. I just saw her leaving!" and after seeing her troubled expression, "Come on, you don't have to be embarrassed. It's not your fault." He paused and then continued, "I thought you might have a vase to preserve the flowers. No reason why you shouldn't enjoy them."

"Why, thank you." Jane blushed. "Come on in! We can carry out this mission of mercy together!" Jane took the flowers from him and entered the kitchen with Jeff following her. She cut the stems and placed the bouquet in a large glass vase filled with water. Jane fussed with the flowers so that they were shown at their best. Red, purple and white in a not too common combination. Jeff steered the conversation toward another topic.

"No festivities for you?"

"You know, with a job and a full class load I don't have much time. Besides, I'm plain...plain Jane. Nobody asked me."

"Don't confuse simplicity with ugliness!"

"Now you're challenging my mind!" Jane was laughing.

Jeff didn't know why he found her so appealing. With no synthetic charm, she seemed to be the opposite of Arlene, with no artifice. With a glowing complexion, her irregular features gave her face an appearance that people would consider 'interesting' but not pretty. Her green-gray eyes twinkled as if the world at large amused her. A word that came to his mind as appropriate for her was "perky."

"There are very few great beauties. They are in Hollywood or work as models. Many of them have no brains at all. You're a real woman."

"Oh, thank you for explaining," and she laughed softly.

They were facing each other in a strange intimacy.

"Actually, if you took the time to look at yourself in the mirror, you'd find that you're quite cute."

"Flattery...flattery. What are you up to?"

He didn't know the answer to that. But he spoke up driven by an impulse he didn't quite understand. He knew that he wasn't pushed by the desire to get even with Arlene. Perhaps, he simply didn't want to let the evening go to waste. Perhaps, after the cold shower of rejection he was charmed by Jane. "Would you care to go to the dance with me?"

"Come on! You're not giving me much time to think. I don't know you and besides Arlene would be furious...I have to live with her. And I don't have anything to wear. Three strikes against it."

He found himself smiling mischievously. "I'm sure you can take care of yourself. And as far as the dress, there is nothing wrong with what you're wearing. We would not be going to a debutante ball."

"Men...men. They have trouble understanding the simplest issues. Let me put on something better."

"You know, extensive cleavage is not necessary!"

Jane rolled her eyes in a pantomime of despair. "I'm afraid cleavage isn't my forte. I'll be right back."

As she left the room, Jeff refrained from saying. "Quality not quantity is what counts." He was under the distinct impression that it wouldn't enhance his case.

On their return from the dance, Jane's eyes sparked and the excitement had put color on her cheeks. Luckily Arlene wasn't back yet. Another awkward moment would have been added to their evening. It had been bad enough that she had seen them and Jane had ignored Arlene's fulminating stare.

"Thank you for taking me...and for letting me dance with other boys."

"Why shouldn't you be free to enjoy yourself, we are not dating...yet. And it bolstered my argument. You were the 'belle of the ball'."

"Don't be silly..."

"You don't date and you don't play. Does that leave some room for me?"

"What do you mean?"

"Does it need an explanation? I find you attractive and I like you."

"If you want to keep me company while I study, that can be arranged. But you're just interested in me because Arlene ditched you."

"That might have been true on the first few minutes after we met tonight, but not now. Seriously, most people have to eat. I don't imagine you're an exception."

"This is very silly!"

"I'm a silly man! That's my best feature!"

Jane shook her head. Clearly she was dealing with a hopeless case. "Okay. We can have dinner together once a week but each will pay his or her share."

❦   ❦   ❦

Jeff couldn't say that he understood the series of events that had followed. Arlene accepted the inevitable and no longer snarled at them. He and Jane kept company, most of the time doing what she had suggested, spending time together while studying. Their majors were entirely unrelated. Yet a closeness developed, perhaps aided by their weekly dinner together. Occasionally, after they were done studying or they had returned from dinner, they'd sit together on the couch, with her fitting snugly next to him. He never broke the closeness or tried for anything more intimate. The tenderness and affection he felt for her were hard to explain. He was sure that if she'd wanted more she would have made it clear to him. Sometimes, on parting they kissed on the lips. It wasn't a sexy kiss or prolonged kiss. But at times it shook him to his foundations. What it meant to her, he didn't know.

In an exception to their routine they had gone skiing. Jane was unusually euphoric. Her skiing outfit didn't differ from what she usually wore outdoors except for the boots she had to rent along with the skis. His apparel had been put together from garments provided by his friends. On the slopes she seemed to be in her element. Something to do with early childhood experience, he imagined. She skied with abandon while his performance was tentative and cautious.

She insisted on leaving the slopes earlier than they had planned.

"We can stop over at a motel and ski some more tomorrow," she suggested.

Surprised, he had tried to discourage her. "I don't think you'll find a single vacancy this late in the season."

Surprisingly, there had been a cancellation at a hotel they had seen from the highway and his credit card proved essential.

She whispered, "I hope you brought condoms."

He was surprised, elated and excited. And this is how there relationship took another step forward.

Unfortunately, much later, the time of parting came. She was going to graduate school elsewhere on a full fellowship. As he had suspected all along, she was brilliant. He had taken a peek at some of her assigned essays and was impressed by their depth and clarity.

He certainly was not in a position to make it difficult for her to leave, and he wouldn't have wanted to do that anyway. They promised to write to each other via e-mail and they did for a while. Inevitably, as he'd expected, the exchanges became infrequent and to his regret finally stopped altogether. He couldn't help thinking sadly that she could have been the woman for him.

Preparing for his comprehensive had interfered with most of his activities and perhaps his e-mail answers had been delayed for too long. Jeff had felt terrible having lost contact with Jane. Perhaps she had grown tired of their exchanges. He suspected that she had changed her e-mail provider. He had never really known her mailing address. The feeling that perhaps she just didn't want to be found nagged him. Jane's graduate school was in Boston, where his parents lived. A visit to his parents and an attempt to reestablish contact with Jane could be combined.

Standing in front of the door to Jane's sister, Maureen Doolittle's apartment in Boston, Jeff felt definitely out of place and on a questionable mission. The noises of a family with small children filtered through the door—the high voices, the admonishing adult echoes. He was thrusting himself into an unknown situation. True enough that's how he had gotten to know Jane in the first place, but this time he might not be welcome. Yet the day before, after Jeff had identified himself when he had telephoned, Jane's sister had said over the children voices, "You must be Jane's friend." After hearing his acknowledgment she aid. "Sorry, I can't talk to you now. I'm in the middle of the kids' bath. Why don't you drop by tomorrow morning…let's say after nine? We'll have a chance to talk."

When on the following morning the door finally opened, Maureen seemed to welcome him. "Come on in, come on in. Sorry, I had to be so short with you but duty called. I'm so glad to meet you finally. Jane talks about you all the time." They shook hands and exchanged smiles.

In the living room, a little girl was arranging a collection of dolls in a row for an imaginary tea party. Another child was doing somersaults on the family couch suggesting a bad fall and an imminent fatal denouement. A little boy carrying a teddy bear was solemnly examining the mysterious visitor. Pointing at the children Maureen recited, "Welcome to the circus. The acrobat on the couch is John Jr., who for four days a week is in kindergarten, Marlene is entertaining guests, and Joshua has to have his diaper changed but I haven't got around to it. My husband, big John, is at work but I hope you'll eventually meet him."

Coffee and cookies followed. Somehow, Maureen couldn't get started right away. Marlene needed a quick hug from Mom, and John Jr. came by and pointing with his finger asked, "Who's that?" The explanation that he was Auntie's friend seemed to satisfy them. But Maureen had serious matters in mind.

"I'm so glad you're here. I don't know whether you have heard about Jane's crisis."

"I haven't been in contact with her for a while. That's one of the reasons I'm here. I don't have her address and telephone number and she doesn't respond to my e-mails."

"She's a graduate student of Joseph Corbett…the Joseph Corbett. Jane admires the man. An article came out under his name and his name only, but it's mostly one of the chapters of Jane's dissertation. She was devastated. Corbett insists that it's not his doing. Jane is very confused. I'm sure she'd welcome your input and support. She thinks the world of you."

"Well, I don't know what I can do but I certainly will be glad to do the best I can."

Jane's hug was heartfelt and she had tears in her eyes. He would have preferred the passionate kiss he had fantasized, but was relieved to get such a warm reception.

"I'm so happy you came! I really need you. I'm totally confused."

She explained in painstaking detail what he had heard from Maureen.

"What do you think happened?"

"I really don't know. Joe has always been straight with me. He tells me he had nothing to do with it."

"Who discovered the plagiarism?"

"I did. I browse through the Journal routinely. I brought the matter up with the Dean. The committee he set up recommended Joe's dismissal. I'm sorry I started the ball rolling. Joe is married and has two kids. He'll have a hard time getting another job."

"It would have come out no matter what, so stop feeling guilty…Hm! Hm! Let me think about it. Certainly the fact that it was published where it would be quickly found suggests a frame up. My dad is a professor. He understands academic politics to a T, I'm sure he can direct us."

Jeff always found it strange to see his father, Peter, in his working environment. The office had no resemblance to orderly surroundings of their home. Here books and loose papers and pads half filled with writing seemed to be everywhere—on the desk, on chairs and some even on the floor. His wife, Jeff's mother, wouldn't have tolerated such a disorder. It was also in contrast to his dad's lectures that Jeff had witnessed—meticulously organized and elegantly presented. A lighted computer screen was on the side. His father, sitting at his desk, looked over his glasses. Light brown hair, rather pale with dark blue eyes, he had what Jeff considered a professorial pallor—that of somebody who doesn't get out much and concentrates on pursuits of the intellect—what Jeff liked to say jocularly was the appearance of a cross between a slug and an owl, if that were possible!

"Ah! The prodigal son is here!" The delighted smile contradicted the banal announcement.

"The son who doesn't write much and comes to visit once in a blue moon!"

"Well, don't forget to make an appearance at home this evening. Your mother will be delighted."

"Why don't I take you two out for dinner. That way Mom doesn't have to slave over a stove when she returns from work."

"Actually, it's my turn to cook, so as long as you let me pay we'll be glad to accept your offer for more than one reason—one of them my culinary prowess or lack of. To what do we owe the honor of your visit?"

"Why should there be an ulterior motive?"

"Tararah, tarah! You must admit your visits aren't common. It's not Thanksgiving or Christmas and you seem troubled. I can't help you if it's woman trouble but otherwise I can provide you with priceless advice."

"Actually priceless advice is what I need or rather an opinion right down your alley."

"The academic doesn't have alleys. Just hypocrisies and cul-de-sacs!"

"And you accuse youth of cynicism!"

"No, cynicism requires disappointed idealism and that requires time to develop. Youth is not cynical—just filled with contrariness. But what can I help you with?"

Jeff suddenly found it hard to find words but then blurted out, "Well…It's hard to explain. Do you think that in the pursuit of tenure an academic would be willing to commit a crime?"

"Well, well, well! I wonder what's bothering you. A crime, eh?" Peter seemed deep in thought for a minute or so. "I'm sorry to say that it would be entirely possible…including plagiarism and perhaps in some selected cases even murder. For some reason some academics consider tenure to be the crowning glory of their ambitions, not the guarantee of low wages and countless meaningless tussles which it actually represents. Plagiarism is the most common breach of ethics, I'm sure. Probably happens most frequently. Particularly if you have a brilliant graduate student! I'm not sure about murder." After a while he continued, "In my own department we had a woman who found advancement and tenure by flying the feminist flag, while sabotaging the advancement of every other woman in our department. I have heard it referred to as the 'queen bee syndrome.' And then to gather sympathy, by a strange coincidence she was anonymously threatened by phone with bodily harm every time she was up for a promotion. And it worked!"

"I take it, you're saying 'yes'."

"You're very perspicacious today! I also think you're talking about the Corbett case."

"How do you know?"

"It's been in the news for a while. Sure, not on the first page. After all what happens in a university is not of general interest and might not even make the papers. No beautiful actresses or juicy divorces are involved! But, this time the events had an interesting twist. Poor Joe Corbett, possibly in search of a promotion, ends up fired."

"Well? What are your thoughts?"

"I very much doubt the substance of the accusations. Although Corbett is not in my field, I have heard he's a very serious scholar, highly regarded and he really didn't need one more publication even one as brilliant as this one is. Unfortunately, whatever happened will make him lose his position and possibly even block a possible new job."

Jeff was pleased to hear that Jane's work was so highly rated by his father but this wasn't what he was searching for. "So what do you think happened?"

"Hard to tell, isn't it. My wild guess is that somebody was trying to impede his promotion and sent the article in for publication without his or Ms. Robertson's permission. These days everything is handled impersonally through the web."

"Sounds a bit far-fetched."

"Not at all. Many are the ones who are discarded from a faculty for petty reasons, sometimes even by trickery. He might have argued with the wrong colleague. Or somebody favored somebody else. Limiting the number who can be considered for tenure is a frequent administrative trick to match the limited budgets. But this doesn't explain your stake in this matter."

"Well, if you have to know, Jane Robertson is a good friend of mine."

"Ooh! *Cherchez la femme!* I knew there was something under all this talk."

Jeff felt himself blush—it was unfortunate that he was so transparent! His father continued, "So, it's that serious!"

"I don't know. I like her a lot."

"Well you know my opinion about the Corbett affair. What does she think?"

"She seems to agree with you about Corbett's innocence, although she really doesn't know what happened. She says he was always very helpful and kind to her and couldn't have suddenly changed into a monster. She has the highest regard for his thinking and honesty.

"You know, since you can't offer me advice about women, if you two don't pick on her I'll bring Jane with me to our dinner. She really needs a break from her troubles."

"Why would we pick on her? We'd love meeting someone who might be able to civilize you."

❦   ❦   ❦

The suggestion to include Jane in their dinner plans was a natural impulse but perhaps misguided. The invitation might send the wrong message. His relationship with Jane was in limbo. Shouldn't a meeting with the parents of a

possible mate be arranged only when a relationship is on solid ground, perhaps after wedding plans are in the offing? Wasn't he being insensitive and pre-
sumptuous? He would have hated to ruin what was left of their friendship. On
another vein, the possibility of Jane being less than welcome or perhaps subject
to an unfair interrogation also upset him. He had heard horror stories from
some of his friends. And anyway, Jane might veto the idea of meeting his parents. He wasn't leaving her much time to decide.

With a good deal of trepidation he asked her and she seemed very pleased.
Whether it reflected that they were still very close friends or even indicated a
romantic attachment on her part, he wasn't sure.

From the moment Jeff and Jane approached the restaurant table where his
parents were already sitting, they seemed delighted to meet her. The choice of
an upscale restaurant and the formal way his parents were dressed, not the
usual jeans and t- or turtle-neck shirts, suggested that they wanted to make a
good impression. They got up from the table smiling and shook her hand.
From then on they seemed charmed. Jeff had never seen them so taken with
anybody. He felt as if his own presence was entirely superfluous.

Jane was witty and charming. Her affection for Jeff was also evident and
warmed him, dissipating any doubts he might have had. Her recollections frequently included his contribution to the stories.

Meeting his parent cleared the ambiguity in their relationship.

Once back in Jane's apartment, Jeff and Jane still had to deal with the
conundrum of how the plagiarism had occurred.

"You don't know how grateful I am that you showed up. I was pretty
depressed until then. How long are you staying?"

"Now that I've moved in with my parents, as long as we need to understand
what happened. I have friends, other TAs, who have agreed to take care of my
classes. You convinced me that Corbett is not involved. Where does that leave
us?"

"Suspecting the rest of the campus, I suppose."

"No, not at all. Who had easy access to your dissertation? I presume only
the members of your thesis committee."

"I'm afraid that doesn't help very much. Besides Joe, there is Bono—an old
grouch. He hates Joe but I can't see a tenured professor close to retirement
doing something like that. That leaves two others. Michael Orwin, a contemporary of Joe's. The two of them are buddies. It's just like they share an office
since they are in the same suite. I doubt he would do anything like that. They
have so many interests in common! Besides, they identify with each other.

They have the same problem. Orwin will be considered for tenure and promotion next year so that until now they must have felt they were in the same boat. Goldstein, I don't know at all. He is a professor from another institution, part of the committee as required by our rules."

"Well, that cuts down our inquiries. Not a whole campus but only four."

"Why don't we start by eliminating Joe as far as we can. I can check his laptop. Even if he erased his electronic communications, the University's computer center should be able to revive them."

"Can you do that?"

"Sure, Joe authorized me to use anything in his office."

"While you do that, I'll start with Bono. I don't know how to go about it. Would you mind an awful lot if I tell people that I'm your fiancé? It would give me some official standing."

"Don't you think you should propose first?" And then an embarrassed, "Never mind! I was just pulling your leg."

Jeff thought he should start by finding out what could be done. The University police chief, John Morgan, was not encouraging. He was relegated to a small office. Jeff wondered whether he was the entire police force, since he hadn't seen anybody else in the complex. Morgan was not an impressive man. With dark eyes, undisciplined brown hair surrounding a pronounced, bald spot, he looked like a thousand other men Jeff had encountered.

"I don's see how I can justify a search, much less examining the contents of a laptop computer. Technically, of course I could do it. All the labtop computers of the faculty were provided by the University and still belong to the University. Likewise, I have access to every office in all buildings. But that doesn't mean I'm willing or even capable of doing anything without a clear just cause. The fallout would be otherwise enormous. I don't head the Gestapo!"

In the hospital waiting room, Jeff was suddenly aware of what the TV set was reporting, the volume turned down to just a whisper. There had been a car accident on Highway 95. A man, Michael Orwin, had no serious injuries and had been released from Beneficial Hospital. A woman with him had been taken to the hospital by ambulance and was seriously hurt. Her name was not released pending notification of family.

The thought that quickly formed in his mind was mixed with anger and he knew that he had to act on it—half intuition, half deduction. Jane's injuries were not from an accident. He suddenly knew it was an attempted murder.

After a short search in recondite folds of his pant's pockets, he found the quarter for the telephone call. The voice at the other end was not encouraging.

"Chief Morgan is not available now. Is this important?"

"I would say so."

"Is it urgent?"

"Definitely."

Jeff had to settle for leaving the number of the payphone with the hope that the policeman would call him promptly. He didn't know what else he could do. Morgan was just the chief of the campus police of Jane's university but at least Jeff knew he would listen.

After a while, the ringing woke him up from his grim reverie. Morgan was on the phone and Jeff made his case. The policeman didn't make any promises.

"I'll look into it. You might be right. But you know that it's my neck which is at risk."

There was nothing that Jeff could do but wait, either for a call back from Morgan or to be allowed to see Jane.

Jeff finally was able to see Jane. Still woozy, her face was covered with bandages and behind them her eyes seemed somewhat unfocused. An intravenous drip was still connected to one of her arms. Jeff had been told that she had a broken leg, several broken ribs and facial damage. One of the ribs had put her life in danger since it seemed to have pierced the pericardium but the operation had taken care of that and stabilized her.

"What happened, Jeff? They say I was in a car accident." Her voice was almost a whisper but he was pleased that she had immediately recognized him.

"Yes, that's what happened. Do you remember how it happened?"

"No. The police interrogated me but I wasn't much help."

"Just rest. Apparently everything should be alright."

"Please, Jeff, don't leave…Hold my hand!"

"I'll stay here as long as they'll let me. As a husband apparently I have the right to."

He expected some sort of comment from Jane about his newly invented status but she didn't respond.

❧   ❧   ❧

Jane was beginning to recover. She had even been disconnected from all the tubes that had surrounded her. Maureen had visited but once reassured by Jane's improvement had to get back home. Jeff was delighted by the progress. He conversed with her about anything not related to her "accident". She was somewhat worried about the state of her face but had been assured that if she needed plastic surgery, it would be a minor matter.

So far only family had been allowed to visit. It was the way Jeff wanted it. He was worried that somebody might try to harm her when he wasn't there.

Chief Morgan came in person. Jeff hadn't left Jane's bedside. He gestured to Jeff to come outside in the corridor.

"Well, your hunch was right. Orwin erased it but the University computer center was able to revive the e-mails and attachments in record time. They clearly show that he sent in the article. I guess that's enough to expose him and get him fired. But I'm not satisfied with that."

"What gave him the clue that Jane was testing the computers?"

"He must have seen her walk off with Professor Corbett's laptop and suspected that he was second in line. He probably couldn't figure out how to destroy his computer without arousing suspicion."

"The big mystery to me is how could he have arranged an accident without killing himself."

"Oh, that could be rather simple. His car is an old model; there is only one air-bag for the driver. Also the passenger-side safety belt doesn't work. It was attempted murder alright. There was no braking as seen from the tire marks. It just crashed into the abutment. Furthermore, Orwin was not intoxicated. The policemen on the scene checked that out. What puzzles me is the motivation."

"I'm sure I can help you there. Both professors are essentially in the same field. It would seem unlikely that the University would promote both of them. If Corbett left, Orwin's chances of promotion would be higher." After a pause, "What can we possibly do? We have no evidence of an attempted murder."

"Ah! He who attempts murder is likely to try again some time in his life. I don't want the perpetrator to escape. It's also the weakness which provides a way of catching him. I have replaced his laptop computer so that he has no reason to think that we are onto him."

"What are you proposing?"

"He'll show up as a visitor. I have a good idea of what he is going to try. His mother is a diabetic, so he has access to syringes and insulin can kill. All he has to do is put a big dose in the drip when he thinks nobody is around. It would even delay Jane's demise to giving him time to disappear. We can rig a drip so that it is not connected to Jane and then arrange a suitable reception."

"Come on, Morgan. That's all supposition. If he comes, and I hope he doesn't, he may have in mind some other entirely different way of hurting her. I won't allow you to put her in danger! We can just let him know that we already have the evidence of his trickery in the supposed plagiarism. Then he would have no reason to hurt her."

"You won't allow it? You know, you're really only her pretend husband. Besides, she should have some say-so. She was the one hurt. I'll go directly to her and see what she thinks."

The whole story was presented to Jane. She was silent for a few seconds, then her eyes were ablaze peering out from under the bandages. "Let's get the bastard!"

Jeff hadn't changed his mind but Jane's vehemence was such that he didn't feel he should or could talk her out of it.

It all proceeded as planned. Orwin made his appearance as a visitor. Bringing flowers and a box of candy, he greeted Jane as if they were old friends. He expressed that he was overcome with grief for having caused the accident, after having offered to drive her home. He stayed for a long time until the two of them were alone. After she seemed to dose he proceeded to spike her drip with a syringe.

Jane was delighted to see his amazed expression when one policeman barred the door as he attempted to leave and another put him in handcuffs with a leisurely Miranda warning.

Jeff ran in as soon as the visitors had left and with tears in his eyes gave her a hug.

"Don't leave me again. I still need you," she said.

THE LAST MAN LEFT

The end of the nineteenth century had held such promise! The first successful laying of a telegraph cable across the Atlantic, completed in 1866, was old hat. Other marvels had quickly followed. The feats of engineering were astounding. The Suez Canal connecting the Mediterranean Sea to the Red Sea was completed in 1869. The Panama Canal was started in 1882. However, encountering many difficulties, it was completed much later. Yet its significance was well understood much earlier. The Brooklyn Bridge, one of the wonders of the world and an amazing feat of engineering, had been finished in 1883. But the progress wasn't just in engineering. Ways of transmitting sounds electrically had been discovered. In 1875 regular telephone lines were established—between cities beginning in 1877, then between New York and Chicago in 1892. Transcontinental telephone service would have to wait, but its completion was obviously imminent. The world appeared to be entirely changed—new and enticing.

Firmly at the beginning of the twentieth century, Irma felt that despite this enormous progress, much of the nonsense of the past persisted. She was considered a spinster by many. Almost thirty and without a husband she basically had no future. But she was not ready to accept the appellation or the stereotype accompanying it. To her, "spinster" connoted a haggard, shapeless, colorless creature only tolerated by most. In contrast, she was far from spent and dressed as well as she could afford, which required some magic and the assistance of her mother who could perform miracles with a needle. But Mother tended to preach, like most mothers did. "Why aren't you married yet?" The answer was simple. She had never been asked. It wasn't as if she wasn't interested or she had abjured marriage, but apparently she was too independent and particular.

Years before, she had been able to attend college, which had required a substantial financial commitment. Her father had been alive then and her family's economic position had been much better. She had graduated without snatching a worthwhile marriageable man as most of her classmates had. Irma had toyed with the idea of teaching school, which would have been a position as poorly paid as her present one. Although children delighted her, she found the restrictions on a teacher's personal life too obtrusive. She would have had to present a drab exterior and accept all the prohibitions and limitations of a capricious and hypocritical public.

The secretarial job at the factory owned by the Orbinell family, she was able to carry off. But, it was uninteresting and boring in extreme. There was one way in which her life was made at least bearable. The Orbinells had organized an amateur theater in their mansion, and Irma was able to she insinuate herself into that small group. She read well, had a nice voice and wrote many of the skits or short plays they used. The Orbinells were as rich as Croesus and with pretensions of grandeur. That combination would have been amusing if it didn't represent a sick reality of our society. Although they resided in Guildtown, they had a house in New York City and a so-called camp in the Adirondacks. On their estate the Orbinells had built a pavilion dedicated to the performing arts. A number of relatives and rich friends participated in its activities. The family included three homely daughters. There was a son who didn't reside with the family and whom Irma had never met. Fortunately, the Orbinell girls were not without theatrical talent, explaining the family's enchantment with the art.

The stars in the short plays the group performed were almost always two of the Orbinell sisters, Faith and Endurance. The younger sister, Penelope, was usually left on the sidelines unless she wished to impersonate a dog or some other small animal. Occasionally, Irma was allowed a short role but being part of the group was enough entertainment. Besides, writing amusing skits, designing costumes and sceneries at least removed her mind from the deadly routine of work. Since the demands were modest, she found herself equal to the task.

Irma might have resigned herself to her fate, which was not totally unpleasant, if it hadn't been for the appearance of Gene Sestre. Mr. Sestre had been one of the engineers involved in the building of the Panama Canal after the United States had taken over the enterprise from a French company. Exactly what he had done was not clear to her. She presumed he was involved in the construction of the dam to create a lake since the reason for his coming was to study the feasibility of constructing a dam near Guildtown. This endeavor supposedly would supply the factory with power and the body of water created by the dam would provide recreational facilities.

At least twice, she had seen Mr. Sestre, or at least a stranger answering the description she had heard, strolling along Main Street and looking through the windows of the many stores that lined it. He wasn't a youngster—she judged him close to her age. Aside from some very young men, he seemed to be the only single man available in the small world of Guildtown. Gossip about his presence and accomplishments buzzed through the town. He apparently was well recognized professionally and still unmarried. Although, of course, the most daring of the gossips suggested he might have been involved with many women—after all he was a mature man and not bad looking.

Gene Sestre had complete faith in science and engineering. These could move mountains, figuratively or in reality. After all, he had been involved in just such a task. He also knew for a fact that his knowledge of women just succeeded in confusing him. No doubt this had to do with his past experience. In Philadelphia, where he had spent his distant youth, he remembered sparring socially with young women of his social class, although he wasn't sure what that actually was. His studies hadn't left him all that much time and, besides, until he was established in his profession any relationship certainly couldn't lead him to anything stable. In Panama the daughters of fellow engineers were forbidden territory. In the small expatriate world it could lead to unpleasantness with repercussions in his job. He had developed a serious crush on the wife of one of the other engineers, but fortunately it eventually had faded although at its peak it had caused him considerable pain. The exotic well-to-do Panamanian young women of the cities, Colón and Panama, were well protected by solid walls and other obstacles. The dusky women readily available he had considered, but rejected the idea as unacceptable. Some unmarried men or men unaccompanied by family had arrived at more stable domestic arrangements. Gene decided he wasn't prepared to put bastards into the world. He would feel responsible for them and find himself rooted in that tropical, uncomfortable, disease ridden and mysterious world.

Now in Guildtown, he was still confused and facing the same impasse as when he had been a downy-cheeked youth.

❧   ❧   ❧

In the back of her mind, Irma had some fanciful thoughts about the new man in town. They really were more like daydreams. She knew her chances of even meeting him were almost nil. Silly thoughts! Silly woman!

Nevertheless, Irma was looking forward to a new and perhaps interesting experience. The Orbinells had invited her to dinner, apparently a special occasion. There wasn't any hidden significance to her invitation, completely out of line with the Orbinells snobbish view of the world. She suspected that it reflected their need to balance the group. There weren't that many available women in Guildtown with a college education and the capacity to carry on an interesting conversation.

Ah! Everything simple turned impossibly complex. What would she wear? She didn't wish to impress anybody but at the same time, being embarrassed could be the unacceptable alternative. There was also the possibility of not being able to maintain a satisfactory level of chatter. After all, her experience at social events was limited to those at her college.

She wasn't disturbed by the giggling and whispering of the Orbinell girls in the little theater, which probably was about the forthcoming dinner. She felt very comfortable with the three girls and was sure of their friendship. They frequently confided in her—their imagined adversities, their fights, the meanness of their governess. None of those real tragedies, but they needed somebody to entrust with their growing pains.

The uniformed maid led her to a large room. Mrs. Clara Orbinell welcomed her at the door. Irma had only met her a few times. Her hostess was far from beautiful but had a certain dignity. Mr. Orbinell, tall and with a severe mustached appearance, was also there and nodded. A flustered Irma was introduced to the group and almost failed to understand that she was being offered a glass of sherry. To her surprise, the mysterious Mr. Sestre was present. Irma noticed that all the women were fashionably dressed and was happy that her mother's latest creation was a good match. Irma found herself engaged in very ordinary conversations and felt herself relaxing. State Senator Botham was friendly without the pomposity Irma expected in a politician. She had heard that his support was needed for the proposed dam. She found herself describing life in Guildtown. Despite its isolation, the town had witnessed visits of some notables. Surprisingly, the incomparable Sarah Bernhardt had made a short stop in 1893. Mark Twain had visited at the turn of the century and his drolleries still reverberated in the town.

Irma glanced at Mr. Sestre, hopefully discreetly. He wasn't handsome but better than ordinary looking. His air of masculinity pleased her. Unfortunately, he seemed attached to a Mrs. Witham. Since there was no Mr. Witham present, Irma guessed she might be a widow and an effort at matchmaking was being made by Mrs. Orbinell. She was surprised to find that her guess irked her. She found herself appraising her possible rival. Mrs. Witham was unfortunately beautiful and beautifully dressed. She spoke animatedly to Mr. Sestre who listened to her attentively. Irma realized that if she was competing with her, she didn't stand a chance. She also imagined that a middle-aged man, Tom Louiston, apparently the new principal at the high school had been entrusted to her care. She felt that she might have been selected purely to balance the group, because Mrs. Louiston had not yet joined her husband, although she seemed to be much on his mind. He kept referring to his wife and suggesting that she would find the new town delightful. She found him a pleasant enough man and was not surprised to find herself seated next to him at the table.

She heard nibbles of the conversations around her. Louiston was soft spoken and he assured the group that the schools had been well administered and he found his new assignment challenging. Irma found herself discussing the importance of discipline in the schools with the principal. Apparently, many of the guests, Mrs. Witham in particular, were fascinated with Mr. Sestre's background. His contention, met with skepticism, was that the real enemy of progress in building the Panama Canal had been, not the obvious jaguars and snakes, but the lowly mosquitoes. Mr. Sestre seemed to be convinced that both malaria and yellow fever were carried by mosquitoes and the diseases could be defeated in part by using mosquito netting. Quinine worked to prevent malaria but had to be used judiciously. Not surprisingly, Mr. Orbinell was interested in different issues. He thought that President Roosevelt was undermining the very businesses that formed the underpinning of the American economy by interfering with them. Irma couldn't help smiling internally. She wouldn't have expected less.

The meal was delicious and served with ceremony and zest. The soups came from two colorful hand-painted ceramic tureens which the Orbinells had picked up on one of their recent trips to Italy. Two maids in uniform distributed the food in bowls or plates and a young girl removed them when they were finished. Throughout the meal, Irma heard some guests murmuring accolades. The food was certainly delicious. The meat dish was a sort of stew.

She thought somebody whispered "bourguignonne" and imagined that it was the name of the dish. The taste was entirely new to her experience which was mostly American fare. Because of the conversation around the table, the pace was leisurely. Irma had never tasted a French dinner wine before and found it interesting. She had to limit her drinking, since she rarely had been exposed to alcohol and after the first two glasses she could already feel a faint buzz.

The pastries, the climax of a sumptuous meal, were divine. The coffee and its aroma were different from any she had encountered before. Afraid of what more alcohol would do to her, she only sipped the brandy that followed. All in all it was an interesting experience.

The parting of the various guests developed in some mysterious and disorganized fashion. The polite goodbyes stretched out for a while. Mrs. Witham had the use of her own carriage since she lived in a Elmton, a few miles away. The assistant principal, a dark-haired, skinny non-descript man dressed in black, had come and was waiting to take Louiston home. Surprisingly, outdoors as Irma prepared to walk home, she found Mr. Sestre next to her.

"I wouldn't dream of letting a woman walk back alone in the middle of the night!"

"Oh! I assure I have done it many times when I worked on the Orbinell's stage productions. Guildtown is quite safe. But I appreciate having your company."

It was actually darker than usual and she was pleased not to trek home alone.

"Yeah, I have heard about the Orbinell's theater. I understand you are mixed up with all that."

"Somebody has been gossiping about me!"

"I wouldn't call it gossip. The information comes from three of your admirers—I would think very reliable sources: Faith, Endurance and Penelope! They seem to adore you! They even talked their mother into inviting you."

"Well, adoration seems to be stretching the point! But they are very dear to me."

"I spent some time with them while visiting the Orbinells—the family and Mrs. Witham."

"Well, they finally released you!"

He laughed, seeming to know what she was referring to. "Mrs. Witham is really quite charming!"

"But?"

Sestre laughed. "No buts. I have an inkling that I'd be interested in somebody less perfect."

"Are you flirting with me or insulting me?"

He laughed again. "God forbid. I'm not really sure what flirting means and I certainly didn't mean to insult you. I wouldn't accuse you of being less than perfect. Give me some credit!"

They continued chatting leisurely. The occasional silences were without strain. Irma to her surprise felt completely relaxed with the man she had been dreaming about. She was sorry when they arrived at her house after what she felt was a too short walk The porch was lighted as she expected.

"Thank you very much for your company. I would ask you in if it weren't so late. I wouldn't want to wake up my mother."

"It was a pleasure. May I call on you?"

"I don't see why not."

They didn't shake hands but they looked into each other's eyes.

Irma suppressed a chuckle as she entered the house. Her mother would certainly be up to hear her account of the dinner party—a rare occasion in their lives. She felt unexpectedly buoyed by her encounter with Sestre.

Her mother listened carefully and was obviously delighted by the details of the dinner party and her trip into luxury. Not so about Mr. Sestre, however.

"Don't waste your time with that man. He'll just play you for whatever you're worth and then drop you. He's too important. And look at him! Still a bachelor and approaching middle age. Mark my word, what he would be interested is a rich woman…a rich widow perhaps."

Irma was not interested in that train of thought. Elation filled her. He obviously was interested in her.

After Gene Sestre's return from Panama—a vacation, a trip to Saratoga, America's playground. Then a whirlwind of activity in New York City. Stern and Rowen, the engineering firm, had offered him a partnership. He wasn't sure whether he was ready for and demurred. Then the consultation with the board of supervisors of Guildtown to explore the possibility of building a dam came up. Actually, the board meant Arthur Orbinell, Sestre was told—the man owned the town. Then he had been introduced to many women in a social vortex which had just confused him. He met many he admired but none he could speak to without feeling totally out of place. Most of them, he felt, were just too young or too refined for him.

When he had finally gone to Guildtown, the boarding house he had been directed to had freed him of the necessity of worrying about his daily needs. Arthur Orbinell had invited him to stay in his mansion, but Sestre felt that he could concentrate on his task without too many distractions if he resided elsewhere. He was happy that his host had accepted his plans without difficulty. He immediately became involved in the problem and accumulated the needed data in the office provided in the factory. A study of the probable location of the proposed dam, the cost of the necessary materials and labor were not very promising. To relax he took long walks, through the town and the countryside. These were more hospitable than those in Panama or in New York City.

He doubted the Arthur Orbinell would be interested in sinking at least two million in the project, although a bond issue was a possibility. But before he could give an official estimate and a more concrete discussion, Sestre was drawn into another social round. Pushed toward Mrs. Witham, a very wealthy widow, he felt she was much the same as the women he had met in New York. Irma Healy was a relief—common sense and a pleasant personality. Somebody he could talk to without artifice or ceremony. He guessed that her personality hid strength and kindness.

Gene Sestre had been overwhelmed by his experience with Irma. It was the first time he had what could be considered a love affair. He had no reservations about being head over heels in love with her. She was not the kind of woman to allow herself to be involved physically with a man without love. They had been together only a few times, but he felt she reciprocated his feelings. Irma, he was sure, was all he wanted in a woman.

His report to the Town Board was presented. The fee he'd collected was substantial. He was free to make other commitments. A trip to New York for a few days to discuss joining the firm of Stern and Rowen was necessary. He hadn't wanted to propose to Irma until a solid basis for their financial future was assured.

When he presented himself at Irma's house on his return, he came in for a surprise. Her mother, who had opened the door, was totally silent, subdued with no words of greeting. She seemed frightened, her eye-lids were swollen as if she had been crying. Without a word she pointed toward Irma's bedroom and quickly disappeared. Irma was packing ready to leave Guildtown.

"My God! What happened?"

Irma was close to tears. "Ma…dear Ma…screwed me completely." Then she was silent.

After a minute or so Gene broke the silence again. "Is this something you can share with me?"

"I suppose, if I find the strength." Gene waited, looking at her. He judged her as lovely as ever but deeply disturbed. Her lips were trembling and she seemed to find it hard to speak. He put his arms around her but she was rigid and unresponsive and he let her step back.

"She went to Mr. Ordell at the factory complaining that you were corrupting me. The idea was to force you out of town. As if Mr. Ordell would care about what you do! Essentially the only thing it accomplished was getting me fired. We don't have any financial resources. I have to go to New York to get a job. There is nothing here. Mom will have to join me later after we sell the house."

"Irma! You know it was nothing like that. I love you."

Silence followed. Her expression seemed to say, "So?"

"Irma! That doesn't change anything. I want to marry you."

"Look, it's noble of you but I don't want you trapped into something you don't want. I knew what I was doing. I can take care of myself. I'm not even pregnant. Marriage is for a lifetime."

"That's exactly it. That's what I want."

"Well, I'm going."

It was obvious that he couldn't stop her. "May I help you carry your bags?"

"The coachman will be here soon. He will help me."

Gene was dismayed by what was happening. A feeling of helplessness filled him. Sometimes there are ways of talking yourself out of corners. Then he discerned a ray of hope.

"I'm going to New York too, I have a job there. Once you find work and are established, will you marry me if I propose?"

Irma managed a laugh. "At least you're persistent. If after three months you don't change your mind, I'll give you my answer then."

As Gene was leaving, he turned and said, "Don't be too hard on your mom. Old people sometimes have a different view of the world. They can't help it."

❀   ❀   ❀

Mrs. Recoust, the boarding house landlady, had emerged from her ground floor apartment, batting her eyelashes mechanically in her usual annoying tic. A short, gray-haired woman in her sixties, in dark clothing and almost entirely round, she had been always good natured and ready to exchange friendly words. Suddenly, she had an air of hostility Irma hadn't seen before.

"You'd better be gone by the end of the week. I can't put up with the goings on. Your boyfriend, in and out, in and out. I can't put up with this. This is a respectable house."

"Oh, Mrs. Recoust you know that you can't put me out."

"I certainly can and if you don't leave I can lodge a complaint with the authorities. They'll do the job for you."

"You know you can't throw me out just like that."

"Yeah? Why not?" Her air of belligerence has escalated.

Irma smiled, "Because if you chase me out, I won't invite you to my wedding."

Mrs. Recoust closed her mouth in surprise and shook her head. "I got myself in trouble didn't I? What's his name?"

"Gene Sestre."

"What kind of a name is that? Sounds like a foreigner." And then turning to return to her haunts and before closing the door, she remarked "Make sure you do invite me though. I'm counting on it."

SWORD, SABER AND FOIL

I, Marco Fenestrini, am a man of the sword…saber and foil too. Not like a man who "lives by the sword and dies by the sword." Not at all. I'm a disciple of Messer Martinone and I have run his fencing academy, which I'm to inherit, since 1816. He was the best fencer in the world until the years and arthritis caught up with him. Now I'm the best.

Martinone dug me out of Orvieto when I was a young boy and carefully saw to my training and education. I lodged with him and his wife who became like a second family to me. They had no children, while my father had too many. A comrade-in-arms of my father from the last war, Martinone explained to me that many are the skills required for success if that's what I wanted. These include good Italian and French with little foreign inflection or regional accent, speaking politely, writing, reading, reckoning and such.

In a way, my occupation makes me an impostor. Despite being blessed with unusual skills, the result of good teaching and lots of practice, I probably will never raise one of my weapons in anger.

Many of my clients want to improve their prowess for pleasure, physical exercise, or the thought that the skills will affirm their manhood, or they actually intend to use the art for dueling or murder. But then that is all out of my hands.

My clients are all men—except for one mysterious woman. I don't even know her name. She's a refined and very attractive lady. You can't mistake her for anything else. Her clothes, reflecting the latest fashion, are gorgeous. She doesn't speak dialect and although she knows Italian she seems to favor an impeccable French. I imagine that she is wealthy. At least she doesn't hesitate to spend. I was wondering what she was doing in my establishment when she sat down in one of the chairs lined along the wall and watched Signor Albalino trying to get past my guard with his foil. To give him credit he was clumsier than usual, being thrown off by the presence of a spectator, a woman to boot and such an unusual woman at that.

As you undoubtedly know, it is not socially acceptable for a woman, much less a lady, to engage in the manly art of fencing, so she arranged to come late at night when she could come without attracting attention. I taught her with the doors locked. She got to be very good, much better than many of my usual clients. The first time, there were some clumsy moments. I didn't know how obsequious I should be. I had never dealt with women of her class and the fraternity of the sword is much less conscious of rank than the rest of the world. Another difficult moment was caused by the fact that she had to change into more suitable clothes—disrobe and dress in a corner with all the lights turned off. This, however, quickly became routine.

You might say that my story started when a man intercepted me as I was going to the tavern, as is my custom, at about 2:00 in the afternoon for a small dinner. I invited him to sit with me and share in the repast or drink a glass of wine. He was dressed all in velour and gilt. He accepted the wine but didn't want to eat. I didn't know whether the surroundings were too plebeian for his taste. He waited until the owner, *signor* Mandolini, took our order and went back to the kitchen and then he spoke.

"I have been sent by Armando, the eldest son of the Duke. My name is Bertoldo." Puzzled, I nodded. "He has been told about your prowess with the sword and would like to test himself with you in a friendly encounter." Another nod seemed necessary.

"You have to come to their summer residence for one day. You can expect two gold coins for your effort."

The offer was generous but then it could have been a prank. The nobility was not adverse to practical jokes, particularly if the butt of the diversion belonged to the common people. Perhaps because my expression reflected my thoughts, two ducats were pushed toward me. Now the man was talking!

A more experienced man could have seen the dangers but I didn't' and judged the matter too mundane to bother my patron, Messer Martinone, for advice. We shook hands over the deal. Another mistake. Any large commitment should be done in writing, but since I was collecting the money in advance, I didn't feel that formality was all that important. Detailed instructions followed: where to go, when to go and what to expect.

On that day, I continued my activities at the academy. When my commitments were over, in the late afternoon, I was about to lock up. A woman called out from the door. I approached her to find out what she wanted.

"Signor Fenestrini, I have to talk to you about an urgent matter."

She was well dressed and when she spoke she had only a trace of dialect in her voice. She was pretty in a fresh unsophisticated way but bore anxiety on her face. I didn't think it was appropriate to ask a lady into the academy but I didn't know what else to do.

Inside, she closed the door and continued. "I'm in the Duke's household. I'm Serafina. You might have heard of me. You shouldn't accept the proposal to exhibit your skills. It's a plan to dispose of the Duke's eldest son, Armando. They are hoping that in the heat of the game, with all the young men present and cheering, one of you will get killed. Armando is awfully hot-blooded. Either way he wouldn't be able to succeed the Duke. If he kills you, the Church and the populace will not find him acceptable. If you kill him, of course, their aim will be accomplished even more quickly. The idea of the game is a masquerade to hide a conspiracy. Please don't go."

"My dear lady, your story sounds far-fetched. Anyway, I have already made a commitment."

"I see that you're even stupider than you look," she said with venom in her voice.

I bowed as if I had received a compliment. I felt sorry for her. She seemed close to tears. I wasn't sure whether her story had substance or not, but I felt it necessary to fulfill my side of the bargain. And possibly I might have more skill than she realized.

"I'll be very careful. You know the saying, '*han fatto il conto senza l'oste*'—'they added up the bill without counting on the innkeeper.' Perhaps it will apply here."

Serafina burst into tears and left. I tried to stop her by holding on to her arm, but she broke free.

After renting a horse—I didn't have one of my own—I started early in the morning. Luckily, the Duke's family and retinue weren't at their summer residence in the mountains but at the one only a few miles from town. Although the summer residence lines imitated a castle, I don't find it as impressive as that in the town, which actually has towers and a moat.

Bertoldo was waiting for me at one of the side entrances and led me to the courtyard through a dark corridor. The light in the open space following the darkness made me blink. The many young people, men and women richly dressed, were feasting—as I saw when my eyesight adjusted to the bright light. The gathering looked much like a country fair except for the elegance of the attire of the participants and the multicolored standards that were flying in the breeze. Many must have been curious about me because they looked up.

I was offered wine and food but I turned them down politely. The men holding the trays were surprised. But I knew well that as long as I wasn't hungry, an empty stomach and a clear mind were essential.

After a long wait, Armando made his appearance. The crowd cheered. With a smile, he bowed to the assembly, in a pantomime of a thespian and then bowed at me. I had no idea whether he was making fun of me or if it was an expected part of the ritual. He was tall, with blonde curly hair, a light complexion and well-proportioned features like those of the little cupids you see in paintings. Not a good sign. Such men frequently feel they need to prove their manhood.

Two men-at-arms chose the swords and looked at me for my approval. I would have preferred my own, which I carry whenever I travel, but I had left it in its scabbard, attached to the saddle of my horse, having expected the use of blades with a safety at the tip to avoid injury. The tips, however, were not provided, vaguely confirming Serafina's warning. Of course it is possible for two experienced fencers to hold back the blade at the last moment but this is rarely done in a public display. I didn't feel like protesting so I nodded. Still a foolish youth, I felt an objection might be taken as a mark of cowardice.

Facing each other, we saluted by lowering the blade first to the left, then the right and the middle. To me any encounter is a high-stakes game. I'm never off guard, never angry or excited. These served me well. Armando immediately thrust. I hadn't encountered that ploy since I was a child. The movements needed for a response are engraved in my mind. I moved to one side and with a twist of my wrist held his blade to the side with mine and then also thrust. I didn't have any intention of hitting him. I was trying to say: "Don't be an idiot, you're not dealing with an amateur."

A flurry of thrusts from my opponent followed. Encouraging yells came from the crowd with each assault. Armando moved fast basing his attacks mostly on the footwork of advance and retreat. He was well-coordinated but his style would exhaust him in short order. There was no doubt in my mind that he wouldn't hesitate in killing me. Once, he thrust fully expecting to hit my exposed neck, which of course had moved. I swallowed hard, the confrontation had acquired the character of walking on a tightrope over an abyss with disaster waiting on either side. I easily could have killed him several times but that obviously would have been a disaster.

I don't know what arcane instinct possessed me, but suddenly I knew what to do. When my opponent was getting visibly tired, I started scoring, trying to hit and rapidly retract so as just to touch or leave only very superficial wounds. First his left arm, then his right. I hit toward the heart, then the left shoulder and then the right shoulder. It must have been clear to him that I was completely in control. I stepped back staring at him and lowering my sword but ready for any movement, and said, "Sir, it's clear that we are equally skilled and there is no point in continuing. I have to congratulate you, my noble, very brave and skillful adversary and thank you for giving me, a humble citizen of our town, this opportunity to show my ability."

It was lucky that Armando understood the true meaning of my message and put his blade down. Had he tried to take advantage of my vulnerability, I would have had no choice but to kill him.

There was a moment of silence and then applause and pandemonium. The revelry started again but after a few minutes the noise suddenly stopped. Everyone turned in a single direction and so did I. The old Duke was there. Although his eyes were ablaze his words were gentle.

"It's always a great pleasure to see youth enjoying itself. Soon it will have to face serious facts and events and it is then that it will have to prove its mettle. But please, for now enjoy, enjoy."

I felt a firm hand on my elbow. "The Duke wants to see you. Please come with me." Dread enveloped me. Just when I'd felt I was safe again!

I was led to a sumptuous, yet cheerful room. Damasks with painted hunting scenes hung on the walls. The Duke looked taller and more menacing than he had in the courtyard. Behind him I saw several women, among them Serafina.

"*Signor* Fenestrini, come forward. I have to talk to you." Then he continued. "I came back not too long ago. Unfortunately, I had been traveling. My ladies were watching the spectacle from this window. When I came in, if I could have interrupted I would have but I was too late. Serafina explained to me what was happening. I owe you. A first born is always special to his father even if he's an idiot. You can rest assured that heads will roll. But in your case I have other plans. Is there anything you desire? It would be a just reward."

"Your Grace, having brought this affair to a satisfactory conclusion is enough."

"Well, then I must decide for you. My treasurer will give you thirty ducats before you leave. You can also pick any one of these ladies, except of course, my daughter Giovanna. They all come with a small dowery if you do the right thing."

I found myself blushing profoundly. "Your Grace, such an honor is totally unnecessary!"

I had been told that the Duke had a very strange sense of humor about such matters. He took delight in keeping all of his illegitimate children under his roof and when he controlled their destiny he wasn't always kind.

"I think you should take Serafina. She also has a devious mind—like yours."

Unfortunately, both Serafina and I were embarrassed and blushed fiercely. Possibly, the Duke misunderstood the meaning of our response. "Ah! I see you're well acquainted already. So be it! And now you can all leave; I have to close this unfortunate affair as quickly as possible."

Suddenly Serafina and I were left alone. She expressed herself forcefully.

"This is ridiculous! I have much better prospects. I don't have to be stuck with a man who is hardly above the level of a servant. My dowery isn't that small."

I was stung by her opinion of me, but who was I to disagree? "I agree with you completely. And I certainly wouldn't consider marrying somebody I hardly know!"

In retrospect the words were unfortunate and open to misinterpretation. She stepped back with fury on her face. I have no idea how she got hold of the short whip, the kind used by riders. It barely missed my left eye wielded with no less fury than what had shown on her face. The pain was considerable and for a few moments I felt blinded. My hand came back bloody from my face. There was little I could do in response. Besides, she seemed to have left the room. A long time ago I had learned the secret of survival is often to do nothing. She was back soon enough with tears in her eyes.

"They won't even let me talk to him!"

"Well, it seems simple enough. I leave and you stay."

There was a look of horror on her face. "You can't disobey His Grace! It would have dire consequences. He has quite a temper!"

It would have been a comedy if it hadn't didn't affected profoundly the future of two young people. Serafina had to accompany me in a coach provided by the household attended by her maid and with an enormous amount of possessions. My mind questioned whether my humble abode would have enough space to contain all her worldly goods. In fact, it was remarkable that I even had a house. I stayed for a long time as a guest in a boarding house—much more convenient for my needs. Unfortunately, the lady of the house took it into her mind to share my bed whenever her husband, a big unpleasant brute, was absent or drunk. The liaison was not unpleasant, although she was no beauty. But it cost me a beating which I could have easily avoided if I had chosen to use my dagger instead of my fists. Martinone and my father took pity on me and advanced me the cash for a house of my own.

The sun was setting when we left. I would have preferred to have travelled before dark to avoid a possible interception by brigands, although the area frequented by the Duke's men was considered safe. Close to the horizon the sky was aflame contrasting with the darkening green of the trees. There is a touch of pleasure even in adversity.

Fortunately, we were not accosted by either friend or foe and arrived at my house without incident. I had been ready to use my sword which I had held on the ready, although it would have been of doubtful use against a pistol.

I helped unload the coach. Serafina expressed surprise that I didn't have a servant to help us. I made sure that everything was alright and then I attempted to leave over her objections.

"Where are you going?"

"I can't stay with you in the house. Your reputation would be shattered. You might want to get married to some deserving soul later."

"You'll live to regret it if you go against the Duke's wishes. He made it clear what he wanted!"

"Well, there are more important things than the Duke's wishes. In my estimation, marriage requires love and peace of mind."

"You're like a child! That's not reality!"

"I'll be back in the morning and I'll bring breakfast. I'll spend the night at the academy." I cringed internally at the thought. I would have to sleep on the floor and as I remembered I'd have no blankets.

I brought pastries and bread, fresh from the bakery in the morning. Serafina's maid, after going to fetch fresh water from the communal fountain, had made coffee and tea and had found the butter. We sat around the kitchen table. Serafina didn't seem concerned with that. I guessed that's what she had done when in the Duke's household. She appeared calmer at breakfast.

"So! What do you propose we do? Mind you, I'll go along with you only if you take the blame for not obeying the Duke."

I had given it considerable thought during a sleepless night. "Thirty ducats are a lot of money. They would last me two or three years and much more since I derive a good income from the academy. I propose to give you half. You could live on that for a while and have your own home."

Serafina snorted. "What can a woman alone possibly do? And I won't be welcome at the palace where all my friends are."

"I've thought about that. There is a dry goods store for sale. Ribbons, cloth and the like. Emma Ticino is too old to run it. The store also dabbles in dressmaking. It's smack in the middle of the social life of women of all social strata. You would never be lonesome!"

"That's what you think of me? You want to make me a miserable dressmaker?"

"It will be what you make of it. You can hire people to do the manual work. That's what Emma Ticino does. And I understand you have considerable experience with cloth and women's fashions. Your maid is quite emphatic about that. You can provide the design and taste. Or you can try to find a husband. Under the circumstances it might be difficult with only fifteen ducats and no dowery. But you're welcome to try."

"You are a first-rate unfeeling bastard, aren't you?"

I thought that was best left unanswered.

As providence would have it, Serafina reluctantly followed the path I suggested. She quickly became by all signs a princess in all but title. All women, including some of the nobility, deferred to her taste and her recommendations. I saw her rarely but was pleased to see her bloom, convinced that she was better off than she would have been if had she waited for the Duke to find her an oaf of a husband.

In my personal life, I went my own way hoping the Duke had forgotten me. In fact, he was kept busy with the threat of conspiracy and rebellion. An active group of Carbonari had come to his attention and there was discontent among the citizenry. Many were inflamed by the absurdity of a united and republican Italy. It would seem that the Emperor of France had planted many seeds that were to germinate later after his death.

Friends introduced me to a young, and I was told rich widow, Liliana Marvola, who had two small daughters. I was charmed by them and we quickly became more than friends. She broached the subject of marriage first.

"I think you should propose marriage. It's obvious that we love each other and people are beginning to talk. I wouldn't worry too much about that, but I have to think of the future of my two daughters."

"Indeed, you're right. Will you marry me?"

"I will but on one condition. You'll have to give up your mistress."

"Mistress? What are you talking about?"

"Everybody knows you have a mistress. How else could she have climbed to such a pinnacle of financial success."

I frowned and it took me a while to realize what she was alluding to. "You mean *Madame* Serafina? She is not my mistress although we have become good friends."

Liliana was obviously annoyed, "You must think I'm a naive idiot!"

I became full of anxiety, worried that my explanations would not suffice. "No, Liliana, you're wrong. Let me tell you what happened from the very beginning.

"As you know, I'm a man of the sword...saber and foil too. Not like a man who "lives by the sword and dies by the sword." Not at all. I'm a disciple of Messer Martinone and I have run his fencing academy since 1816. He was the best fencer in the world until the years and arthritis caught up with him. Now I'm the best..."

THE TALLY

An enormous warehouse of high ceilings, polished wooden floors. Every bit of space covered with tastefully displayed furniture and rugs, arranged in microcosms each representing a style, an imagined household. Rugs, couches, tables, chairs and beds carefully selected for dramatic effect—the choices in each group skillfully blended to form a pleasing whole, ranging from the rustic in one spot to gentle curves and polished elegance of yesteryear in another.

"Damn good gimmick," thought Roger. A tall man, clean shaven and with light brown hair, he was with his friend. Bill, having just married Laura, was looking over what was needed for their household. To their acquaintances, the marriage had been totally unexpected. The two had known each other forever, but had never thought of each other as material for romance, much less marriage. Roger, who knew them both well, couldn't imagine how it had happened. A highly improbable event, he thought, especially since cupid had to hit both of them, not just unexpectedly but simultaneously. Roger liked them both and wished them luck.

Bill was an ordinary looking fellow. His face was neither handsome nor ugly. His sandy hair surrounded a bald spot the size of a silver dollar on the back of his head. He was what might be called medium-sized and had a smile which frequently played on his lips. He was a pleasant fellow, Roger thought.

Roger was there merely to pass the time. Bill had asked him to come and keep him company. The final decision required the presence of his new wife, Laura.

Actually, Roger was not interested in furniture. Having been divorced for two years, his attempts at domesticity no longer included refurbishing his bachelor pad. He found himself looking over the woman who was showing them around, a saleswoman or hostess of sorts—reasonably attractive, in her late thirties, small breasted, well clad in a gold and brown printed silk blouse and a straight brown skirt meant to flatter her legs. No wedding ring, but a tasteful ring holding a small emerald-like stone. Her chestnut hair was skillfully arranged to denote spontaneity, a look that Roger thought might be expensive. The almost invisible lines on her face and a perfectly molded nose suggested plastic surgery. For some reason these details carried for him a subtle message—a woman who would be an easy target for a determined man. After breaking up with his latest, Roger was interested only in a liaison with a minimum of complications. Romance lead to situations he wished to avoid.

Before leaving, Bill folded and pocketed a sheet of paper with some of the specifications and prices the sales woman had jotted down for him. For his part, Roger made sure he had one of her cards with her phone number and e-mail address, which specified that Evelyn Batros was a sale's associate. Of course, there was no way he could know whether she was unattached.

At a party, Laura had once summed up Roger's philosophy in relation to women: heartless and only in search of pleasures. She had dubbed him the ultimate hedonist, a modern day satyr. The words had been said with a smile and after an obviously satirical description of his physical attributes. Nevertheless, the charge which had elicited universal laughter should have stung. It didn't, simply because Roger recognized it was at least partially true. The pain of the still-remembered marital conflict and divorce and the lesser pain of more recent encounters with the opposite sex were still on his mind and had led him to a very egotistic philosophy. He was not the kind of man who pretended to be what he wasn't.

When he phoned Evelyn at the store, she sounded eager, undoubtedly savoring a possible sale. Her voice indicated less enthusiasm however, when he made it clear that she was the interest of his attention. Not surprising, Roger thought, the world is full of possible missteps for a single woman. Her responses suggested that she was unattached.

"Look," he reassured her, "I'm harmless, I work for the law firm of Fulton and Fulton. Give me a chance. Meet me for coffee at the *Orchestra*." Roger didn't tell her that he was one of the partners of the firm. No point in planting thoughts in her mind. She finally agreed to meet him The proffered reassurances seemed to work, although her acceptance was unenthusiastic.

The bustling coffee shop just a few blocks from the furniture store provided the necessary protection of a large group of people and the privacy it provides—people with company insulate themselves from the crowd, either out of habit or the need to concentrate on the conversation they are holding with their friends.

They met at the door of the *Orchestra*. Over coffee and pastries, Roger poured on the charm. He was respectful but flirtatious—well informed but a good listener.

"I called Fulton and Fulton," she volunteered.

"I'm glad you did. Now you know!"

They had dinner together a couple of times. On the third date at the door of her apartment, Roger kissed her passionately, holding her body close with his hands on her buttocks. Her trembling told him all he needed to know. She had told him she had no roommates, so he pushed his way in and closed the door behind them. The two of them tumbled onto her bed. He found her pliable, yet not reluctant to take exciting initiatives.

The affair was a pleasant one. There wasn't much they had in common, and at least on his part, there was little intimacy apart from their shared sexuality. Roger took her to a few plays or movies. At the rare party, they'd met some of his friends. She was self-contained, polite but not one to volunteer opinions or engage in discussions.

Not surprisingly Roger noted that sooner or later he would become bored with her. Better break up before the inevitable became obvious.

He met her at her apartment and instead of their usual sexual banter, he got ready to announce what was on his mind. Breaking up had always been unpleasant but he knew what had to be done. Before he could marshal his thoughts, Evelyn spoke up.

"Roger, it's been great fun and I wish we could continue but I'm afraid you won't want to stay with me any longer. The fun would be over. I have been diagnosed with a serious disease, not contagious mind you." She smiled and then continued, "I don't want to draw you into something I'm sure you wouldn't want."

The thought that she had anticipated him was amusing. The excuse was palpably false. He thought, "Score in your favor. Great style!"

Playing along with her excuse was only natural. There was no point in allowing the situation to become a confrontation. After all she was letting him off painlessly.

"I'm sorry to hear this. May I ask you the nature of your condition?"

"Well, I don't mind telling you if you will refrain from commenting. It's ovarian cancer. As you might know, it is almost always fatal." The latter was issued with a grimace and a smile.

"Aren't you overdoing it?" he thought.

There wasn't much he could do or say after that. He kissed her a chaste goodby and wished her luck. In his car he almost burst into laughter but contented himself with an amused smile.

He didn't know what had compelled him to ask for her at her place of work. The woman on the phone explained that Evelyn's health had forced her to quit and she no longer was with the firm.

The lawyer in him made him go one step farther. He had an easy-going relationship with the Hawk Detective Agency often retained for such matters by his firm, and had his friend Louis Contini (dubbed by his friends, 'Hawk') look into the matter. He was still reluctant to accept her story. Although Hawk couldn't possibly get the medical details, he did find out that she was under the care of an oncologist and was about to be treated at the hospital.

That the explanation she had given him was true was unexpected. Furthermore, it saddened him at least for a few moments; he genuinely liked her. But then these things happen and it was none of his business. Evelyn's problem was supplanted in his mind by happier thoughts. Roger had in fact noted a woman who attracted him strongly, Roberta, ironically someone he had met at a party when he had been accompanied by Evelyn. On their first date, with some careless comments Roberta had started a train of events that he couldn't have predicted.

"I have been told the woman you used to date, Evelyn, is very sick and she has nobody she can turn to."

"Hm, I'm surprised. She is a very pleasant woman. I would have guessed she have had lots of friends."

He dismissed Evelyn's problem. But then somehow thoughts about her returned to torment him. What compelled him to call her was not clear to him. But he did call her and went to see her.

"You're all alone? Don't you have relatives, close friends?"

"Roger, it's sweet of you to worry about me, but I think I can confront my problems by myself. I'm accustomed to being alone. I have faced many crises alone."

"You have health insurance I imagine."

"Don't kid yourself, a job such as I had depended on commissions and had no benefits. That's the way the world is run. But then there is always Medicaid."

"Well, let me know if I can help."

"But you shouldn't get involved. You know that we really weren't close friends even if we shared some good times."

He was relieved that he wouldn't have to follow up on his offer. His past had let him avoid any serious commitment to helpless causes.

A few days later the jangling of the phone forced him to pick it up just as he had returned to his apartment. Evelyn's voice was so charged with anxiety that he had trouble recognizing it.

"I'm terrified. I can't do it on my own Roger. Could you accompany me when I go to the hospital. Just for the checking in."

Evelyn seemed to have regained her composure when he arrived. The checking in was routine. She had to wait until they found a hospital room for her for after her recovery. He found the registration process deeply disturbing. This was not a casual medical procedure. She should have been able to choose the best possible hospital.

He found himself in a totally unfamiliar role. Holding her hand he spoke softly of things in the world familiar to them. He concocted a few amusing anecdotes which brought a smile to her lips. Obviously, the moment for him to leave came soon.

For some reason, he found himself incapable of sleeping. Evelyn's misfortunes and her courage, even if sometimes the latter faltered, were of such magnitude and so unfamiliar that they were almost outside of his comprehension.

To his own surprise he found himself at her side when she went into the operating room and then after a tense wait when she was released into the recovery room.

❋   ❋   ❋

Roger didn't know what was driving him. He went to see her once she left the hospital. She came to the door and smiled.

"Please come in! Forgive me if I have to stretch out."

He had brought flowers knowing fully well that it was an empty gesture. She had spread herself out on her couch and looked pale and tense. She must have wondered why he was there. He spoke without preliminaries. Her quandary had been eating at him since the last time he had seen her.

"You should get the best of care. There are hospitals that specialize in cancer. Sloan-Kettering in New York comes to mind."

"Roger, you know that I have no money, no insurance."

"Evelyn, this is no time for the usual way of doing things. You don't have the money, but I do."

"How could you possibly do that? We are just friends. You must have other responsibilities."

"Look, I have much more money that I can possibly spend—no child support, no alimony payments, no debts. I really don't know why I accumulated so much. Please let me do this for you!"

❦   ❦   ❦

Roger stayed with Evelyn to the bitter end. After weeks of pain, her death came during a peaceful moment. He was grateful that she had died when not in the throngs of pain, relieved by the drugs.

He didn't return to work for at least a week and avoided his social world for more than a month. Laura insisted that he come to dinner. She and Bill hadn't seen him for a long time. Without going into detail, Roger explained that he had been upset when a friend of his had died.

At the door a cheerful Bill greeted him. Another couple was present that Roger also knew and introductions were not necessary. Bill directed him to a table with drinks.

Sipping on a drink before dinner and after casual conversation, Laura remarked to Roger, "You are different. Something changed."

"I'm a few months older."

"No, you are more serious, more thoughtful," and then she said with a smile, "Maybe you finally grew up!"

Roger thought, "A person is just a tally of all his experiences, all the emotions he has been subject to." He really didn't know what he could tell Laura. But he noted that in her eyes, he no longer was a hedonist. Perhaps that summed up all that had happened to him.

POINT OF VIEW

Adrianne thought that Benjamin Worth, lean and humorless, had the appearance of an ascetic. She could only think of him as Mr. Worth. Pale and tall, his mouth was forever pursed as if in disapproval. He was colorless in more ways than one. Rarely did he join in the revelry which sometimes broke out spontaneously in the office or the boardroom when something amusing happened or after a tense moment. He didn't invite confidences and neither did he convey any personal information. Everybody knew that he was married but little else. Years before Mrs. Worth had attended their Christmas parties, Adrianne had been told—a colorless presence, just like her husband. Mr. Worth seldom spoke out unless his opinion was solicited and then it was frequently bland. He dressed conservatively but without a thread of imagination. How he had climbed so high in Wolfson Plastics was hard to understand. Perhaps because he was conscientious and hard working. Surprisingly, those attributes still counted.

Adrianne had to give him credit. He never revealed any antagonism to her presence, even when she had just started with the firm and had been the only woman. This was rare in a man's world. Neither did he show any antagonism when she climbed the company ladder. It had been her dream, possibly culminating soon with her becoming head of the whole shebang. Still, she considered Mr. Worth an anachronism who had lived past his usefulness, although she would never voice her opinion.

Mr. Sullivan, the boss of bosses, clearly agreed with her unspoken evaluation.

"Christ! He's been gone for a full week, 'family sickness.' This just won't do. You'll have to take over his accounts. Here is the paperwork. But go see him first at his home. Not every detail is ever fully spelled out."

Adrianne was talking about that unpleasant task with Edward. They were having dinner at a fancy restaurant, still at the stage of reading the lengthy menu. She thought that a foray into an elegant and pleasant environment might revive their relationship which was getting somewhat dull. They had lived together for three years and it was beginning to feel, God forbid, like marriage.

They had agreed a long time ago never to discuss their work when going out on one of their outings. But she couldn't help herself.

"Ady, it sounds to me as if the prick is getting ready to fire the poor bastard!" Ed had never liked Sullivan. "These days, you have to have youth and pizzaz or you don't count!"

She knew there was a lot of truth in what he said. In fact, the two of them, Ed and Adrianne, were considered by most to have those attributes. Always elegant. Good looking and sophisticated.

"Ed! I didn't know you felt that way."

"Well, from what you tell me Worth carries his load well and he has been doing so for many, many years. What is it? Twenty, thirty."

"Oh! I forget. Somebody told me once."

The waiter had come back and his presence interrupted their discussion. Ed ordered scotch on the rocks—Chivas Regal, he insisted as always. "How pretentious," she thought, whiskey is whiskey. She was happy with the house white wine.

They didn't speak about the matter again. After they ordered their food they went on to a discussion of the play they were to see shortly, Wendy Wasserstein's *The Heidi Chronicles*.

Unfortunately, the unpleasant task of talking to Worth didn't go away. She phoned first. Worth's response was not exactly forthcoming. "Well, any day is as bad as another. Come this afternoon."

He opened the door wearing a frayed shirt and shapeless pants. He looked overwrought and overtired. "Come on in, come on in. I'll see what I can do to help you, although I'm not exactly in the mood for business."

The house was drab, furnished with odds and ends from another period. The two of them sat in the living room. A door giving to a bedroom was ajar. "I have to listen, Elaine is not doing well, not well at all." He explained, "my wife." They sat on the couch and Adrianne placed the papers on a coffee table after pulling it close to them.

Worth plunged right in, "The Lepssis account..."

A pained call came from the bedroom.

Adrianne could hear a plaintive female voice asking, "Can't I have more now? It hurts like hell!"

Worth excused himself, got up and hastened to the room. Adrianne couldn't hear his response but the tones were soothing, affectionate. He must have acquiesced because he was gone for some time. Adrianne leaned over so that she could see. She got a glimpse of the patient who appeared emaciated beyond imagination. Then Worth's back blocked her view and she sat back.

When he was back he spoke to Adrianne softly. "It's hard to guess what is best for her, more pain or morphine. Cancer. She's dying. I probably erred and gave her more morphine. She wants to die at home. I have to respect that. I'd want the same."

Then he leaned over toward her. "When you have been married for forty years, it's just as if you're dying too." And then with moisture in his eyes, he said "I just wish I could share some of the pain. We've shared everything else."

Adrianne didn't know what was moving her. Pity? Sympathy? Impatience?

"Look, it's best if I leave. Obviously, it's not the right time for business."

❦   ❦   ❦

That evening, sitting in the kitchen she waited patiently for Ed to return. He was supposed to bring food from the Chinese restaurant. Normally, she would be hoping he would bring their chicken with cashews, her favorite. But with all that was worrying her, she didn't even think about it.

Ed put the bags on the kitchen table. Adrianne hardly noticed the enticing aroma that emanated from the package. He turned toward her.

"Oh, oh. I see that you have something on your mind…Something bad."

"Ed, I quit Wolfson." She knew fully well the implications. She was not likely to find a comparable job in town and would have to move to New York or Chicago. Either way she was likely to lose Ed. After all his career was going very well where he was.

Ed's face was blank. "Tell me what happened."

"It happened as you predicted. Sullivan wanted to fire Worth. I objected. He said he would anyway. I waved the ultimate threat, that I'd resign if he did that to Worth. Well, I resigned. It's not a question of a disagreement, it's a question of principle. They'll have a hard time without me. He offered me to head my section, raises, etc., etc. I didn't buy. The irony, of course, is that eventually he'll have to rehire Worth. There is nobody else besides me who knows the ropes."

"Ady, I'm proud of you."

He hugged her and kissed her.

"Yeah! But where does that leave us?"

"We'll do fine. You'll get another job easily elsewhere."

"What about you?

"I'll be fine too. I can get another job easily."

"You really want to move?"

"Not particularly. What I want is to be with you."

Adrianne was overwhelmed by a strange feeling. She didn't know exactly what it was but it felt good.

"Well, where should we look first?" she asked.

MASQUERADES

Terry had always found that one string of events leads to another. Teaching in the Community College was not the most interesting job in the world. There was of course the rare moment when everything came together. His thoughts would flow freely in appropriate vernacular and the class would respond. But that wasn't often. The burden had been lightened by his volunteering in a middle school. For some reason the jeering, disrespectful students could be interested in chess. Terry had put together and trained one of the best teams in the state. They still jeered, used four letter words and spoke as if the world was made of shit. It existed just to bore them or keep them out of anything worthwhile. But they must have enjoyed the game. They didn't have to stay after school, or come to the park on weekends—unless they'd wanted to play. Besides these activities, Terry was always happy to explore something unusual. His experience one evening dragged him into a complex adventure.

Terry's adventure never should have happened. He would have been happy to avoid the miserable corner of city where he had gone. As usual Arthur's instructions had been abominable. Terry couldn't find that damn jazz place where a group displaced by Hurricane Katrina was supposed to be performing. He was to meet his friend there, like him a jazz enthusiast. These days, good live New Orleans jazz was hard to come by. The spontaneity, the improvisation were what delighted him. He was early and decided he might as well wait to resume his search. Once time went by, he might be able to hear the sound of the instruments from the street.

The bar where he finally entered wasn't the kind he was familiar with. At least from the outside and at night they all seemed about the same. Had he noticed its unauspicious interior immediately, he probably would have left. The uninterrupted buzz of men's voices and the occasional loud expletive—several tattooed men with muscular arms in sweat stained t-shirts sitting

- 182 -

at the tables. Beer bottles prevailed. The words that could be distinguished were laced with profanities and sexual innuendo. Although not brightly lit, the room was not enticing. The floor of naked wood planks was scuffed and grayed by time and abuse from what he could see and strewn with cigarette butts and unidentifiable debris. The smell of cigarette smoke, stale beer and a faint hint of old urine prevailed. It must have been one of the few places where smoking was still allowed. Terry knew it had been a mistake to enter but then he hadn't known whether the other bars in the vicinity were any better. He'd have to remember to tell Arthur that the whole area sucked. Terry had ordered a beer from the bar and with the bottle in his hand sat down as far as possible from the crowd.

Perhaps he shouldn't have been surprised by drama that unfolded before his eyes. After all, this was a place where he felt anything might happen. First harsh, angry words laced with obscenities were exchanged between a man and a woman. The woman was slight and pretty in a tawdry way—too much makeup, clothing in loud colors, much cleavage, long exposed legs—and stringy brown hair. Her face might have been pretty if it hadn't been twisted in anger or fear. She couldn't have been much older than twenty. Her opponent looked much like the other men, his muscles bulging, his hands big and dangerous. He suddenly seized her and yanked her out of her seat to force her to leave with him. Struggling, she protested but the man's threats seemed to forestall any forceful yells for help. Had she cried out, Terry was pretty sure nobody would have paid attention anyway. Whoever she was, she had moxie. There was no reason for him to get involved. A whore is just a whore. They made their choice a long time ago.

Terry always considered himself the ultimate cynic, ready to limit his involvement in situations that didn't concern him. Yet for some inexplicable reason, he found the scene deeply disturbing. On top of that he had always had the strange delusion that he could handle violent confrontations handily. He knew it wasn't true, but his responses were from pure instinct. Strength and skill were just two of the factors, but chance also played a role—too much perhaps. His teacher, Takimura, had warned him that you never can predict the outcome of a physical encounter. Besides, in this case how could he be sure that the resort to force wouldn't start a riot? The men present didn't seem adverse to violence.

Terry's words came out between clenched teeth. "Can't you tell? She doesn't want to go with you." But he hadn't forgotten all of Taki's teaching—"do the unexpected." Terry didn't wait for an answer. His left hand seized the man's arm and twisted it. His right foot swept the right leg so that the man lost his balance and fell. Terry grabbed the woman practically lifting her. He was surprised to find her so light. They were out of the door before the element of surprise was over. He didn't stop until he had put some distance between them and any possible attacker. The woman's feet hardly touched the ground. The easiest way of disappearing from the well-illuminated street was to enter another bar. Taverns seemed to stretch out along the street, one following another.

He dragged the girl inside with him. The new bar was dark and quiet, more suited to a rendezvous or a tryst. That's were he should have gone in the first place. The woman kicked him as he sat her down at a table.

"What makes you think I want to be with you, motherfucker!"

Terry chuckled, "I can take you back if you want." That seemed to temporarily silence her.

"Who the fuck are you?"

"Why? I'm a knight in shining armor. Can't you tell?"

"More like a dickhead in shining condom."

Terry signalled the waitress who was approaching them for two Buds.

"Enough with the flattery! Where do you want me to take you?"

"I thought you might want some nooky. I guess you're not up to it."

"That's exactly true."

As the waitress brought two beer bottles, his companion let out a sigh. "Take me home."

"Finish your beer first if you haven't had too many already. We dickheads don't like to waste good drinks."

Her apartment was not too far. A car ride of a few minutes. He insisted on going up the creaky stairs with her. After opening the door with a jangling of keys, she surprised him with a kiss and disappeared slamming the door shut. He wiped his mouth with the back of his hand. God only knew what her mouth had touched! Although he could still chase down the location of the elusive jazz bar, he didn't feel in the mood for it anymore. He'd have to devise appropriate excuses for his friend. The truth seemed too far-fetched. It wasn't until much later that he found that his credit card billfold was missing. He chuckled to himself. That was what the kiss was about! What a chump! He certainly had taken the prize! Knight in shining armor! More like a naked ninny. Now he had to cancel all his credit cards!

His life returned to its usual routine and the peculiar incident receded from his mind. His teaching at the Community College was demanding even if it paid very little. What can you expect with only a master's degree? The kids from the chess group weren't meeting that week. Too bad, one of the girls, Charlene, was developing very nicely and had the makings of a champion. Terry enjoyed watching her progress—her determined little face furrowed in concentration.

In the evening, the telephone jingled as he was at his desk looking over some essays and wondering whether he was really wasting his time teaching. Very few of his efforts seemed to show meaningful results. Parroting from his lectures or Google seemed to prevail. The phone caller ID on the screen said "police." What the shit! He thought it could only mean trouble and he was right. He picked up the receiver. "Yes?"

The woman's voice didn't sound familiar. "This is Arlene."

"Do I know you?"

"I'm the damsel in distress you rescued!"

Ah! Maybe now he could avenge his loss of the credit cards.

"Yeah! What do you want?"

"I need more rescuing."

Terry was ready for a tart reply but he had detected a note of desperation in her voice. "Hm!" was all he could say.

"I need bail. It's only two hundred dollars but I don't have it…Please Terry? I'll be forever in your debt."

"What happened?"

"They arrested me. All bullshit!"

"I bet!" he thought. Of all the nerve. She probably got his name from the credit cards she had stolen.

"Well Arlene, what's in it for me?"

Arlene giggled, "Please come to the police station with the money, it's the right thing to do. As I said, I'll be forever in your debt."

Terry didn't know why he went to the police station. For some reason she intrigued him. The police would probably think he was her pimp! Her makeup was smeared; her hair and clothes were in disarray. She was prettier than when he'd first seen her. Her relief was palpable and there was hope in her eyes. That would be his only reward, he suspected.

He took care of the formalities. The money he had put aside for his vacation would have a sizeable dent in it. They climbed into his illegally parked car. The aged dark Toyota sedan looked almost respectable under the light from the street lamps. He was relieved to see no ticket on his windshield. The fines had become rather steep. Three in a month were more than enough.

"Where to?"

"Oh! Christ, I got no place to go!"

"What happened to your apartment?"

"Some goons are waiting for me there."

"Oh, oh. What did you do now?"

"Not a damn thing."

"You sure are a strange person. Shall I drop you at a motel?"

"You know I don't have any money. What's wrong with your place?"

"No way!"

That's just what he needed. Sharing his space with a prostitute! If she had argued or cried he certainly would have dumped her then and there. He stole a covert look in her direction and when illuminated by oncoming cars or the street lights, all he saw on her face was despair.

"Alright. But just for one night. And it's understood that we won't have anything to do with each other and tomorrow you get going."

In his apartment, first she required a sandwich, and luckily for her the makings were not too stale. It took a short while to prepare decaffeinated coffee for the both of them. He poured the brew in two mismatched mugs. She looked tired but he wasn't yet in the mood to let her off the hook.

"You stole my credit cards!"

"I had no way of knowing what I had taken. I wanted to know who you were. I didn't use them. Honest!"

Terry knew this was true. He let silence settle between them and then he spoke again.

"You'll have to tell me the whole story soon. Or you can go to hell!" She ignored his request and he let silence dominate for a while.

"You must be some kind of a dweeb. I see nothing but books and papers. Nothing to lighten up."

Terry ignored the comment. "You can have my bed, but take a shower first. I don't think you're at your best. I'll sleep on the couch. I want the bed and the bathroom to be your limits."

When the coffee was gone, he pulled a blanket out of the closet, turned off the lights except in the bathroom and slipped out of his pants. Leaving the door open, he hunkered down without difficulty. After hearing splashing in the bathroom, he heard the bed springs creak so she must have gone to bed too.

He must have been asleep for no more than a few minutes when he awoke with a start hearing her fussing in the bed—tossing and turning.

"Something the matter? Bed bugs?"

"Can we talk?"

"You had to wait until I was asleep? Why now? Is it really necessary? I'm tired."

"I haven't lied to you but I certainly tried to fool you. I don't feel right about it. And I might have put you in danger."

"What are you talking about?"

She turned the light on. She had wrapped herself in her sheet and with her wet hair, looked very young, very serious and vulnerable.

"I'm not a ho!"

"Is that why you waked me up...just to proclaim your virtue? They framed you when they arrested you for soliciting?"

"No. I solicited alright, right under the nose of a cop. It was the only way I could get away from some nasty men who were stalking me."

"Alright, enough of that. Start the story from the beginning and explain who you are."

"Actually, I'm Marion Gaytin. I'm a freelance reporter. You might have seen some of my stuff in *The Daily Chronicle*."

"That's your real name? Not a pseudonym? And you aren't yanking my chain?"

She reached into her purse and handed him her driver's license. Even the photograph matched.

"Okay, okay! Now start from the beginning."

"Check me out first. I published an exposé on the importation of juvenile prostitutes with the connivance of some immigration officers. It was a big hit. Check it out on Google. I see you have a lap-top on your desk."

"I'll take your word for it even if you don't have a very good truth record. Do you want me to believe that Marion Gaytin couldn't come up with two hundred dollars?"

"I don't carry my credit cards or much cash when I'm being Arlene, and I certainly didn't want the cops to know me as Marion Gaytin. I even hide my driver's license. Can you imagine what the media would do if they knew I'd been identified or arrested as a hooker?"

"Okay, tell me the whole story."

"I'll tell you the absolute truth but there isn't much to tell. I decided to look into prostitution in our fair city and the possible tie-in with the police. I guess I was a bit naive. I wanted to interview the women and get the whole flavor along with the tragic details. Sometimes as 'Arlene' I dressed like them and fre-

quented the same places. I recorded most of the conversations on my miniature tape recorder. The last one was with a woman named Mauve. Accidentally
I overheard the involvement of two policemen—nicknames, precinct, everything. Something like protection money changing hands along with intercept-
ing narcotics for their own purposes from minor dealers. As fate would have it,
I have no record because my tape recorder had run out of tape! But somebody
else must have been listening. The next day I heard on the boob-tube that a
prostitute answering Mauve's description had been murdered execution style.
And I'm damn sure it was Mauve. I have been on the run ever since. And don't
think I haven't been racked with guilt about what happened to Mauve."

"Does that explain my first rescue?"

"I don't know. The man dragged me into that bar. Either a john who
couldn't take 'no' for an answer or he wanted to take me some place for
another reason. Maybe my adversaries don't know exactly what kind of threat I
represent. After that, everything was reasonably cool until somebody broke
into my apartment. I have a draft of my report on my lap-top. I transferred the
information on the tapes to my computer at work but the actual tapes were at
home. The last time I went back, I saw the lab-top was missing…I ran like hell.
The rest you know."

"So they might have followed us from the police station."

"That's my fear, yes. That's why I am so worried and couldn't sleep. I'm
sorry to have involved you."

Terry laughed bitterly. "Don't you worry, sweetheart. The classroom and
teaching has given me a deep understanding of crime and punishment—the
devious and the profane!"

"I'm really sorry!"

"Let's worry about that later. Now we have to do something."

Terry sat back in deep thought and didn't say anything for a long while.
When he saw that Marion was about to speak, he held up his hand to silence
her. Did he believe her story as unlikely as it was? He did, although it was with
the part of his brain that held his intuition and not reason. What should they
do? His intuition spoke up again, they should get the hell out of there. He
finally was ready to speak.

"First of all let's see whether there is one of your friends waiting outside.
Maybe they don't care whether we can see them or not. I don't know why we
haven't heard from them already. Perhaps they are waiting for us to fall asleep."

He turned off the light and went to the window pushing the shade so that
there was a sliver of street view. His car was a block away. He'd been lucky to

find a space there. That's where they would have to go to escape. There was nothing to see, but that didn't mean that whomever was stalking them wasn't in one of the parked cars or hiding in one of the entrances of the apartment houses. He or they might have entered their building already. Shit! How can you tell. But then he realized it really didn't matter. He had to imagine that they were there and then make his move. A faint, just like in chess. All very predictable.

"Get dressed we got to move!" Marion grabbed her clothing, almost dropping the sheet she was holding, covering her. "Oh, shit. Not in your old clothes, they must be filthy. Let me see. Take one of my shirts. My shorts should fit you loosely and cover most of your legs which would be good. I find them damn distracting."

Terry also slipped his pants on.

He knew exactly what to do. Whenever the volume of the abominable music coming out of the apartment of the college kids above his had been too high, Mrs. Panquiss would call the police. On that night, the students didn't seem to be in or had succumbed to the cloud of weed Terry had occasionally smelled on a warm day when all windows were open.

"Okay, are you ready?" He looked at her and saw her reluctance. "You can't expect to look elegant in my clothes. And it's best if you look sexless considering your questionable past. Nobody will recognize you in your present duds!"

Marion retaliated by holding up her index finger in the well known vulgarity. Terry quickly looked through his tapes, found one he didn't like, pushed it into his machine and then turned it on at top volume. The loud and annoying music was deafening. If this didn't work, he'd have to think of some other ploy. He winked at her and over the overwhelming sound he said, "Clears your sinuses. Doesn't it?" He didn't think she had heard him, but then it really didn't matter.

He heard or was he reading her lips? "What's going on?"

"Wait and see," he answered,. leaning down and practically speaking into her ear.

Soon they heard sirens. As usual given the circumstances, the men of the Third Precinct wanted to make a dramatic entrance. They must regard it as a game when Mrs. Panquiss calls. Besides, they can yell at some fresh college kids that only know how to be obnoxious! If they were lucky, one of them would take a swipe at a guardian of the peace and the policemen would be able to do more than warn them.

Just as Terry had thought, just before the police arrived, a car parked in front took off with squealing tires. With Terry's prodding, the two of them were down by the entrance in no time at all. He restrained Marion with one hand, then stepped out, waved at the policemen with a big smile and yelled, "They sure know how to make a big racket!" and the two of them went to his car. A few blocks away he stopped the car and turned toward his passenger.

"We have two choices. We can go to my mom—she lives out of town and she can put us up for a while or I've got enough money left for one night at a motel."

"I think going to your mom would be a terrible mistake!"

"Why is that?"

"By now they know who you are."

"Oh, she wouldn't be that easy to trace. Sure, if they had lots of time, but not quickly. She goes by her maiden name and lives many miles from here."

"Look, mothers have a way of interfering. They have their own agenda which is not likely to work. I have thought about going to the police, but I have no evidence. They are likely to ignore me. Besides, don't forget that policemen are involved."

"I completely agree about not going to the police. But you're wrong about my mom."

"Oh?"

"She is more like Ma Barker than your stereotype. She's on this side of the law but she's a tiger. In my case, in the remote past, principals, social workers and career counselors didn't stand a chance."

"Who's Ma Barker?"

"One of the gangsters of the thirties."

"Aren't you being a bit tough on her?"

"Maybe. But tough she is."

"From what you say you must have been quite a handful."

"That I was. But let's get back to our problem."

"Okay. It will be Mom then. I'll take your word for it. And what about your dad. You must have a dad!"

"He died some time ago."

Following silence, Terry turned the car key and they were on their way.

❦   ❦   ❦

Terry's mother let them in without delay. They were expected since Terry had phoned her from the road. She had been simply told that her son's companion was called Marion. As soon as the older woman took a look at Marion and her ludicrous clothing, she hugged her and exclaimed to her son: "What have you done to the poor girl!"

"That's all the clothes we had, Mom."

His mother laughed. "Don't tell me why. Not into my tender ears. Well, we have to remedy this immediately. I'm sure I can find something of Liz's upstairs that will fit Marion once I fuss with it."

She disappeared up the stairs. Marion lifted her eyes and shook her head in mock despair as if to say, "Told you so." Terry couldn't resist the challenge.

"You'll be surprised to find out that her priorities are always correct."

"Who's Liz?"

"She's my sister. She's in college now."

His mother came down the steps slowly, she had a t-shirt and a pair of blue jeans.

"They won't be perfect, but after I get done with them they should be presentable. Try the jeans," and then pointing, "use the bathroom over there."

When Marion came out, wearing the garments, Mom quickly pinned the bottom of the jeans and with needle and thread she hemmed them.

"You can replenish your wardrobe later." Then she continued, "You're Marion Gaytin, of course. I have been reading your columns. One of them had your picture. You can call me Norma."

Terry smiled triumphantly as if to say, "See, she's not the dope you thought."

Norma continued, "I must say I think they are first rate. And the personal risks you took! I guess now this is more of the same. You two tell me what it's all about."

Norma listened carefully to Marion's story and Terry's interjections. She laughed at Terry's musical trick as if to say "that's my boy" and he was still a teenager. And then came her questions. Did Marion know the names of the policemen? Fortunately, Marion at least remembered their aliases and their routes when collecting their take. Whether their routine changed after Mauve's death was another matter.

Terry was not too discouraged by the lack of information. "My bet is that they'll go back to their routine after one or two weeks. Anyway, I have an approach that might work, you know like one size fits all, as they say when you go to buy new men's socks."

Norma interjected, "Ooh! I think you have something very ugly in mind."

"The uglier the better! As far as we know they aren't altar boys and it would seem they killed Mauve."

"Can you tell us?"

"You can guess since I need your help. Can you call your friend Douglas at the Forensic Laboratory and ask him what is a smelly impurity often present in impure heroin that has been seized in raids? As I remember from my chemistry lab in college, when you isolate and purify a compound, there is always something left with it, it could be alcohol, acetic acid, acetone or something like that."

Marion wanted to hear the rest of his plan.

"It's best if I keep them to myself right now. Besides, I'm going to play it by ear. But first we'll wait a while, maybe one week, maybe two. Mom is going to lend us money. You can replenish your wardrobe and we can relax. I'll have to find somebody to replace me in my classes and I'll call one of my chess buddies to take care of my chess group. I'm in the mood for a lot of swimming at the municipal pool. If you feel the same way, Marion, you're welcome to join me!"

Two weeks passed happily. The two of them behaved as if they had been friends all along. Terry was sure that Norma, like all moms he knew, would hope it was the beginning of a romance. She was tired of waiting for grandkids with few hopes left, even though her daughter Liz could easily be an alternative source.

For the ploy he had in mind, Terry insisted on going alone, to Marion's intense irritation.

"I'll be doing something highly questionable. Probably legal but still questionable. You should keep your slate clean to remain a credible journalist. Let me do the dirty work."

❦   ❦   ❦

"For shit sake," Marion screamed. Terry had never seen her so angry. "Here I try to attract your attention, we go dancing together, we go swimming together. I try to be sweet. Absolutely nothing happens. You take off for two days and where do you go? To a whorehouse. Don't tell me that isn't sick!"

"Marion, I tried to explain. It's part of my plan. It was business."

"Sure. That's what whorehouses are—businesses."

"Look, I didn't go there for sex."

"Oh, sure. You just had to get fucked as part of your fucking game. Don't tell me you didn't get laid!"

"I didn't get laid. I had to do something to justify my presence there. I told her I just liked to look at her naked. That I was going to pay her anyway."

"And that's better? And who was the paragon?"

"What has that to do with this? She told me her name was Stephanie."

"For shit sake! Here your mother was convincing me that you're a real human being, kind and sensitive. I thought I was beginning to care for you. And all you were doing was playing with me, shitting me. I despise you."

Along with the discomfort and anxiety over the enormity of their misunderstanding, Terry felt a warmth he never would have expected. No woman had ever told him she cared for him. They might have said how much fun they had with him, but that is an entirely different matter.

"Please, sit down. Let me tell you what actually happened. I care for you too. I didn't realize how you felt or I would have said it earlier. So please don't jump to conclusions."

Terry had timed himself to arrive at the whorehouse at about the same time the police duo usually came to take their cut. He was carrying a briefcase with ersatz heroine. The madam gave him hell for bringing the case into the house and he had to leave it in the hall. After selecting Stephanie from the available women, he had stayed with her as long as they would let him—forty minutes maximum. When he came out, the briefcase was gone. When he remonstrated, a man the madam had summoned threw him out bodily. And that was the end of the story. Would the trick work? He was sure that if they actually examined the powder they would know it was a fake. If they didn't, they must have had somebody who was ready to buy it from them. And then, hopefully all hell would break loose.

"So? What do you think that will accomplish?"

"I'm not sure. Maybe nothing. Maybe they will be put out of commission by their usual buyers for trying to cheat them."

"It seems to me that all it will accomplish will be to confirm that I know too much."

"They know that already."

The atmosphere between them remained glacial and they went their separate ways, mostly ignoring each other. Norma must have wondered what had happened but she was wise enough not to ask questions.

♣   ♣   ♣

Terry had to go back to his previous life. If there was danger so be it! He had to pick up teaching where Arthur had left his class. One evening, the radio had been on as the notes he had in front of him came to life. His lectures were usually freshly prepared every year. But this one time he had to make an exception, since he didn't have enough time. He could use what he had presented last year.

Something in the news broadcast caught his attention. The male voice seemed devoid of emotion. Two policemen had been killed execution style. After the first announcement, the event was described in some detail. One of the biggest manhunts in the city's history was on. The suspect was a minor narcotics dealer. The news focused on the details of the victims' personal lives. They were both married. One had two small children. The older one had two sons in college.

Terry remained motionless. Thoughts were swirling through his mind. Buster, isn't that what you wanted? How does it feel to kill two men? And you're a sneak too. Your hands are totally clean. How does it feel to have killed? How does it feel to be a coward?

He found himself trembling and sweating. His thoughts were in turmoil and there was no way of quieting them. He moved around the rest of the evening like an automaton. Didn't eat. During the night he hardly slept.

In the morning somebody was pushing his door bell insistently. He felt like ignoring the summons. Then he suddenly got up and opened the door. Marion was there, more attractive than ever. She seemed to know what he felt. Terry had no idea what was taking place but he found himself sobbing, in the softness of her embrace. They moved together into his house holding each other.

"Like all men you're a pompous fart but when it comes down to something important, you're sweet and sensitive just like your mom says." She led him to his chair and went on her knees holding him. "Look, you can consider it self-defense. They were looking for us and it wasn't to play tiddledywinks. Besides don't forget they killed Mauve. I was a complete ass for getting into a fight with you over nothing. Please forgive me."

Technically it was the end of the adventure. In reality for the two of them it was just the beginning.

ABOUT THE AUTHOR

Henry Tedeschi has taught at the University of Chicago, University of Illinois Medical Center (Chicago) and the State University of New York at Albany. He has written numerous technical articles, several book chapters, a monograph and a textbook in Cell Biology—two printed editions (Academic Press and W.C. Brown) and one edition on the web. Born in Italy he was sent to boarding school in Switzerland when Mussolini's racial laws prevented him from attending school in Italy. He spent several formative years in Argentina. He left at age 17 when he immigrated to the U.S. to attend college. He has written fiction and poetry all his life for his own pleasure. He enjoys writing, particularly short stories. He finds writing fiction opens a window into observed details of human behavior, times and places that are otherwise ignored. He has written two mysteries (*One Day at a Time* and *Double*) and three collections of short stories (*Long and Short Stories, More Long and Short Stories* and *Three for the Road*). The collection in *Long and Short Stories* ranges from suspense and mystery to whimsical. They portray a triumph of human values over vicissitudes imposed by situations over which the protagonists have no control. The second collection, *More Long and Short Stories*, emphasizes the drama and sometimes the comedy of the human condition. Each has a different focus, from the difficulties inherent in encounters between men and women, growing up and aging to the problems of academic life and its frequently unrecognized traumas. *Three for the Road* contains longer offerings—two are based in New York, one in the 1820s and another in the 1870s. A third is contemporary and takes place in a South American country under the rule of a cruel dictatorship. All three are stories of suspense and adventure.

978-0-595-40099-7
0-595-40099-X

Printed in the United States
82637LV00003B/307-324/A

9 780595 400997